Ever[illegible] GUILTY PLEASURES . . .

For prim and shy Daphne Wade, the sweetest guilty pleasure of all is secretly watching her employer, the Duke of Tremore, as he works the excavation site on his English estate. Anthony hired Daphne to restore the priceless treasures he has been digging up, but it's hard for a woman to keep her mind on her work when her devastatingly handsome employer keeps taking his shirt off. He doesn't know she's alive, but who could blame her for falling hopelessly in love with him anyway?

Anthony thinks that his capable employee knows all there is to know about antiquities, but when his sister decides to turn the plain young woman in gold-rimmed glasses into an enticing beauty, he declares the task to be impossible. Daphne is devastated when she overhears . . . and determined to prove him wrong. Now a vibrant and delectable Daphne has emerged from her shell, and the tables are turned. Will Anthony see that the woman of his dreams has been right there all along?

Laura Lee Guhrke

Guilty Pleasures

An Avon Romantic Treasure

AVON BOOKS
An Imprint of HarperCollins*Publishers*

This is a work of fiction. Names, characters, places, and incidents are products of the author's imagination or are used fictitiously and are not to be construed as real. Any resemblance to actual events, locales, organizations, or persons, living or dead, is entirely coincidental.

HarperCollins*Publishers*
77-85 Fulham Palace Road
Hammersmith
London W6 8JB

ISBN: 0 00 774039 5
www.avonromance.com

This edition published 2005
First Avon Books paperback printing: February 2004

Avon Trademark Reg. U.S. Pat. Off. and in Other Countries, Marca Registrada, Hecho en U.S.A.
HarperCollins® is a registered trademark of HarperCollins Publishers Inc.

Printed and bound in Great Britain by Clays Ltd, St Ives plc

For my literary agent, Robin Rue.
Your support of my career
and your faith in my work
mean more than I can say.
Thank you, Robin.

And ruin'd love, when it is built anew, grows fairer than at first, more strong, far greater.

William Shakespeare

Chapter 1

Hampshire, 1830

No one who glanced at Daphne Wade would ever imagine that she had a guilty, secret pleasure. Her countenance was plain, made more so by the spectacles perched on her nose. Her hair was light brown and fashioned into a functional bun at the nape of her neck. All her dresses were varying shades of beige, brown, or gray. Her height was average, and her figure was usually concealed beneath a loose-fitting work apron of heavy canvas. Her voice was low and pleasant to the ear, with nothing strident in its tone to evoke anyone's attention.

No one judging her by her appearance would dream that Miss Daphne Wade had the rather salacious habit of staring at her employer's naked chest whenever she had the chance, although most women would have agreed that Anthony Courtland, Duke of Tremore, had a chest worth looking at.

Daphne rested her elbows on the sill of the open window and lifted the brass spyglass. Using the instrument was awkward when she was wearing her spectacles, so she pulled them off. After setting the gold-rimmed pair on the windowsill, she once again raised the spyglass to her eye. Through its lens, she scanned the archaeological site in the distance, searching for Anthony amid the workmen.

She always thought of him by his Christian name. In speech, she called him "your grace," just as everyone else did, but in her mind and her heart, he was always Anthony.

He was talking with Mr. Bennington, the excavation architect, and Sir Edward Fitzhugh, the duke's closest neighbor and quite the amateur antiquarian himself. The three men stood in a huge pit of excavated ground amid the crumbling stone walls, broken columns, and other remnants of what had once been a Roman villa. At the moment, they appeared to be discussing the mosaic pavements beneath their feet that had been uncovered by the workmen that morning.

The moment she froze the spyglass on Anthony's tall form, she felt that familiar twist of her heart, that addictive mix of pleasure and discomfort. It was a combination that in his presence always tied her tongue and compelled her to withdraw into herself until she seemed part of the furniture, but when she watched him like this, she always longed to be the subject of his full attention. Love, she thought, should be a pleasant thing, warm and tender, not something that hurt one's heart by its intensity.

Daphne felt that intensity now as she watched him. When in residence at Tremore Hall, he was wont to spend two or three hours each day working alongside Mr. Bennington and the men on the excavation. Sometimes, if she was not on the dig and he found the August afternoon exceptionally warm, Anthony was compelled to remove his shirt. Today was a very warm day.

To Daphne, he almost seemed a part of the Roman excavation around him, for Anthony was one of those rare men who looked like a living statue. With his uncommon height of over six feet, with his broad shoulders and sculpted muscles, he could have been a Roman god carved of marble, were it not for his dark brown hair and tanned skin.

She watched him as the three men continued their discussion of the floor, and she felt that odd, melting sensation that came over her every time she saw him this way, a sensation that somehow made breathing difficult and made her heart race as if she had been running.

Sir Edward bent to move a heavy stone urn that was blocking a portion of the mosaic from their view, but Anthony stopped him and lifted the urn himself. Daphne was delighted by this gallantry, which only served to reinforce her high opinion of him. A duke he might be, but he wasn't so overproud that he would stand by and let a much older man like Sir Edward injure himself.

Anthony carried the urn to the cart nearby, placing it beside a crate filled with broken pieces of wine amphorae, bronze statues, fresco fragments, and other discoveries. At the end of the day, the pieces would be taken to the antika, a building nearby where artifacts were stored, until Daphne could repair, sketch and catalog them for Anthony's collection.

The sound of footsteps coming down the corridor toward the library brought Daphne out of her clandestine observations. She pushed the ends of the spyglass together, collapsing it. As she moved away from the window, she shoved the spyglass into the pocket of her skirt. By the time Ella, one of a dozen maids in the duke's employ at Tremore, entered the library, Daphne was seated at her desk with a text on Romano-British pottery open before her, pretending to be hard at work.

"Thought you'd like some tea, Miss Wade," Ella said, setting the teacup and its saucer on the edge of Daphne's large rosewood desk, beside the stacks of books on Roman antiquities and Latin.

"Thank you, Ella," she answered, trying to sound absorbed in her book as she turned a page.

The maid turned to leave, saying over her shoulder, "Didn't think you could see a thing, miss, without them spectacles. Seems t'me they don't do you much good sitting over on the windowsill."

The maid disappeared into the hall and Daphne

lowered her flushed face into the open book before her. *Caught again.*

Still, could anyone blame a plain, quiet, self-contained young woman who spent most of her time buried in ancient artifacts and Latin lexicons for being in love with her employer when he was so utterly splendid?

Daphne straightened in her chair with a sigh and rested one elbow on the desk. Chin in her hand, she stared into space, dreaming of things her rational mind knew could never happen.

He was a duke, Daphne reminded herself, and she worked for him. She had been employed by him for nearly five months now, and he paid her the quite generous salary of forty-eight pounds per annum to repair frescoes and mosaics, to restore antiquities, and create a catalog of the collection for a museum he was building in London. It was a demanding position with a demanding employer, but she was happy. She did every task he required of her not only because that was her job, but also because she was in love with him, and loving him was Daphne's guilty, secret pleasure.

Anthony leaned back in the copper bathtub with a contented sigh. God, he was tired, but the work had been worth it. That bedchamber floor he and the men had unearthed earlier in the day had some extraordinary pavements.

They had also found an entire wall of fresco pieces, damaged and crumbling, but also quite erotic. He must remember to tell Marguerite about them, especially the one depicting the master of the house as if he were the god Priapus, with his penis on one side of a scale and bars of gold on the other. No need to tell Marguerite which side was shown to be heavier. Mistresses always understood that sort of joke.

"Your grace?"

He opened his eyes to find Richardson standing beside the bathtub holding the jar of soap and a fresh pitcher of steaming water. Anthony leaned forward in the tub and allowed his valet to wash his hair, savoring the tangy scent of lemon soap and the pleasure of being rid of a day's worth of dirt and limestone dust.

Once Richardson had finished, Anthony rose and stepped out of the bathtub. He accepted a warm towel from his valet and began to dry his body as Richardson left the dressing room.

Thinking of Marguerite made Anthony realize it had been months since he had last seen the dark-eyed, dark-haired beauty. She had been his mistress for over a year now, but he had scarcely had half a dozen opportunities to visit her. The excavation here at Tremore had been dominating his attention of late and had kept him away from the cottage he provided for her just outside London.

Anthony tossed aside the towel and combed his hands through his still-damp hair as he walked into the bedchamber, where Richardson was waiting for him with fresh linen and a dressing gown of black and gold jacquard silk. He raised his arms and his valet slipped a cambric shirt over his head as the door opened and a footman entered the bedchamber.

"Lady Hammond is here, your grace," the servant said with a bow.

"Viola?" Anthony was not expecting his sister, and he glanced over his shoulder at the footman in surprise as his valet began to button his shirt. "When did she arrive?"

"A quarter of an hour ago, sir."

Anthony muttered an oath, thinking that if Hammond had shamed Viola with another scandal, this time he'd have the fellow's head. "Tell the viscountess I shall be with her in a moment, and have Madeira and port sent up."

"Very good, sir. Lady Hammond said she would await you in her sitting room." The servant departed, and Anthony thrust his arms into the sleeves of his dressing gown. A few minutes later, he left his own room and headed down the long corridor to his sister's suite at the opposite end, where a footman waited there to open the door to him. He entered his sister's sitting room, stepping into a baroque fantasy of pink velvet, white brocade, and gold leaf that suited Viola's golden blond beauty and lavishly feminine temperament down to the ground.

Anthony's worry that her visit brought bad news was dispelled the moment he caught sight of her, for she immediately began to laugh. The sound made him pause, and a half smile curved his mouth. He was glad to hear her laughing. It was better than listening to her cry over her disgrace of a husband. "What is so amusing?"

"You," she said, rising from her settee to come toward him. "You look like some decadent Turkish potentate in that dressing gown, with such a frown on your face that I imagined you about to order someone's tongue cut out."

"No one's tongue," he answered, taking his sister's outstretched hands into his own. "Hammond's head did come to mind."

Viola gave him an affectionate kiss on each cheek and turned away. It did not escape Anthony's notice that she would not meet his eyes. "You do not need to do anything so drastic, dear brother," she told him, returning to her seat on the settee.

"You mean he is finally behaving himself?" Anthony moved to sit on the striped pink and white brocade chair opposite her.

Before she could answer, a maid entered the room, carrying a tray that held port, Madeira, and two glasses. She placed the tray on the table beside Viola and departed.

"You want port, of course," Viola said, and began to pour the wine.

"He is behaving himself, is he not?" Anthony leaned forward, accepting the glass of port from his sister's hand. "Look at me, Viola, and tell me the truth."

Viola met his gaze. "The truth is that I wouldn't know. Hammond does not keep me informed of his activities, but I did learn yesterday that his most recent interest seems to be sea bathing."

Anthony could tell from her voice that nothing

had changed. "Hammond is at Brighton?"

"His arrival, of course, compelled me to depart from there at once."

Anthony frowned. "You cannot be forever avoiding him, Viola. For good or ill, he is your husband, and you have scarce spent two weeks in his company this past year. The gossip is rampant. Even here in Hampshire, I have heard rumors—"

"Speaking of rumors," she cut in, "I have been hearing quite a bit of gossip about you of late." She raised her glass and gave him an inquiring glance. "Can it be that I am soon to have a sister?"

Her words irked Anthony, not because she was asking such a question, but because he did not enjoy being the subject of gossip and speculation.

"Ah," he said, and took a sip of port. "Word of my recent trip to London reached the seaside pavilions at Brighton, I take it?"

"Did you expect it would not?" she countered, smiling. "The oh-so-eligible Duke of Tremore, a man who never dances at balls, who would not be caught dead at Almack's, who avoids young ladies of impeccable background as if they all have the plague, suddenly takes the ducal emeralds to London to be cleaned. Most of our friends are in agreement that this bodes well for a duchess. Are you finally going to marry? Please tell me yes. Nothing would delight me more than knowing you have found someone to make you happy."

He studied his sister over the rim of his glass for a moment without speaking. How could any woman with a husband like Hammond retain any optimism about happiness in marriage? "I am going to wed, yes," he confirmed.

Viola gave a cry of delight. "How wonderful! I have been going over names in my mind all the way up from Brighton, but I cannot imagine who could have captured your heart when you have been buried here since March. Who is she?"

"Can you not guess? One choice stands high above the rest. Monforth's eldest daughter, Sarah."

"Ugh!" Viola fell back against the velvet pillows of the settee with a groan. "You cannot be serious."

"Monforth is a marquess with impeccable connections. Lady Sarah would make an excellent duchess. She is well bred and has a substantial fortune. She is also healthy, gracious, and quite beautiful."

"And she is as intelligent as a fence post."

He conceded that with a shrug and reached for his glass. "I don't intend to have intellectual discussions with her," he said as he took a sip of port, "so what does that matter?"

"Oh, Anthony!" Viola rose and circled the table to sit on the arm of his chair. "Lady Sarah cares nothing for you."

"And your point?"

"She seems as sweet as honey, but it is a facade," Viola went on, contempt in her voice. "The only things she really cares about are money and position. You have both, and she would sell her soul to have you."

"Yes," he agreed dispassionately, "she would."

"Then why?" Viola cried. "Why, when you are

in a position to choose from among hundreds of young ladies, would you pick someone as shallow and calculating as Lady Sarah Monforth? She could never make you happy."

"God, Viola, I am not getting married expecting to be made happy by it. It is the sensible course. I would prefer not to marry at all, but I must secure an heir, and I cannot afford to postpone the inevitable any longer. I am choosing the young lady who is most suited to the role of duchess, a young lady who will make no demands upon me beyond my support."

"I see what you really mean," Viola said slowly. "You have chosen a woman who will not care that you have no respect or affection for her, and who will not be hurt that you do not love her, as long as you supply her with a generous allowance and she supplies you with a son."

"Exactly so."

"Oh, Anthony, really!" Viola cried in dismay and jumped to her feet. He watched as she began to pace back and forth, and neither of them spoke. She seemed lost in thought, and he hoped she was accustoming herself to his decision.

Finally, she stopped pacing and looked at him. "Have you proposed to Lady Sarah yet?"

"No," he answered. "She is in Paris with her mother. They are to spend the autumn there."

"Good, then I have time to change your mind."

She gave him that beguiling smile that ever since their childhood could get nearly anything out of him she wanted, but this time Anthony was unmoved. "I have no intention of changing my mind.

If your expression is anything to go by," he added, noting how quickly her smile faded, "the end of the world is at hand. You seem quite upset about this."

"Of course I am upset," she answered, and resumed pacing. "You are about to make an irrevocable choice that will ensure nothing but misery for you. I should die if you were unhappy."

"Viola, you are being far too dramatic, as usual. I am quite content as I am, with the life I lead, and I see nothing about marrying Lady Sarah that would mar my current contentment."

"Giving up Marguerite for Lady Sarah would mar any man's contentment," she answered with such wry humor that he couldn't help a smile.

Marguerite was no secret, but discussing one's mistresses with one's sister was not quite the thing. On this occasion, however, Anthony felt he must make Viola understand his intentions. "I am not giving up Marguerite."

Viola stopped pacing once again and stared at him, shocked. "You cannot possibly be thinking to keep her after you marry?"

He met the rebuke in her eyes with a direct stare. "Why not?"

"Oh, Anthony, I loathe Lady Sarah, I confess it, but such a course is so unbelievably cruel, and I cannot believe you would do such a thing."

He stiffened at the rebuke. "You forget yourself, Viola. My choice of bride is not your concern, and neither are my mistresses."

"Oh, do not attempt all that ducal hauteur with me, Anthony," she shot back. "I am your sister, and every single day of my life, I endure the pain of marriage to a man who has nothing but contempt for me. How can you justify this when you know how I have suffered?"

Viola always did tend to express her emotions with a great deal of drama. "I know that," he answered calmly, "and it wounds me deeply. For the pain he has caused you, I would throttle Hammond with my bare hands if I could, but your situation and mine are very different."

"How?"

"Sarah will not give a tinker's damn if I keep a dozen mistresses as long as I keep her in funds. She has no affection for me, nor I for her. You, on the other hand, still have some tender regard for Hammond, and that is why his behavior causes you pain. Although why you still harbor any affection for him is one of life's inexplicable mysteries, since he is a blackguard whose treatment of you is deplorable."

"And it is my own bitter experience that impels me to abhor your selection of Monforth's daughter. I want you to be happy with your wife, happy enough that you do not need the companionship of women such as Marguerite Lyon, happy enough that you need not schedule your life to be wherever your spouse is not. I cannot help but believe that it is possible to be happy in marriage, despite my own poor choice."

Something in the soft romanticism of her words irritated him, for they brought memories to the surface, memories he thought both he and Viola had buried for good. He ruthlessly shoved those memories back down deep and concealed his irritation with an air of indifference. "How you can remain such a romantic, Viola, never ceases to astonish me."

"Perhaps because I believe our parents were blessed to have loved each other so passionately, while you believe they were cursed."

Anthony felt his fingers curl around the delicate crystal glass in his hand so tightly, he was surprised it did not shatter. He set the glass down with care. "Love is all very well," he said lightly, leaning back in his chair, "but it has little to do with marriage. Look among our acquaintance. All of them are in love. Just not with their spouses."

Anthony's careless tone brought his sister back to his side. She sat down again and took his hands in hers. "Do be serious. Will you not at least try to find someone you could love?"

Anthony studied her face for a moment, and he did not know what to say. Viola had married Hammond for love. Despite Anthony's misgivings about the match, he had not been able to deny Viola her heart's desire, and the resulting union had been a disaster. He had no intention of making his sister's mistake and marrying for love only to be made miserable by the union.

"I beg you to at least consider my opinion," she went on. "You deserve better than Lady Sarah. You deserve a wife with a kind and generous nature, a woman filled to her fingertips with passion for you, a woman who cares for you more than your rank or your fortune."

All this high-blown sentimentality was bordering on the ridiculous. He jerked his hands free of hers. "God, Viola," he said with some impatience, "I do not require passion of a wife."

"Well, you should. Besides, Lady Sarah doesn't love you. I doubt she is capable of the emotion."

"So what?" He met his sister's dismayed gaze with a hard and determined one of his own. "Since when has love ever been necessary to matrimony?"

Viola stared at him for a long moment, then she sighed. "Perhaps it is not necessary," she said, and rose to her feet. "But it would be nice."

Chapter 2

"So these are his grace's latest treasures?" Sir Edward smiled at Daphne over the pieces of jewelry she had laid out on the library table. There were armbands of gold, several pairs of pearl earrings, a few cameos, and an exquisite necklace of emeralds set between hammered gold leaves. The jewels glittered in the morning sunlight that poured through the windows of the library. They made a dazzling display against the white cloth that protected the table.

"Very fine emeralds," he pronounced, studying the necklace through his monocle.

"They are not so fine as the ducal emeralds, I dare-say," Mrs. Bennington pronounced as she leaned her short, stout frame over the table a bit to have a closer look. Her rubicund face scrunched with disappointment. "When Bennington told me about these Roman jewels, I was so excited to see them, but now that I have, I find them rather a letdown. So crudely made. Why, no young lady would wear these!"

Daphne laughed. "But Mrs. Bennington, these are not to be worn. They are for the duke's museum. His grace intends that museum to be open not only to the wealthy and privileged, but to everyone. Is that not a noble goal? All British people, rich or poor, shall be allowed to see their history."

"She sounds just like Tremore, does she not?" A feminine voice floated to them from the doorway.

All three of them turned to see the woman who entered the library. Daphne pushed her spectacles up the bridge of her nose to have a clearer view and recognized her at once from the portraits in the gallery. This was Anthony's sister. The portrait did not do her justice, for on canvas she seemed only a pretty blond woman with hazel eyes like her brother. But in reality, one could imagine that her face had launched the thousand ships at Troy.

Lady Hammond smiled at her and Mrs. Bennington in a friendly way, then nodded to the man at the end of the table. "Sir Edward," she said, her hands outstretched in greeting as she walked toward him. "What a pleasure to see you again so soon."

"Lady Hammond," he answered, taking the woman's hands into his own. "I so enjoyed dining here at Tremore Hall last evening, and your presence made it especially delightful."

"I enjoyed it as well, Sir Edward. I was fascinated

by your discussion with his grace about this excavation of his."

Daphne would have loved to participate in such a discussion, but that was unlikely to happen. Being an employee of the duke, she never dined with Anthony or his guests. She took her meals with the Benningtons in a separate dining room, but it would not have mattered in any case. She had spent her evening fulfilling a request Anthony had made of her just before dinner.

Would you be able to have those pieces of jewelry finished for me by tomorrow morning, Miss Wade?

It was a time-consuming and tedious process to clean and repair jewelry, but she had willingly spent her evening and half her night in the antika accomplishing it.

The viscountess noticed the pieces laid out on the table. "These must be the emeralds my brother was talking about last night. It is hard to imagine that they were buried right on our land all this time. Are they really over fifteen hundred years old?"

"Over sixteen hundred, actually," Daphne answered, causing the woman to turn in her direction.

"Lady Hammond," Sir Edward put in, "you must meet Miss Wade and Mrs. Bennington. Mrs. Bennington is the wife of the project architect, while Miss Wade—"

"Does everything!" the viscountess put in. "Or so I have been told. Sir Edward was singing your praises last night at dinner, Miss Wade. Even Anthony admitted that you were quite the best antiquarian he knew."

"He said that?" Daphne felt a warm little glow at the idea that Anthony had been singing her praises, but she did not show it, far too afraid of having her secret feelings for him revealed. "I am gratified to hear it."

"I should hope so, dear, for that is high praise indeed," Mrs. Bennington put in. "Mr. Bennington tells me the duke's good opinion is very hard to earn, for it is always given with the strictest honesty."

"Quite true," Lady Hammond agreed. "He is always frank in his opinions, sometimes brutally so, but he said Miss Wade is a most excellent mosaicist and restorer. How did you ever come to learn such things, Miss Wade?"

"I suppose you could say I was born to it," she answered. "I have lived and worked on excavation sites all my life."

"Speaking of excavations," Sir Edward went on, "I must go down to meet his grace at the site. He wishes to show me the hypocaust."

"A hypocaust sounds most impressive," the viscountess commented, "but what on earth is it?"

They all laughed, but it was Daphne who answered. "A hypocaust is a sort of cellar beneath the house that slaves kept filled with hot water. It made the tile floors warm in winter and heated the house. Quite a practical design."

"I must see it then. Anything that would keep

one's feet warm in the wretched English climate would be a sound idea."

"We could do with more of them, Lady Hammond, I am sure," Sir Edward answered. "But forgive me, I must go." He bowed to her.

"I shall go with you," Mrs. Bennington declared, "for I must speak to my husband."

"Of course, dear lady, of course." Sir Edward offered her his arm, and they departed.

After they had gone, Daphne turned to the viscountess, who was studying her with frank interest. The moment their eyes met, the viscountess smiled. "My brother has always wanted to excavate the ruins here at Tremore. How did he come to hire you for this project, Miss Wade?"

"My father was Sir Henry Wade, one of the most knowledgeable Roman antiquarians in the world. I was his assistant. The duke had been corresponding with Papa for several years. He would often purchase antiquities we uncovered, and Papa always offered any rare finds to his grace first. Your brother eventually hired us to come to England to work on this villa for him, but Papa died very suddenly. We—" She broke off, and swallowed hard. Nearly a year had gone by, but it still hurt to talk about Papa.

She took a moment to collect herself, then went on, "We were just finishing our work on Volubilis in Morocco and preparing to come here when he died. The duke had already paid our passage to England, and I decided to come anyway. His grace was so good as to hire me to assist Mr. Bennington.

My knowledge does not compare to that of my father, of course, but I do the best I can."

The viscountess returned her attention to the jewelry. "These are beautiful pieces. I would not have thought ancient jewelry could remain in such pristine condition as this."

"It doesn't, I assure you," Daphne said, laughing. "The necklace was in pieces when the duke himself uncovered it yesterday, and several of the jewels had fallen out of their settings. I cleaned the lot, then put the pieces back together and sketched them for his grace's catalog."

A slight frown marred the other woman's face. "No young lady should have to work so hard."

"Oh, but his grace wants the museum open by mid-March. I don't mind the work. I enjoy it, and these pieces are extraordinary historical finds. Valuable jewelry is rare, for it is usually stolen long before an antiquarian has the chance to uncover it."

"You must be a remarkable woman, Miss Wade. I cannot fathom what would be enjoyable about what you do. Repairing jewelry, restoring mosaic floors, and piecing together clay pots would not be my idea of enjoyment, especially under my brother's supervision. He is impossible to work for, I have no doubt."

"Oh, no," Daphne cried. "He is a very good employer. If it had not been for Anthony, I—" She stopped, realizing she had said his Christian name aloud.

The viscountess did not appear to notice her slip

of the tongue. She looked down and caught sight of the drawings Daphne had made of the jewelry. She picked up two of the sketches to study them. "You make a drawing of each item you find? For a catalog, I believe you said?"

"Yes," she said, relieved. "I do a sketch of each artifact. They will form the permanent record of his grace's collection."

The viscountess studied the drawings for a moment, then set them aside. As she did so, she caught sight of Daphne's sketch book, which was also lying on the table, and she opened it.

Remembering what was inside, Daphne made a move to stop her from going further, but it was too late. The viscountess was already looking through her drawings.

"I do not believe you would be interested in those, Lady Hammond," she said, feeling a hint of panic. "They are not for the catalog. They are just my scribblings, and quite unremarkable."

"Miss Wade, you are too modest. These are lovely."

Without snatching the sketch book away, there was nothing Daphne could do but watch as the viscountess studied her drawings of the excavations and the workmen. One by one, she examined each page and set it aside, coming closer and closer to the ones tucked away at the bottom of the pile.

Just when Daphne wished she could crawl under the nearest floor carpet, Lady Hammond finally reached the drawings of Anthony, and she paused an inordinate amount of time over the last one, an image of him standing amid the excavations without his shirt. Daphne felt her cheeks heating with mortification, and she tried to look at anything in the library but the other woman's face.

After what seemed an eternity, the viscountess put the last sketch down. She replaced the drawings back inside Daphne's worn, leather-bound portfolio precisely in the order she had found them. "You have great talent," she said, and closed the book. "The last one is especially fine. A very accurate likeness." She paused, then added, "My brother *is* quite a handsome man, is he not?"

"I suppose so," she said, trying to sound indifferent. "I have always made it a habit," she said, struggling for some semblance of dignity, "to do drawings of each person involved in an excavation. It helps record the event for posterity's sake."

"Of course." The very gravity of the other woman's voice told Daphne she didn't believe it for a moment, but she did not point out that posterity hardly required a drawing of Anthony without his shirt.

The tap of decisive, familiar footsteps in the corridor outside the library told Daphne who was coming, and she circled around to the other side of the table, never more thankful of a distraction in her life. She grabbed a soft, damp chamois, and by the time Anthony came through the door, she was polishing a gold armband, rubbing away any last tarnish from its surface.

"Anthony!" Lady Hammond greeted him over one shoulder. "I did not expect to see you until dinner."

"I came in search of you, Viola," he answered, crossing the room to stand beside his sister. "I thought you might wish to see some of the antiquities."

"With pleasure."

Anthony proffered his arm to her, but instead of slipping her own arm through his, the viscountess pointed to the jewelry. "Look at what your Miss Wade had done. I understand these pieces were in very poor shape yesterday, yet you would never know it to see them now. Miss Wade is extraordinary."

He looked over at Daphne, and his smile took her breath away. "Yes," he agreed, "quite extraordinary."

Her heart skipped a beat as he circled the table to her side. She watched him anxiously as he made a careful perusal of her efforts, and she hoped he would find no flaw with them.

He looked up, his beautiful hazel eyes meeting hers. "Excellent work, Miss Wade."

Pleasure washed over her like the sun. She swallowed hard and nodded, unable to think of a thing to say until he had walked away.

"Thank you," she finally managed to call out as he moved toward the door, arm in arm with his sister, but he must not have heard her words, for he did not turn to look at her again.

The viscountess did, though, glancing over her

shoulder at Daphne for a moment. There was something in the other woman's face, a speculative and thoughtful expression Daphne did not attempt to interpret. Instead, she returned her gaze to the wide shoulders of the man walking out the door.

Excellent work, Miss Wade.

Those four simple words were enough to keep her walking on clouds for the remainder of the day.

Chapter 3

One of the many things for which Daphne admired Anthony was his practical good sense. When the duke had decided to begin excavations on his estate two years earlier, he had ordered that a cottage be built near the site that would act as the antika room for the dig, the place where artifacts could be kept until they were completely restored and taken to London.

The antika had three spacious rooms. One acted as a storehouse for all antiquities awaiting Daphne. Another served to house them after she had finished their restoration. The third room acted as her workroom, and Anthony had designed it well. Plenty of windows let in the natural light. The stone walls and floor kept the interior cool in summer, a fact which Mr. Bennington found very appealing, but which mattered not at all to Daphne. She found England pleasant in summer rather than hot, and a far more desirable place to be in August than the deserts of Morocco.

A pump and a drain had been installed, and several massive oak tables held her works in progress. One of those works was a mosaic pavement she was about to begin restoring.

Preoccupied with her task, Daphne did not observe Lady Hammond standing in the doorway until the other woman gave a slight cough.

"I hope I am not interrupting something of vital historical importance," the viscountess said, smiling. "My brother was giving me another tour of the site this morning when we were suddenly interrupted. The workmen, it seems, have discovered a statue of great significance."

"Really? What statue?"

Lady Hammond waved her hand in a dismissive gesture. "I have no idea. My brother was diverted to this new find, and I saw my opportunity to escape."

Daphne was puzzled. "Escape?"

"Yes, indeed. When Anthony's conversation turns to history and Roman antiquities, I confess I am bored to tears. Suppressing the desire to yawn yesterday as he showed me an endless array of clay pots and bronze hand-axes was difficult enough. Today's tour of stone walls, broken roof tiles, and layers of dirt twenty feet high was too much for me, and I was compelled to run away. You are like Anthony, no doubt, and find such things fascinating.

But I am not an intellectual person, I fear, and I cannot bear to devote myself to tedious discussions of broken wine amphorae."

Daphne wondered how anyone could call such discussions tedious. In her daydreams, she had impassioned discussions with Anthony about such things every day, discussions that never happened in reality, of course, because she was usually at a loss for words whenever he was near.

"So," Lady Hammond went on, breaking into her thoughts, "I left my brother and wandered in this direction. I spied you through the doorway and thought I might pause a moment for a visit with you. If you do not mind?"

Daphne hesitated, still feeling an acute sense of embarrassment about the sketch the viscountess had found the day before. No one liked having their deepest secrets revealed, especially to a stranger.

As if reading her mind, the Lady Hammond said, "I must warn you that I am very tiresome about secrets. I keep them."

A look of understanding passed between the two women. "That is an admirable quality," Daphne answered. "Your friends must be grateful for it."

"Some of them, perhaps, although it causes my less discreet friends much vexation."

Daphne could not help laughing at that. Anthony's sister had a forthright friendliness she liked, and she beckoned her into the antika room. "I would be glad of your company."

"Good." Lady Hammond came inside and

crossed the room to the table. She looked down at the dirty slab of tiled limestone on the table. "What is it you do here?"

"I am restoring a mosaic. Watch." Daphne pulled on a pair of heavy leather gloves, then retrieved a glass bottle containing deutoxide of hydrogen from beneath the table. She pulled out the cork and slowly poured a generous amount of the liquid over the tiled surface. As the accumulated grime began to wash away, the image of a woman appeared, a naked woman lying on a shell-shaped boat.

"Isn't she lovely!" the viscountess cried, studying the image. "Do you know who she is?"

"Venus," Daphne answered at once. "The Roman goddess of love. This square was in front of the door into the main sleeping quarters of the master and mistress of the house. Because of this mosaic, the fact that they shared their sleeping quarters, and from other artifacts found at the site, I believe that this couple's marriage, though arranged, became a love match." She paused, looking at the image, then added, "I would like to think they were as happy as my own mother and father."

"Was your parents' marriage a love match, then?"

"Oh, yes. They had a depth of affection and companionship of which few can boast. I was only a child when my mother died, but even then, I knew how much in love they were."

"You believe love is important in marriage, Miss Wade?"

Daphne looked at the viscountess across the table, astonished by a question for which the answer seemed so obvious. "Of course. Doesn't everyone?"

"No, my dear," Lady Hammond answered with a hint of irony in her voice that Daphne could not fathom. "Not everyone does. I have heard the opinion of late that love and marriage are two separate things, that they need not ever have anything to do with each other. What do you think of that?"

"Whoever expressed that opinion must be a sadly cynical person." Daphne picked up a small bristle brush and bent down to drench it in the pail of water beneath the table. She straightened. "What other reason is there to marry?" she asked, moving the brush over the tiny tiles to remove the remaining grime from the grout lines.

"Children are an excellent reason."

"Really?" Daphne paused, unable to resist giving the viscountess a look of feigned astonishment over the rims of her spectacles. "I did not realize one needed vows and a ceremony for the actual children to begin arriving."

The other woman gave a smothered half laugh. "A wicked observation, Miss Wade. In society, such a statement would make people think you quite shocking."

"Wicked perhaps, but also sensible. If children are the goal, then love between the partners would ensure plenty of them."

To Daphne's surprise, the other woman's smile

faded and her expression became almost melancholy. "Yes, I suppose it would," she agreed, then shook her head. "But let us continue our discussion of marriage. Aside from children, there are other practical considerations, do you not agree? Family alliances. The accumulation of wealth. To gain greater position and power in society. There are many people who feel those are more important than love when choosing a marriage partner."

"What purpose do those considerations serve if one is unhappy? I would think that to marry without love would bring a lifetime of pain."

The countess drew in her breath so sharply that Daphne was startled. She once again looked up. "Lady Hammond, are you unwell?"

"No, no." The other woman lifted her hand in a gesture of reassurance. "I am quite well. It is just that love itself can bring its own measure of pain, Miss Wade."

Daphne paused, her fingers tightening around the brush in her hand as she looked into the other woman's eyes. "Yes," she admitted, "I suppose it can, if one is not loved in return. But surely the joy of the experience is worth the pain."

"Is it?" Lady Hammond murmured, and her lips twisted into an ironic sort of smile. Her gaze moved past Daphne as if she were staring into a far distant landscape. "I wonder."

Daphne felt a sudden empathy for the other woman. "So do I," she admitted, "but it did sound quite noble and poetic when I said it."

The two women looked at each other and both of them began to laugh.

"I knew the moment we met I was going to like you," the viscountess exclaimed, still laughing. "We must become friends."

Daphne smiled back, both pleased and touched by the suggestion. "I should like that, Lady Hammond. I have not had much opportunity to make friends, having moved about so much in my life."

"You must call me Viola, and I shall call you Daphne. Flower names, you see? We already have something in common."

"But not a love for clay pots."

"No. In that respect, you are much more like Anthony, though what the two of you find so fascinating about shards of pottery baffles me."

"Well, it is the pottery that truly reveals the history of a site—"

"No, no!" Viola held up one hand, stopping her. "I have heard this all before. I was running away from it a few moments ago, remember?"

"So you were. Very well, I shall not impose a discussion of Samarian ware, cream ware, and buff ware upon you."

"Good, for I should much rather hear about you. Sir Edward told me you were born on the island of Crete?"

Daphne could not help being flattered. She was so seldom the object of anyone's attention. "Yes. My father was excavating at Knossos. I do not remember much about the excavation. I do remember how hot and dry it was. My mother often described to me the meadows and woods of England. It sounded like paradise to me."

"Both your parents were English?"

"Oh, yes. They met when he was in England to give a lecture on his findings at Knossos. He had been made a Knight of the Bath and was in London to receive the accolade. After a whirlwind courtship, they eloped and returned to Crete together."

"And what of the rest of your family?"

"I . . ." She hesitated, then said, "My father was an orphan."

"And your mother's family?"

Daphne stilled, the brush in her hand pressing against the mosaic so hard that its bristles were nearly flat. The mention of her mother's family brought back the memory of that horrible day in Tangier and the letter she had received from a London attorney two months after her father's death.

Thank you for your inquiry to Lord Durand regarding a certain Lady Wade, whom you have declared to be the wife of Sir Henry Wade and formerly Miss Jane Durand, daughter of his lordship. Your declaration is impossible, for the Honorable Miss Durand remained unmarried until she died at her father's estate in Durham, in 1805, when she was but twenty years of age. There is no possibility whatsoever that she could be your mother, and Lord Durand regrets that he can be of no assistance to you in this matter. Any further attempts to gain money or protection from his lordship shall be futile.

Remembering that letter brought back all the fear she had felt then, the sick knot of fear that came with knowing she was all alone, her money running out, no one to help her and nothing of value left to sell. Nothing but a passage to England.

Daphne shoved memories of that day in Tangier out of her mind. She did not want to discuss her mother's family or the shame of being unacknowledged and unwanted. "Mama never talked of her relations."

"She must have said something to you."

Pressed, Daphne admitted, "I know that my grandfather was a baron, but I know almost nothing else. My mother died when I was eight, and my father and I never discussed it."

"A baron. Do you know his name, at least, or where he lived?"

"No," she lied.

"But this is shocking! What manner of father leaves his daughter without family, means, or protection upon his death, and does not even tell her the names of her connections?"

"My father was not so harsh as you imply!" Daphne cried, compelled to defend her parent. "He was a vigorous man, and he could not know he was going to die so suddenly. He was the most loving father anyone could have, and you insult me by saying otherwise."

Viola fell silent. After a moment, she said, "You

are correct to scold me, Miss Wade. I am quite chastened. My only excuse is that it makes me heated to see a young lady left so unprotected and made to work, but it was not my business to inquire into your affairs. Please accept my apology."

She did indeed seem contrite, and Daphne relented. "Of course."

"Did you remain on Crete after your mother's death?"

"No, we left the island only a few months later. Papa could not remain there. Too many memories. He was heartbroken when Mama died."

"And did his grief obsess him?" Viola asked, a strange note of hardness entering her voice. "They were happy, but when she died, did he abandon his duties, ignore his children? Did his grief drive out his sanity?"

Daphne was astonished by this sudden, strange turn in the conversation. "What odd questions you ask! He grieved, of course, but never so much that he abandoned his duties. He never ignored me, nor lost his sanity."

The other woman shook her head as if coming out of a private reverie. "I confess I was thinking of someone else. I am so sorry. Where did you go when you left Crete?"

"Palestine. We have also excavated at Petra, Syria, Mesopotamia, Tunis, and Morocco. Large excavations usually take many years, but after my mother's death, my father was never able to settle in one place for very long."

"But what of society and company?"

"I have not had much of that. An occasional dinner with friends of Papa's in Rome, but that is all."

"No parties? No balls?"

"I'm afraid not." Daphne shook her head, smiling. "I do not even know how to dance. There is not much demand for balls in the midst of the desert. I am more accustomed to the company of donkeys, camels, Arabs, and stuffy old antiquarians."

"Your life has been a fascinating one, Daphne, but there are so many pleasures you have missed."

"Perhaps, but I have loved every moment of my life. I do miss my father, but I think he would have liked it that I came to England after he died. He wanted me to see it. That is why he finally agreed to the duke's offer to come here."

"Have you seen London?"

"No. I traveled by spice caravan from Marrakesh to Tangier, then a ship to Portsmouth, and straight on to Tremore Hall from there."

"A spice caravan!" Viola burst out laughing.

Daphne looked at her in puzzlement. "Did I say something amusing?"

Still laughing, the other woman shook her head. "Amusing? Oh, Daphne! You say the most extraordinary things in the most matter-of-fact way, as if traveling by caravans is quite commonplace."

"Well, it is commonplace," Daphne said, laughing with her. "Although perhaps not here in Hampshire."

The other woman's amusement faded away and she looked at Daphne thoughtfully. "Morocco,

Palestine, Crete. I cannot help but think you find Tremore Hall quite dull in comparison?"

"Oh, no! To me, living here is luxury beyond belief. I must confess that I find sleeping on a feather mattress far better than a canvas cot in a stone hut or desert tent."

"Heavens, I imagine any woman would! You like it here, then?"

"I do. When I reached England, I had the odd feeling I had come home, though I had never been here before. Everything in England is so fresh and green, so beautiful after all the arid deserts in which I have lived. It was all my mother said it was. I do not ever want to leave."

"And what do you think of the estate?"

"I have not seen much of it, I'm afraid. I have been so busy with the excavation work, I have not had a chance to explore, although I have walked through the gardens on occasion. It is a splendid property, but a bit intimidating when you first arrive."

"Yes," Viola agreed. "I know what you mean. When I was a girl, I had been at boarding school in France for several years, and when I came home, I was struck by just how intimidating it was. I had forgotten. Anthony will not let me change a thing, though. Family history and all that."

"I can see his point."

"You would, Daphne, for you also see the point of clay pots. If it were your home, you would be like Anthony, no doubt, and refuse to redecorate a thing."

Daphne caught her breath at the sudden wave of

longing that swept through her at the other woman's offhand comment, but she shoved that feeling aside at once. This was not her home. She did not have a home. "I would change one thing," she replied, forcing lightness into her voice. "I would remove those hideous gargoyle finials from the main staircase and consign them to a dustbin."

"They are awful. When I was a little girl, they gave me nightmares. Perhaps when Anthony marries, his duchess will have them tossed into a dustbin so their children are not frightened."

An image of Anthony and his duchess with their children came into Daphne's mind, and she banished it at once, tucking her chin to hide her expression.

"I am sure you wish to marry, Daphne," Viola said, breaking into her thoughts.

"I . . ." She took a deep breath and bent down beside the table to dip the brush in the pail again. "I had not thought about it," she said as she straightened. She resumed her task and did not look at the woman opposite her. "It is unlikely to happen."

"Why do you say that?"

"I recognize that I am a plain woman, and rather on the shelf at twenty-four. I have little opportunity to make new acquaintances. And, if I did marry, it would only be for a deep, true, and lasting love. So, you see," she added, glancing up with a little laugh, "the odds are against me."

Viola did not reply, but Daphne could feel her new friend's gaze on her as she returned her attention to her work, and it was a long time before the other woman broke the silence.

"It is a shame you've not seen London."

Daphne looked up, startled by the change of subject. "I would like to, one day. Do you and your husband live there?"

"It depends on the time of year," Viola answered. "I spend my autumn and winter at Enderby, our estate in Chiswick, which is just outside London, while Hammond stays at Hammond Park in Northumberland. In the spring, we lease a town house for the season together. In the summer, I go to Brighton and Hammond returns to Northumberland. It is an arrangement that suits both of us quite well, for we are only required to spend a few months together each year, and that is enough for the sake of appearances."

Daphne was rather shocked, but she did not show it. She also felt a wave of compassion for her new friend. "I see," she murmured.

"I make Enderby quite lively in winter," Viola went on, a brittle sort of brightness coming into her voice. "I give many house parties and surround myself with company, for I do not like being lonely—" She broke off and gave a half laugh. "Listen to me, sounding so self-pitying. I am quite ashamed of myself. My only excuse is that you are a very good listener, Daphne."

"There is no shame in being lonely," Daphne said gently. "I, too, know what that is like. For much of my life, I have lived in desert tents miles from anywhere, places where I was the only Englishwoman within fifty miles. Papa and I stayed in Rome during the winter, and while he spent his time with other scholars and antiquarians, I would wander about the libraries and museums, reading anything about England I could find. History, politics, society, customs. I should love to see London one day."

"Oh, Daphne, I wish I could show it to you! It is the most exciting city. I should love it if you could come with me when I go to Enderby. You would be such good company for me, and Chiswick is only an hour's ride from London. Why, if you stayed for the season, you could come into town with us, and I could introduce you into society. We might be able to find your mother's family."

"That is impossible," Daphne answered. Anthony was here, and she could not imagine leaving Tremore Hall for a long time to come. "I have far too much to do."

"Anthony's museum opens in March. Could you not come after that?"

"No, for I will still need to carry on with excavations here even after the museum opens. I doubt we will be completely finished for at least five years."

"I understand, but it is such a shame." Suddenly, Viola gave a cry of vexation. "Oh dear, I must go back. If my brother discovers I have run away from this excavation of his, he will be so disappointed in me. He is always trying to persuade me to intellectual pursuits."

Viola started for the door, but turned in the doorway to look at her one more time. "By the way, Daphne, beauty does not mean a thing, you know."

Daphne watched as her new friend vanished through the doorway, and she smiled a bit ruefully. “Beautiful women always say that,” she murmured to the empty doorway.

Chapter 4

Anthony leaned one hip against the pianoforte, studying Viola's expression in the candlelight as she stared into space and tapped out a soft melody on the keys. He did not fail to observe the half smile that curved her lips. "You look quite pleased with herself," he said, "and whenever you look like that, I begin to worry. What are you thinking about?"

"Venus," she answered, and looked up at the man standing beside her.

His eyebrows rose at such an oblique answer. "The goddess of love? What makes you think of Venus?"

"Did she ever arrange marriages between mortals?"

His eyes narrowed with suspicion. "Are you

planning to fight my marriage to Lady Sarah and arrange for me a better one? Pray desist, Viola, for you know my feelings on this."

"No, no." Viola stopped playing long enough to wave one hand carelessly in his direction, then resumed her music. "You have made your choice, and I know when it is futile to attempt to change your mind. I suppose," she added with a sigh, "that when one looks at it in a prudential light, it is the best decision for you. You are the Duke of Tremore, after all, and should marry high for duty's sake, even if your choice is without love and affection. No, I have moved on to arranging a possible match for someone else, a match that provides me a far better chance of success. Daphne's."

"Daphne?" He frowned. "I do not recall—"

"Miss Wade."

He stared at Viola as a vague vision came to his mind of brown hair raked back in a bun, spectacles, dreary dresses covered by heavy work aprons, and an inability to speak without stammering.

"You intend to arrange a marriage for Miss Wade?" he asked, astonished.

"If I can persuade her to go to Enderby with me, I shall introduce her to some eligible young men, and we shall see what happens."

"You will do no such thing."

The vehemence of his tone rather startled Viola. She stopped playing again and looked at him, wide-eyed. "Why, Anthony, you sound quite heated. I had no idea you would mind so much."

"I do mind. Miss Wade has work to do here, vital, important work. I won't have her go off gallivanting about Chiswick and London with you. What happens to my museum and my excavation?"

"That excavation is all you think about these days. There are some things in this world that are more important than your Roman villa."

"Nothing can be more important than uncovering history." He could hear the passion he felt for the excavation in his own voice as he spoke. "Viola, this site is one of immense historical significance. It is the best site of Roman ruins ever uncovered in Britain, and it is on my estate. We are learning things about life in Roman Britain that we never knew before. The artifacts we uncover here will be of tremendous benefit to scholars and historians, and the museum in London will allow all British people to learn about their heritage. This is a piece of our history."

"I am not concerned with history, dear brother," Viola said, with no understanding at all of what he was attempting to achieve. "I am concerned with the life of a young lady of good family who has been forced by circumstance to seek employment, is allowed no life of her own, and has had no amusements or society in her entire life. Why, she does not even know how to dance. It is appalling how neglectful her father was of her comfort and care."

Viola paused for a quick breath, but before Anthony could point out that history and serious antiquarian study were far more important than dancing, she went on, "And now, Daphne is forced to earn her living. A young lady working herself to exhaustion scrubbing mosaics and piecing clay pots back together like a servant. Worst of all, she has no future prospects for her life except more drudgery."

Anthony frowned, displeased by the accusatory note in his sister's voice, as if Miss Wade's so-called drudgery were his fault. "The work Miss Wade does for me is crucial to the success of this project, and she is paid quite well for her efforts."

"Her future seems precarious to me."

"Hardly. The museum in London will be open in mid-March, but it will take far longer than that to finish the villa. She has employment here for the next five years, at least."

"And after that is finished? When your museum is complete and your excavation is done, what happens to her then?"

"She finds a new position, I suppose."

"By which time she will be nearly thirty, an age which virtually eliminates her chances of ever marrying. Did you know she is the granddaughter of a baron?"

"That is absurd. Her father had no such relations."

"I am talking of her mother's father. She knows no other details about him, or if she does, she did not wish to impart them to me. I do not believe she intended to tell me anything at all, but that bit about her grandfather slipped out. Why she should wish to keep it a secret, I do not understand. Pride, perhaps."

"Or a need for privacy. Some people do value

their privacy, Viola," he pointed out. "In any case, her future is her own affair."

"I am making it my affair." Before he could reply, she went on, "This is no sort of life for a baron's granddaughter, even if she has been left in virtual ignorance of her own background. Since she knows so little of her relations and she has no friends to help her—"

"She seems to have found a friend in you."

"Yes, she has. I like her, and we have become friends. In fact, I am envisioning her as a sort of protégée. I should like to introduce her into society, help her make new acquaintances, and perhaps even secure her matrimonial future. I know quite a few young men to whom I should like to introduce her. She might take a fancy to one of them, and nature will take its course."

"Poor girl."

Viola shot him a look that told him she did not find his dry comment amusing. "Not everyone chooses a wife as you do, Anthony, picking the one least likely to win your heart. Nor does everyone who falls in love end up unhappy. I should like to see Daphne have a season in London, have a romance of her own, and make a sensible and affectionate marriage to an honorable gentleman of good character who will love her and provide for her."

He felt compelled to mention the obvious. "I do not see why you wish to embark upon such a futile exercise. Women like Miss Wade are not made for romance, and they do not marry."

"Anthony, what an extraordinary remark. What on earth can you mean by it?"

"I mean, the girl hasn't a romantic bone in her body. If she had a dowry, or if her connection to this baron were established, her prospects for matrimony would be better, but without them, you are embarking on a hopeless business. One only has to look at the girl to know that."

"I do not know it, and I have looked at her quite a bit in the last day or two. I should imagine any number of well-bred young men would find her quite charming."

"Charming? With that horrible bun she wears and those dreary clothes, the girl's as noticeable as a stick insect on a twig. She is so much a part of the background, I doubt any man would even see her unless she were standing a foot in front of him, and even then, he would forget her the moment she was out of his line of vision. I know I do."

Viola stiffened. "I did not realize that a woman's physical beauty was the only quality that made her worthy of a man's attention," she said coldly.

Anthony felt the sting in those words. "I did not mean it that way."

"What did you mean?"

"Her face never changes expression, and you never know what she is thinking or feeling. Unless she is talking about artifacts, the girl cannot even carry on a conversation."

He saw Viola staring at him in dismay, but he went on, "When she does manage to get out a few words, she cannot seem to string them together without stammering. In truth, I do not know what came over her. The first day she was here, she talked well enough, but she has scarcely said a word since then. Taken all in all, she is the most insignificant creature I have ever met."

"Yet she is so important to your excavations that she cannot leave. Therefore, she must have some desirable qualities."

"She is intelligent, I grant you that, and excels at her work. She can translate Latin, Greek, and I do not know how many other ancient languages. She is an excellent mosaicist and restorer. She draws well. But those attributes hardly qualify her for matrimony. She has no dowry, no connections but a mythical baron, and no feminine appeal to make up for those deficiencies."

"She knows me, and if her grandfather is a baron, then she has two connections, at least. If we can find her grandfather, he might provide her with a dowry. As to her other so-called deficiencies, that is only your opinion. You see her as just another person employed by you, like Mr. Cox, or Mr. Bennington, or one of the servants. I doubt you have once looked at her as a woman."

"Miss Wade is not a woman. She is a machine. An efficient, well-ordered machine. She is never ill, she never makes mistakes. You know, I do not think I have ever heard her laugh."

"Oh, don't be absurd. I heard her laugh only this morning."

"I never have." Anthony paused, trying to think how to describe Miss Wade to Viola from a man's point of view. "When looking for a wife, a gentleman would not want a machine. He would want a woman with some womanly attributes. Miss Wade, unfortunately, has none. It is rather pathetic, really."

"I had no idea that you see her in such an unfavorable light," Viola said slowly.

"I believe any other man would share my opinion about the girl."

"Will you stop calling her a girl?" Viola countered with some irritation. "She is twenty-four. She is a woman."

Anthony thought of the shapeless apron that concealed any womanly shape Miss Wade might possess. "If you say so."

"I do say so. Everything you have mentioned is a flaw of upbringing, not character or beauty. I think Daphne could be quite pretty, with some proper advice from me. She has lovely eyes and a beautiful complexion. A bit too tanned for fashion, but surprisingly light if one considers she has lived so much of her life in the desert. She has a nice smile, she is intelligent and well-read, and I can assure you, that though she might be a rather serious young woman, and is perhaps a bit shy, she is quite capable of laughing."

"You had better find her connections, then, for plain, shy, serious young ladies who fade into the wallpaper do not catch husbands otherwise. They become spinsters. An unfortunate dictum, but true."

Viola gave him a cold stare that told him more

clearly than words what she thought of his opinion, and he felt a hint of self-reproach. Perhaps he was being harsh, but really, Daphne Wade was as drab as an English February. He decided it would be wise to give no further opinions on the subject. "It hardly matters, so let us not argue. The girl is not going anywhere until my museum and excavations are finished."

A stick insect on a twig.

Daphne felt frozen, her hand still poised to push open the door leading into the music room. The door was slightly ajar, and the conversation she had overheard hung in the air like the acrid smell of smoke that lingered after a fire.

No feminine appeal.

She stared down at the wax-coated wooden tablet in her other hand, her mind blank. Upon her soul, she could not remember now why she had been so excited to find Anthony and show this to him the very moment she had finished translating it. She couldn't even remember what it said.

Hugging the tablet to her chest, she turned away from the door and ran, unaware of where she was going, unable to force the coherent thought of a destination to the forefront of her mind. She was too dazed to think, too numb to feel, but she could hear, over and over again, the carelessly brutal opinion of her uttered by the man she adored.

Miss Wade isn't a woman. She's a machine. It's rather pathetic, really.

Like a moth blundering in lamplight, Daphne

stumbled her way through the maze of Tremore Hall's many corridors, only instinct guiding her to the refuge of her own bedchamber on the other side of the house.

Once inside the privacy of her own room, she slammed the door behind her, dropped the tablet heedlessly to the floor, and clamped her hands over her ears, but it was a futile gesture. She could still hear Anthony's words ringing in her ears, muted only by the sound of her own sobs as her heart fractured into pieces.

Chapter 5

The human heart must be a strong and resilient thing, Daphne decided when she awoke the following morning. She was surprised to find that she was no longer in the throes of wrenching heartbreak and pain. Instead, in a strange way, she felt as if she had been reborn.

She had spent the entire evening and most of the night crying into her pillow and nursing her broken heart. She had shed countless tears for the pain of Anthony's insulting words. She had told herself, more with defiance than sincerity, that this Lady Sarah he intended to marry was welcome to him. She had called herself all kinds of a fool for her unrealistic illusions. Most of all, she had grieved for the painful destruction of the hope in her heart, hope for Anthony's affections, hope that she had not even acknowledged to herself until his opinion of her had shattered it.

Now, though a vestige of pain still lingered, Daphne did not feel sad or foolish. She felt free.

As she dressed, she tried to understand herself, and she realized that it was as if a great weight had been lifted from her. She had spent the last five months trying to be what Anthony wanted, trying to anticipate and fill every need or desire he expressed to her, working like a slave to please him, and all it had gotten her was his indifferent scorn.

Daphne sat down at the dressing table in her room and stared idly at her reflection as she brushed out her hair. A rueful smile tipped her mouth. Anthony had called her pathetic, and she looked rather a sorry mess just now with her face all puffy from crying, but the only pathetic thing in this scenario was how much of herself she had wasted on him.

Anthony's words had been harsh, but they had made her understand something about herself, something that she had never seen before.

Since her mother's death, she had spent her life needing to be needed, trying to fill the void in her father's heart with the love her mother's death had taken from him, trying to be his partner in his work, trying to be the antidote to his grief. Here, she had tried to do the same with Anthony, desperately wanting him to need her, wanting him to make her feel valued, appreciated, loved.

As noticeable as a stick insect on a twig.

Now, in the light of a new day, she vowed that

things would be different. She remembered Viola's questions in the antika yesterday, and she realized they led to a much more fundamental one.

What now?

Daphne turned in her chair and surveyed the room around her, a room that was ornate to the point of opulence. The gold and green damask draperies around her bed, the paneled walls and fireplace mantel of carved rosewood, the elaborate moldings of angels on the ceiling, the malachite-topped dressing table where she sat, and the painted urns of peacock feathers. Like all the other rooms at Tremore Hall, it was large and overpowering, conveying immense wealth and a true sense of history, but it was a house with little warmth. *Rather like its owner*, she thought. He thought to marry without any sort of love or affection. How cold he must be, and how blind she had been never to have seen that aspect of his character before.

Daphne returned her attention to her reflection in the mirror, met her own gaze, and made her first decision about her future. She had to leave Tremore Hall. She could not stay here. To be near that wretched man, to continue to work for him like a slave for the next five years, knowing the disdain with which he regarded her, was an intolerable prospect.

But where else could she go? What could she do? She had done excavation work all her life. For the first time, she began to wonder if there were other possibilities for her future.

I should love it if you could come with me to Enderby.

Daphne remembered the viscountess's words of yesterday in the antika. She also went over what she had overheard of Viola's plans for her, and she felt a spark of excitement. The viscountess had admitted being lonely. She envisioned Daphne as a sort of protégée, and wanted to find her a husband. Perhaps she would agree to allow Daphne to stay with her for a time, introduce her to people, help her form some connections. Who knew what might happen? With the viscountess to guide her, she could gain a great deal of experience with the ways of good society, ways she had only read about in books.

Perhaps this opportunity would enable her to become a governess to a wealthy family. Or perhaps she should swallow her pride and make another attempt to unite with her grandfather. She might even fulfill Viola's matchmaking hopes and find someone to marry, someone who truly loved her and wanted her.

Daphne decided it was time to stop believing she had no choices for her future. It was time to begin deciding her own destiny. Perhaps it was even time to have a bit of fun.

She would leave here and enter the glittering world of English society. As for Anthony, he could go hang, and his opinions with him.

"I beg your pardon?" Viola set down her quill and stared at Daphne in complete astonishment.

Daphne knew she was being quite bold, but she was desperate. "Yesterday you mentioned how you wished I could go with you to Enderby when you leave here. Given our short acquaintance, I know it is presumptuous of me to ask, but did you mean it?"

Viola recovered herself and gestured to the chair opposite the writing desk in her room. "Do sit down, Daphne."

Daphne took the offered chair, crossed her fingers in her lap, and waited for an answer.

"Of course I meant it," Viola said, "but what about your position here?"

"I intend to resign my post."

"I thought you loved it at Tremore Hall." Viola stiffened in her chair and gave Daphne a sharp look. "Has something untoward happened since yesterday?"

"No, not at all," she hastened to assure the other woman, hoping she sounded convincing. She could not bear it if Viola or Anthony learned she had overheard their conversation and the duke's low opinion of her. "I have enjoyed it here, but your words of yesterday about London have made me realize all that I have missed."

Viola leaned back against the mahogany chair in which she was seated. "My dear Daphne, I am all astonishment. I had no idea my words would provoke such a reaction."

There was a hint of dismay in the other woman's voice, and Daphne's heart sank. Perhaps the viscountess's words about friendship had been lightly spoken. Perhaps she had been talking about her with Anthony for obscure reasons of her own. Nonetheless, Daphne knew she had to leave Tremore Hall, and Viola was her best chance of doing so. "Since my father's death, my life has been following an inevitable path over which I have had little control."

"Because you are a woman," the viscountess said, an almost acerbic note in her voice. "We have little control over our lives."

"Perhaps, but I have been turning our conversation over and over in my mind, and I cannot help but feel that it is time I found my mother's family and took my rightful place in society."

"Of course! I said as much yesterday, but you were adamant about staying here. Are you certain you wish to do this?"

"Yes. I have never had the chance to enjoy good society or make friends, for Papa and I were always moving. Here, I am buried in the country working alone all the day long and never meeting anyone."

"Of course you must be very lonely here, and earning a living is beneath a baron's granddaughter. I confess I had been thinking how delightful it would be to reunite you with your family and help you to come out into society. But I had thought your feelings—" She broke off, not voicing whatever she had been about to say. Instead, she looked down, fingering the quill pen on her desk, lost in thought. Daphne waited, silent, hoping the viscountess's seeming reluctance did not mean she would refuse.

After a moment, Viola looked up. "Have you discussed this with the duke?"

"No. I felt I should speak with you first."

She nodded. "I told you I would be delighted to have you at Enderby, and I would not have said it if I did not mean it. However, Anthony will not like it. What will he do without you?"

Daphne bit back the tart reply that Anthony would not waste one moment grieving her departure. "He will be able to find someone else for the post."

"But not someone as excellent as you. Why, only the other night he was telling Sir Edward and me how skilled you are at your work. He admires your knowledge and intelligence very much."

And that was all he admired, since she was a stick insect with no feminine appeal. Daphne did not want to think about his opinion ever again. In the light of a new day, remembering his words made her want to bash him over the head with one of his Samarian wine jars.

"This excavation and the museum he intends to endow with the artifacts means a great deal to my brother," Viola went on. "He intends to retain you until the project is finished, and he will not want you to leave."

Daphne did not care tuppence for what Anthony wanted. "He will have no choice."

"Anthony has been a duke since he was twelve years old. He is accustomed by a lifetime of experience to getting his way."

"He cannot force me to stay."

"Oh, Daphne, you underestimate the power of a duke. News of your departure will displease him enormously, especially when he learns I am the one taking you away."

Daphne's heart sank. "I should hate to be the cause of any rift between you and your brother," she said, trying to hide her dismay. "I understand if you wish to retract your invitation."

Viola considered the situation for a moment, then she shook her head. "I shall do no such thing! To my mind, it is unconscionable that a young woman who is the daughter of a knight and the granddaughter of a baron should have to earn her living. You deserve your rightful place in society, and Anthony is only being selfish. It will be my pleasure to have you at Enderby."

Daphne's relief was so great, she nearly sagged in her chair. "Thank you. I am in your debt."

"Not at all. I shall enjoy your company very much. All I ask is that when you resign your post, you give Anthony a month's notice of your departure. He will need time to find someone to replace you."

Another month here, knowing Anthony's contempt for her, would be hard to bear, but she had no choice. "Of course."

Viola picked up her quill and scrawled something on a sheet of paper. "I shall be leaving here shortly and going to Chiswick. I will anticipate your arrival there in about a month. If you change your mind, write to me at this direction."

Daphne took the sheet the other woman held out to her. "I will not change my mind."

"Do not be so certain of that. This excavation business is very important to Anthony, and he will not like losing you. I know my brother very well. He can be very persuasive when he chooses. And very determined."

Daphne did not reply to that. She was leaving, and there was nothing more to say.

Anthony sank the spade into the ground with care, working to remove the earth without damaging any treasures that might lay buried in the ancient room beneath his feet.

He was probably the only peer in all of Britain who truly enjoyed physical labor such as this, he thought, as he pressed his boot down onto the spade and lifted another shovelful of damp earth. Most of his acquaintances would be shocked to see him now, covered in dirt with his shirt off, his body damp with sweat.

He dumped the shovelful of dirt into the wood-framed screen box beside him, and as he did so, he caught sight of Miss Wade approaching, weaving her way amid the workmen and the half-uncovered walls of the excavation. He paused and reached for his shirt, pulling it over his head as she came up to him.

"Could I speak with you a moment?" she asked. "It is rather important."

"Is something amiss with the artifacts?" he asked as he lifted his arm to wipe the perspiration from his forehead with his sleeve.

"No. This is not about the artifacts. This is a personal matter. Could we speak privately?"

Her words surprised him. For one thing, Miss Wade seldom said more than two words together. Second, he could not imagine her having any personal matters, particularly not ones she would wish to discuss with him. His curiosity aroused, he walked with her to the antika. "What is it you wish to discuss?" he asked once they were inside.

"I—" she began, then stopped and closed her mouth, looking straight ahead, staring into the cleft of his unbuttoned shirt as if she were looking right through him. The sunlight through the windows glinted off the lenses of her spectacles, preventing him from looking into her eyes, and the rest of her countenance, as usual, revealed no hint of what she was thinking. He waited.

The silence lengthened. Impatient to return to his work, Anthony cleared his throat, and that got her attention. She took a deep breath, lifted her face, and said the last thing he would have expected.

"I am resigning my post here."

"What?" Anthony knew he could not have heard her correctly. "What do you mean?"

"I am leaving." She reached into the pocket of her heavy work apron and pulled out a folded sheet of paper. "I have here my letter of resignation."

He stared at the folded sheet of paper she held out, but he did not take it from her hand. Instead, he folded his arms across his chest, and said the only thing he could think of. "I refuse to accept it."

A flicker of consternation crossed her face, a hint

of emotion from the machine. He was even more taken aback.

"But you can't refuse," she said, frowning. "You can't."

"Unless the king tells me no, I can do anything I want," he said, hoping he sounded quite smug. "I am a duke, after all."

That reply only disconcerted her for a moment. "Is your lofty rank supposed to intimidate me, your grace?" she asked in her quiet voice, a surprising hint of anger in it he had never heard before. She slapped the letter against his chest, and when he did not take it, she pulled her hand back and let the paper float to the floor. "I am resigning my position. I will be leaving one month from now."

She started to turn away, but his voice stopped her. "Where are you going, in heaven's name? If you have been persuaded away by some other excavation—"

"I will be staying with Lady Hammond at Enderby. She is going to introduce me into society and help me find my mother's family."

That was just as ridiculous now as it had been last night when his sister had suggested it. There were only seven months before the opening of the museum. Seven short months in which they had an enormous amount of work to do.

Damn Viola's sudden interest in romantic endeavors. She knew how important this excavation was to him, and also how crucial Miss Wade's expertise was to getting it completed. He had no intention of letting this little scheme of theirs go any further.

"I can appreciate your desire to find your connections, Miss Wade, but you can easily make inquiries about your relations from here. Viola will not carry out any plans involving your departure from here without my consent. I refuse to give it, and will tell her so."

A smile he could not help but describe as triumphant curved her lips. "Lady Hammond said that all I needed to do was speak with you and officially resign my post, giving you one month to find a replacement." She gestured to the letter on the floor. "Now I have done so."

"Find a replacement? God, woman, people like you do not grow on trees! You know perfectly well that anyone with your skill at restoration is committed to a project years in advance. It took me three years to get your father. The museum opens in seven months, and you know the villa will take at least five years. Replacing you is impossible at this point. I have assured the Society of Antiquarians that this museum will be opened in time for the London season, so that we might generate as much interest as possible. I will not have the opening delayed a year because you've got it into your head all of a sudden to go off to London in search of a husband and the frivolous amusements of society. You cannot leave until this project is finished. I have obligations to fulfill, and I have given my word."

"You, you, you!" she cried, an outburst that astonished him, not only because she dared to speak to him in such a way, but also because it was the first display of real emotion he had ever witnessed from her. "You may be a duke, but you are not the sun around which the world revolves. In fact, you are quite the opposite, for you are the most selfish man I have ever known. Inconsiderate, too, for you order your servants and staff about without so much as a please or a thank you. You care nothing for the feelings of others, and you are arrogant enough to believe that your rank entitles you to behave that way. I—" She broke off and wrapped her arms around herself as if attempting to contain her emotions. As well she should, for this torrent of inexplicable criticism was both unjustified and unpardonable.

He opened his mouth to dress her down for her impudence, as he would any other person in his employ, but she spoke before he had the chance to do so. "The plain truth, your grace, is that I do not like you, and I do not wish to work for you any longer. Speak to Lady Hammond if you wish, but I am leaving in one month regardless of whether or not you forbid her to help me."

Anthony watched her back as she walked out of the antika without another word, not knowing quite whether to go after her or go after Viola for putting idiotic notions into her head. In the end, he did neither.

Instead, he bent down and retrieved Miss Wade's letter of resignation from the floor. He opened it and scanned the two lines written in her precise and perfect script.

As he refolded the letter, a memory came into his mind of the day she had arrived at Tremore Hall five months earlier. Today was not the first time

Miss Wade had given him cause for surprise.

For a long time, he had wanted to excavate the Roman remains on his estate, and had envisioned a museum in which to put them. Not just a place for the wealthy and privileged to view a part of their history, but one open to British citizens of all classes. There was nothing else like it in London.

Sir Henry Wade had been widely acknowledged as the best antiquarian living, and Anthony had wanted the best for his excavation. He had spent three years trying to persuade Sir Henry to take on the villa excavation and the restoration of its antiquities, to no avail. He had been forced to use other, much less skilled restorers, and he had found their expertise woefully inadequate, but he had persisted in his attempts to persuade Sir Henry to return to England and take over the project, and the man had finally agreed to come.

But it had not been that eminent gentleman he had found waiting for him in the anteroom off of Tremore's great hall that March day five months ago. Standing amid the stone statues, green marble columns, and crystal chandeliers of the anteroom, he had found a young woman with a round, solemn face and gold-rimmed spectacles, a woman who had proclaimed to his house steward that she was Sir Henry's daughter. Dressed in a worn brown traveling cloak, wearing brown boots of heavy leather and a wide-brimmed straw hat, with a plain black portmanteau at her feet, she had looked as dry as the Moroccan desert from which she had come.

In a soft, well-bred voice that displayed no discernible personal feeling, she had told him of her father's death and her arrival here to take Sir Henry's place and complete his excavation.

His immediate refusal should have sent her scurrying for the door, but it had not. She had ignored his words as if he had not spoken at all. She had told him of her knowledge and experience in a recital of concise facts, listing in methodical fashion all the reasons why he should allow her to step into what would have been her father's position.

When he had finally interrupted her, stating in the most icy tone a duke could command that he had chosen her father because he had wanted the best antiquarian available and he had no intention of hiring her without her father, she had not pleaded with him. She had not tried to play on his sympathy or his chivalry with some heartbreaking story about how she had nothing and no one and needed the job. She had merely blinked at him through those spectacles, staring at him with that inscrutable face and looking for all the world like a solemn baby owl as she had replied in utter seriousness, "I am the best available."

His disbelieving laugh had gone right by her, for she had continued, "I am the daughter of Sir Henry Wade, and he was the best. I was trained by him, and now that he is gone, there is no one more qualified for this post than I."

He had never intended to hire her, but he had few options. For the sake of expedience, he had agreed, and for the sake of propriety, he had brought Mr.

and Mrs. Bennington from one of the lodges on the estate into the house, so that Mrs. Bennington might act as her chaperone.

During the five months Miss Wade had been here, he had come to realize that her words had been no idle boast. She knew more about ancient Roman antiquities than he could ever hope to know. She was an excellent mosaicist, and her fresco work was perfection itself. He had wanted the best, and as she had so bluntly told him, he had gotten it.

Anthony came out of his reverie and crumpled the letter in his hand into a ball. Until this project was complete, Miss Wade was not going anywhere. When he had the best, he was damn well going to keep it.

Chapter 6

Viola had predicted Anthony would not like the idea of Daphne resigning, and the moment he came storming into her sitting room scarcely an hour after Daphne's departure, she knew her prediction had been an accurate one. He was frowning like thunder.

"Miss Wade is leaving," he said without ceremony. "What have you been up to?"

Viola looked up from her letters to glance at her maid, Celeste, who had paused in her task of repairing a torn hem on one of her gowns, then back at Anthony. "If we are going to have a row," she said calmly, "I should not like to do so in front of a servant."

Anthony turned to the maid. "Leave us," he ordered, and the girl stuck the last pin into the dressmaker's model, bobbed a quick curtsy to both of them, and left her mistress alone with the duke, closing the door behind her.

Viola studied her brother for a moment, noting his narrowed eyes and the grim set of his mouth. Oh, yes, he was very angry indeed. Even to her, it was a bit intimidating.

"I really don't know what you mean," she finally said. "Daphne came to me and said she had decided to resign her post. She told me of her intention to find her grandfather, move in society, and perhaps begin meeting suitable young gentlemen. She asked for my assistance. What was I to do?"

"Refuse. That seems to be an obvious choice."

"I would not do such a thing. She is a baron's granddaughter."

"Perhaps. We do not know that."

Viola shrugged as if it did not matter. "A knight's daughter then," she amended, smiling. "I like her, we have become friends, and I think she deserves to be given the opportunity to find her family. She is no common servant sent up from the orphanage. She is a young lady, and she deserves to take her place in society."

"Cannot this little venture of yours wait until spring? Or better still, five years or so?"

"How heartless you are, Anthony!" Viola rebuked. "Five years will serve to eliminate her chances in the marriage mart altogether. Besides, she wishes to go, and you cannot blame her for wanting to establish her connection to her grandfather. I told her if she was determined to this course, of course I would assist her, but she needed to speak with you first."

He shot her a shrewd, knowing look. "You encouraged her to resign."

"I did not refuse to help her, if that is what you mean. Daphne must be allowed to claim her birthright."

"That is not what I meant. You talked to her about how exciting London is, how amusing the balls and parties are, offered to help her find a husband and all that rot. God only knows what silly ideas you have put into her head."

"There is nothing silly about a young lady wishing for company and society and wanting to find a husband. She is very lonely here, you know."

"That is hardly the point," he answered. "You know how important this museum and excavation are. You know I have obligations to complete this project. I cannot believe you would do this, Viola."

She spread her hands wide and donned an air of bewilderment. "Anthony, you seem quite put out. I fail to understand why you should care one way or the other. All you need do is replace her."

"Miss Wade is not replaceable. She is vital to the success of this project, and she is not going anywhere for at least the next seven months. Five years, if I have my way."

Viola began to laugh. "My dear brother, you cannot make her stay against her will. Slavery is against the law, you know."

He was clearly not amused. "When I hired her,

she took on an obligation to me through the completion of this project. She intends to break her promise to me, yet she had the impudence to call me inconsiderate."

"She did?" Viola was astonished. Anthony's position was so high that most people, including herself, would not dare speak to him in such a way. "I can scarce believe it."

"Believe it, for that is what she said. I do not say please and thank you, she said. I am inconsiderate, arrogant, and—what was it?—selfish. Yes, that was it. She said she was resigning because she did not want to work for me any longer."

He sounded outraged—baffled, too, without any comprehension of Daphne's point of view. Viola was a bit confused herself. What on earth could have prompted Daphne to speak in such a fashion? She seemed such a serene, steady sort of person. "Anthony, when she told you she was resigning, what did you do? Bully her, I suppose."

"Indeed, I did not. I simply reminded her of her duty to me and my obligation to the Society. She flew into an inexplicable temper, and leveled all manner of insults at my head. Who is she to speak so?"

Though still puzzled by what had prompted Daphne's sudden desire to leave Hampshire, Viola could read between the lines where her brother was concerned, and she no longer needed to wonder what had sparked Daphne's temper on having her resignation refused. He had probably gone on and on about what mattered to him, without a thought for what mattered to her.

Viola almost wanted to laugh. She had a great deal of affection for Anthony, but he did have his faults, which Daphne had clearly not hesitated to point out to him. Despite the other woman's quiet reserve, Viola was developing a high degree of respect for her. Reserved, perhaps, but quite able to speak her mind, and stand up to Anthony.

"What was the girl thinking?" he demanded, turning away to pace back and forth in front of his sister. "Does she not understand her place? God, does she not know what I could do to her for this?"

Viola studied him as he moved back and forth in such high dungeon, and she realized she had never seen him quite like this before. Undoubtedly, he had never heard such criticism in his life, and was so outraged by it that his usual coolness and self-possession had deserted him. Daphne had truly gotten under his skin, probably because everything she had said was true, and deep down, he knew it.

"A duke saying please and thank you," he went on. "How ridiculous is that?"

Viola was too preoccupied to reply. A thought suddenly occurred to her, a thought that seemed incredible at first, but which took hold with such force that she could not set it aside. Oh, how delightful if he could be persuaded to marry Daphne instead of Lady Sarah.

The more Viola thought about that idea, the better she liked it. If Daphne was indeed the granddaughter of a baron, her suitability would be disapproved only by a few high sticklers. Viola knew from that look she had caught on Daphne's face the other day that she was a woman of passionate feeling, despite her outward demeanor. She was head over ears in love with Anthony already. She also seemed to know her own mind, and she had the temerity to stand up to a duke. That boded well for future happiness. Of course, his unfair impression of her had to be overcome, as well as her decision to leave and her new, unexpected animosity toward him, a feeling that puzzled Viola. Where had it come from?

"Oh, good lord!" she exclaimed as a realization suddenly struck her. "Of course. How could I have been so blind not to see at once?"

"That is what I want to know," Anthony's voice intruded, and made her realize she had spoken aloud. "I am quite put out with you, Viola, as well as with her. What were you thinking?"

Viola tore herself away from her dismayed realization long enough to reply, "I am sorry, Anthony, if you feel put out."

Daphne must have overheard their conversation in the music room, their conversation about her. That explained everything. No wonder she wanted to leave with such haste. No wonder she wanted to go into society and find suitors to soothe her wounded pride. No wonder she dared to throw criticism back at Anthony. What woman would not retaliate for the comparison to a stick insect?

"You should have at least consulted me," he tossed out at her as he continued to pace. "She had the gall to say she is leaving because she does not like me, Viola. Deuce take it, who is this chit to like me or not? Who does she think she is?"

"A woman who is not afraid to tell you what she thinks of you, obviously." As much as she hoped her brother could be made to revise his assessment of Daphne, she wondered if it would matter in any case. Daphne had been in love with him, Viola was sure of it, which made her wounded pride all the harder to heal.

Bringing the pair together suddenly seemed a hopeless business, and Viola's heart sank. Daphne was a warm and loving person, and she would make Anthony so much happier than Sarah ever could. "She is entitled to her opinion, Anthony."

He shot her an angry glance as he paced. "You are partly responsible for the entire situation. I expect you to retract your offer to the girl at once."

Viola folded her arms and gave her brother the stubborn look characteristic of their family tree. "I will do no such thing. If Daphne chooses to come to stay with me, I will not gainsay her."

Anthony stopped pacing and faced her with all that ducal intimidation. "You intend to defy me?"

She stood her ground. "I intend to do what is right. Daphne deserves to find her relations and take her place in society. I have offered to help her in that task, and I have invited her to stay at Chiswick with me. I will introduce her into society, assist her to make appropriate acquaintances, and introduce her to eligible young men. I will not take back that invitation simply because you will be inconvenienced. If you do not want her to leave, I suggest you find a way to persuade her to stay. If you can."

The moment she said those words, Viola felt a ray of hope return. Anthony had never been one to refuse a challenge. As she expected, her brother met her gaze and replied, "I can, and I will."

"Might I suggest," Viola added, smiling, "that in persuading her to stay, you make use of the charming aspects of your character? You might have better success in changing her mind if you remember that she is a woman with needs and feelings and dreams of her own. Though she might be an excellent antiquarian, Daphne is not a machine. If you got to know her, you might come to understand her, which would only serve to help your cause."

He did not react to having his own description of Daphne thrown back at him, nor did he seem to appreciate her advice. Instead, he started for the door. "I will keep your counsel in mind."

"Good. Then I think I will go on to Chiswick in the morning, so that I do not get involved in this any further."

"Excellent." He paused in the doorway to look at her over his shoulder. "I shall be down to London in a few months, and will pay a visit to Enderby to see you then. In the interim, if Hammond does anything—"

"I shall inform you at once."

"Good."

Viola watched her brother go, and she hoped her notion to bring Daphne and Anthony together would succeed. Matchmaking was a tricky business, but she thought this match at least had a chance. Granted, Daphne wasn't beautiful like

Lady Sarah, but she was attractive in her own way. She shared Anthony's most important interests in life. She had the intelligence and good sense necessary to run the vast households of a duke with ease. She had passion and a warm, tender heart. Though he did not realize it now, Daphne was a woman who could make him happy. If it came about, theirs would be an excellent match.

She summoned Celeste to begin packing her things. She had done all she could to ensure Anthony's future happiness, and she would have to content herself with that. Perhaps she would write a letter or two along the way to move the pair in the right direction, but love, if it was destined between these two, would have to happen on its own. She knew the best thing she could do for now was get out of the way.

In addition to helping Anthony find a loving wife, there was also the benefit of prevailing over Lady Sarah Monforth, one of the most worthless young women in England. The idea of that sweet triumph made Viola smile.

Daphne watched as a pair of workmen carried a large section of mosaic flooring through the doorway into the antika. She winced as the corner of it hit the door jamb, chipping off a tiny piece of the pavement. "Oh, please be careful."

"Never say please to the workmen," a low voice murmured in her ear. "If you do, they will not respect you."

The sound of Anthony's voice right behind her

almost made her jump, and Daphne turned around. "I appreciate the advice, your grace," she said, "but since I have been around workmen all my life, I believe I can manage to get a pair of them to move a mosaic pavement without assistance."

She walked away, but she could still feel Anthony's gaze on her back as she followed the men inside the antika. "Thank you," she said as they laid the pavement on her largest worktable. "Now, I need—"

"Leave us," Anthony interrupted from behind her.

The two men immediately moved to obey, ignoring Daphne's sound of protest. She frowned at him as the workmen left the building. "I do not suppose it occurred to you to inquire if I had any further need of their help before you dismissed them?"

"No," he answered with characteristic bluntness. "I wanted to speak with you in private, so I sent them away."

"Do you always get what you want?"

Daphne watched his dark brows lift in surprise at her impertinence, and she could not suppress a hint of satisfaction. Being indifferent to him was so easy, now that she didn't care for him any more.

"Usually," he answered. "Perhaps because I am arrogant, inconsiderate, and selfish. Or so I have been told."

Having her own words quoted back to her was a bit disconcerting, but if he expected an apology, he was mistaken.

"All dukes are like that," he went on. "It is the way we are raised, you see. It comes from a lifetime of being surrounded by people who wait to gratify every whim and obey every order without question. Do not expect any duke to behave otherwise."

She bowed her head in deference to his superior knowledge of dukes. "With you as my example, your grace, I assure you I will not."

He made a choked sound that sounded suspiciously like a laugh, and Daphne's sense of satisfaction evaporated. She had wanted her words to sting.

"I see you have found your tongue at last, Miss Wade," he commented, a wry note in his voice.

"I was unaware I had lost it," she answered at once. "To my knowledge, it has remained in my mouth for the whole of my life."

"A fact I am just now discovering," he murmured, and took a step closer to her, but she refused to step back. She returned his study of her with a level, steady gaze of her own.

"Your eyes are not blue," he said, sounding as if he had just discovered something unexpected. "They are lavender."

Daphne's heart slammed against her breastbone and all her newfound confidence deserted her. There was something in his eyes, something in his voice, that hurt, that made her remember the woman she had been yesterday, a woman blissfully unaware of how heartbreak felt.

She drew a deep, steadying breath. That woman was gone, and the woman who had taken her place was not going to feel any pain because of him. Not ever again. "Surely your grace did not seek me out to comment on the color of my eyes."

When he did not reply, she turned away. Over her shoulder, she added, "Whatever you wish to discuss, I hope you don't mind if I work while we talk."

Daphne took his silence for acceptance. She did not make any attempt to guess why he wanted to speak with her. It could be about her resignation, or something to do with the excavation. She really did not care. She just wanted him to go away.

She walked to the table where the mosaic the workmen had brought in lay waiting for her to begin repairs. She examined the pail of resinous cement she had mixed a short while earlier, stirring it with a wooden paddle to make certain it was the right consistency. Satisfied, she lifted the lid of the large wooden tile box that rested on the table to the right of the mosaic. All the loose floor tiles that had been sifted from the excavated ground of the villa where this mosaic had been found were sorted into the various sections of the boxes by color. Now she needed to begin selecting the ones she would use to fill in the missing places of the mosaic.

As she pulled out various half-inch cubes of blue and green marble and compared them to the oceanic background of the mosaic, she waited for Anthony to speak, but when he did not, she looked over at him to find he was still watching her. "You said you wanted to talk with me," she prompted.

"Yes, of course." He seemed to come out of his reverie and walked to her side. "My sister has left Tremore Hall for Chiswick."

"Yes, I know," Daphne answered as she selected

two tiles of serpentine green and cobalt blue from the box. "She said good-bye to me a short while ago as her carriage was being brought round." She could not resist adding, "I shall see her again in a month."

"That is why I wanted to speak with you." He paused, then said, "Miss Wade, despite the fact that you are a woman, I have come to have a high regard for your abilities as an antiquarian and a scholar."

Daphne thought of all the hours she had worked to prove herself and gain his respect. And now, when it was too late, he was finally giving her a tiny scrap of that respect. Was she supposed to be impressed by such condescension? "Thank you, your grace. And despite the fact that you are a duke, you appear to have some actual knowledge of antiquities."

This time, he did laugh, making no effort to smother his amusement. "Yes, you have a tongue, indeed, for now that you are leaving, you are not attempting to curb it for my sake."

No reply was required of her, and she did not make one. Instead, she kept her attention on her work. She began comparing the tiles in her hand to the ones already set in the mortar by the gap she would fill in, choosing those she felt made the best match. As she worked, she tried to ignore the man standing beside her. She wished he would say whatever he had come to say and then leave. It seemed an eternity before he spoke.

"I would like you to stay."

Her left hand tightened around the tiles in her palm, but only for a moment. What he wanted did not matter to her any longer. "No."

Hoping the matter was now resolved, Daphne bent down for a closer comparison of two tiles. "A bit too green, I think," she murmured as she straightened and set the discarded cube aside. She reached toward the box, but before she could select a new tile, Anthony's fingers curled over her wrist, stopping her.

"You cannot refuse to at least give me the opportunity to change your mind," he said.

"It would be a waste of time. I am leaving."

"What has prompted this sudden desire to go?" His thumb caressed her wrist, and Daphne felt her pulse quicken in response. Angry with herself, she pulled her wrist free of his grasp.

"My reasons are not your concern."

"Viola told me about your grandfather. If you wish him to acknowledge you, I can be of assistance in that regard. If you stay long enough to finish my excavation, I would use my influence to bring him to heel."

She would die before she would accept help from him. "I do not need any such assistance from you, your grace. I should like my grandfather to acknowledge me because it is the right thing for him to do, not because he was intimidated into it by a man of higher rank. Besides, I do not want to stay here. I have been working on excavation sites all my life, and I want a change of scene. I want to make new acquaintances."

"And find a husband as well, I hear."

Daphne stiffened at those words. She could not detect any hint of ridicule in his voice, but he must be laughing at the very idea that someone might want to marry her. "I see nothing wrong with that."

"If marriage is your goal, Miss Wade, pray let me dissuade you from it. It is far better in life to remain unencumbered if possible."

"Thank you for your cynical view on the subject, your grace, but it is not a view I share. I would like to believe that marriage is a partnership of mutual love, respect, and companionship, not an encumbrance. And as I have said, there are several reasons why I am resigning my post."

"Then I won't waste words trying to convince you to abandon any of them. All I wish is to convince you to delay them until my excavation is finished, or at least until the museum is opened."

When she did not reply but continued sorting tiles as if he had not spoken, he moved closer to her, close enough that every time she moved her arm, her elbow brushed against him. "I thought you enjoyed your work, Miss Wade," he murmured. "I thought you were happy here."

Daphne went still, seized by a sudden doubt. She had been happy, she had enjoyed her work, work that was comfortable and familiar, work in which she took great pride. She was about to leave all that and enter a very different world. With his words, she couldn't help wondering if she was doing the right thing.

But all that had changed yesterday, her happiness

had been spoiled, and she did not want to work for a man who regarded her with so little respect. "There is nothing you could say or do that would convince me to stay here longer than one more month."

"I will double your wages."

"No."

"I will triple them."

She paused in her task with an exasperated sigh and turned her head to look at him. "Are you simply unable to comprehend the word *no*?"

"I do have a difficult time with that particular word," he conceded.

"I'm not surprised," she answered, resuming her work. "You probably do not hear it very often."

"Rarely," he agreed. "I am arrogant, I daresay," he went on, "and everything else of which you accused me. I admit it freely, Miss Wade. I ask that you overlook my flaws, accept my offer to triple your salary, and stay."

Daphne was not impressed by his insincere attempts at self-deprecation, and she would not give an inch with him ever again. "When it comes to persistence, your grace, the children selling sham lapis beads in the streets of Cairo could take lessons from you, but my answer is still no."

"Can you not stay at least through March? I have promised my colleagues that this museum will be open by the fifteenth of that month. I need the best people I can find for this project. You are your father's daughter, and as you once assured me yourself, you are the best restorer available. I could not possibly find anyone to replace you whose skills are equal to yours."

She was unmoved by flattery. "That," she said coolly, "is your problem."

"True." He took a step back from her and said nothing more. The silence lengthened, and she hoped he had finally accepted her resignation. But after a moment, he spoke again, and his words made her realize he hadn't accepted it at all.

"I would like to propose a compromise."

Chapter 7

The man truly was impossible. Daphne tossed down the tiles in her hand, scattering them across the chipped, cracked surface of the mosaic and turned to face him. "I have no intention of making any compromises with you."

"Hear me out. If you stay, I will not only triple your salary, I will also pay you a bonus."

She made a sound of disdain. "That is not a compromise. That's you thinking you can buy anything you want."

"I usually can. Another characteristic of dukes, I fear."

The prudent, practical side of her character was tempted to ask how much of a bonus, but she did not. "You cannot buy me."

"Proud words, Miss Wade. And what if you do not find your family? If you do not find a husband with whom to have this partnership of mutual love and companionship you seek? What then? You cannot stay with Viola forever."

"Then I will find employment. I will learn all I can of good society and become a governess."

"You already have employment, and the work you do here is far more interesting than that of a governess. I assure you that governesses earn far less than I am paying you and they have a very difficult time of it. You would not wish to be a governess. Trust me on that, Miss Wade."

"I would not trust you on anything, your grace."

"Because you do not like me?"

"Precisely."

He did not seem at all put out. "Then, if I wish you to remain, I am forced to make myself more likeable to you and more worthy of your liking and trust."

"Do not waste your time. I will not stay. If I have no other choice, I will find another excavation on which to work. I am sure your sister knows many wealthy people who have buried Roman ruins on their country estates. I am sure a few of them would like those sites excavated. It seems to be quite the fashion in Britain."

"And you think any of them will hire you?"

"Why would they not?" she countered smoothly. "You did."

"This is ridiculous," he said, impatience with her inflexible resolve creeping into his voice. "Why go off to Chiswick and London when any and all of your goals can be met during the remainder of your time here? You have your Sundays out to make new acquaintances. I am certain Mrs. Bennington would introduce you to the townspeople."

"How exciting for me. And I suppose in the coming months, you would parade suitable young gentlemen of your acquaintance before me so that I might find a marriage partner?"

He didn't blink an eye. "If you like."

"Oh!" she cried, goaded beyond endurance. "You are the most selfish man I have ever known! If you think I would accept such a ridiculous proposition—"

"I will pay you five hundred pounds."

Daphne blinked. "I beg your pardon?"

"Stay until my excavations are finished, and I will pay you a bonus of five hundred pounds."

Daphne sucked in a deep breath. "You are joking. That is an enormous sum."

"It is also a dowry. Many peers are stone broke. Your grandfather, even if he should acknowledge you, may not be in the position to provide you with a dowry, so I have done so. Now, I have offered everything you claim you want. Will you reconsider my offer of a compromise and stay?"

Daphne looked down, staring down at the tops of Anthony's polished black boots. Five hundred pounds was an amount she had never seen in her life before.

What if, despite Viola's influence, her mother's family refused to acknowledge her? What if, God forbid, her parents had not been married and she was illegitimate? She did not know Viola well enough to rely on her should either of those possibilities come to pass. What if she once again found herself with nothing and no one?

She thought of that dingy little hotel room in Tangier where she had stayed for eight weeks after her father's death. Papa had left almost no money when he died. She had sold his books and equipment to support herself as long as she could. When she was down to only enough dirham for another week and the letter had come from her grandfather's attorney with an answer that gave her no hope, Daphne had never been more frightened in her life. The only belongings she had left were a small trunk of her clothes and two passage billets to England paid by the Duke of Tremore.

It had never occurred to her before those months alone in Tangier just what a frightening place the world could be for a woman who had no family, no money, and no one to whom she could turn for help. She had been only a hair's breadth away from destitution, and she never wanted to be in such a precarious position again.

Anthony waited, and she could feel his gaze on her as she struggled to make a choice. She resented the complacency with which he had thrown five hundred pounds in her face, certain she would take it. He knew perfectly well that such a sum was a fortune to her and a mere trifle to him.

Perhaps she should accept. It would be far more

prudent to throw her injured pride to the wind and take his offer than risk the unknown, uncertain future.

Daphne hardened her resolve, shored up her pride, and decided just how far she would go. She lifted her chin, looked Anthony in the eye, and said, "Let me give you my version of a compromise, your grace. I will stay until December first, three months instead of one. I will repair and restore as many artifacts for your museum as I can at a reasonable pace. In addition, until I leave, I will assist you in finding the most qualified person possible to see your project through to completion. In exchange, you will treble my salary for these three months, give me a second day off each week—Thursdays will do nicely—and pay me the stipend of five hundred pounds."

"Only two additional months for triple your wages, five hundred pounds, and another day off in which not to work for it? You must be mad."

"That amount of money is little enough to you. Mad or not, that is my offer."

"Are you certain you do not wish to add some other demands to this compromise? Saturday afternoons free to make calls on your friends, perhaps?"

"Since you have asked, I would prefer less sarcasm and a bit more politeness from you. You may be a duke, but I am the granddaughter of a baron, the daughter of a knight, and the friend of a viscountess. I deserve to be treated as a lady, not as a servant."

He tilted his head to one side, studying her. It was

as if he was considering whether or not he would gain ground by further bargaining. He must have concluded that she was firm in her resolve, for he nodded in agreement. "Very well. I accept your terms, and I will make every attempt to be more polite. I also feel compelled to give you fair warning."

"Warning?"

"Yes. Until December first, not only will I make every effort to remember my manners, I will do everything I can to change your mind and make you stay until the end of my project."

"I am not your slave. You cannot *make* me do anything."

"Persuade you, then, if you like that better. I can be very persuasive when I choose." Suddenly, he smiled at her, and that smile was as brilliant as the sun coming out from behind a cloud. "I want you to stay."

Daphne sucked in a deep breath, appreciating the heady power of that smile, appreciating the considerable charm he could wield without a bit of effort, charm that could make any woman want to please him. For the barest moment, she was tempted to soften and agree to stay longer, but she ruthlessly shoved that momentary madness aside. "And I, your grace," she said without emotion, "can be very, very stubborn."

"We are both warned then," he said, still smiling as he bowed to her. Then he turned away and departed.

After he was gone, the potent pleasure his smile had once given her still lingered, along with the sharp, sweet sting of remembrance. He had looked at her in just that same way the first time she had ever met him.

She had been awaiting him in the anteroom off the great hall, awed by the lavish opulence of her surroundings, unable to quite believe anyone actually lived here. Tremore Hall, she'd thought, wasn't a house. It was a palace.

She remembered how the sound of the immense front doors being thrown back had made her jump. The echo of a man's bootheels tapping against the marble floors outside the anteroom had reawakened that sickening knot of fear in her stomach, that fear of being alone and poor and desperate. Dozens of questions had gone through her mind in those few endless seconds as his footsteps had drawn him closer and closer to her. What if he turned her down? What if he threw her out? If she could not convince him to hire her without her father, what would she do?

Then he had walked into the anteroom, and he had frozen her in place because he was the handsomest man she had ever seen, with dark, curling hair, thick-lashed hazel eyes, and a sulky mouth. But those glimmers of boyish softness were overpowered by his other features. There was no softness in the lean, harsh planes of his cheekbones, the long aquiline nose and the implacable line of his jaw. In that first brief glimpse, Daphne knew this was a man who was master of all he surveyed. If Tremore was a palace, this was the prince.

Daphne was of average height, and he was nearly a head taller than she. In his black riding boots, buff trousers, blue velvet coat, and immaculate white linen, with his wide shoulders blocking much of the doorway where he had come to a halt, he was like no man she had ever seen before. Daphne, accustomed all her life to desperately thin, ragged Arabs who looked far older than their years, had never seen anything quite like the Duke of Tremore. His powerful build and demeanor exuded strength, vitality, and power.

As he had walked toward her, Daphne had willed herself not to move. "Well now," he had said in a voice deceptively soft, "Sir Henry's daughter, are you? Where is your father, Miss Wade?"

Daphne had somehow managed to explain what had happened, why she was there without Papa, and why his grace should hire her anyway. Even now, she did not know how she had managed it, for his hazel eyes had narrowed on her so haughtily during her speech that she'd felt as if she were about to be tossed over the palace ramparts.

He had subjected her to a long, hard stare, clearly wondering if her claim had any speck of validity, his skepticism of her abilities a palpable force between them. Who could blame him? She was trying to convince him she was an expert in antiquities and restoration, and a better one than any man he could find. The duke had a right to be skeptical.

In the end, he had not tossed her over the ramparts.

"You are hired, Miss Wade," he had said, holding out his hand to her. She had taken it, so relieved that she had employment and grateful for the opportunity to prove herself and her abilities.

She had looked into his face and had watched him smile at her. That smile, warm as the sun, had transformed him from disdainful prince to charming man. It had rendered her speechless, that smile. It had threatened to buckle her knees, and had sent her heart tumbling in her breast with a chaotic mix of every emotion she had ever felt, every emotion except the fear that had been tormenting her for months.

Her fear had vanished. With this man, she'd thought, there was nothing to be afraid of. She was safe. She had a place in the world again. That was the moment she had fallen in love with the Duke of Tremore.

But she was wiser now than she had been five months ago, and the echo of infatuation, gratitude, and admiration was gone, like a candle lit, burned for a brief time, and blown out. How foolish she had been.

Daphne returned her attention to her work and told herself that it did not matter how persuasive he tried to be, she was still leaving. He could no longer melt her into a puddle with a smile. The only power he'd ever had over her was his hold on her heart, and that was gone now. There was nothing he could do to make her stay past the first day of December. Nothing on earth.

Anthony liked his days to run smoothly. When in residence at Tremore Hall, it was his custom to keep country hours and a precise schedule. In the mornings, he usually toured various sections of the estate with his land steward, Mr. Cox. He then met with his house steward, his secretary, his landscape architect, and other members of his staff, conducting any business that his ducal responsibilities required. He was usually able to spend a few hours working on the excavation before dinner. He dined at six and was in bed by ten.

But during the week that followed Miss Wade's resignation, Anthony found every task he undertook had the irritating tendency to remind him of his predicament with one of the most valuable members of his staff and how to persuade her to remain.

He was reminded of her when Mr. Cox explained to him the engineering problems with the new aqueducts and suggested that perhaps Miss Wade might have a suggestion or two about how to fix them, since she knew so much about Roman aqueducts.

He was reminded of her by the post, which contained many letters regarding the museum, including one from Lord Westholme, another member of the Antiquarian Society and one of his partners on the project. Westholme had reminded him of how much everyone in the Society was looking forward to the opening in March.

During his call at the vicarage, the vicar had proven quite tiresome. He *would* insist on quoting from the story about the rich man and the ewe lamb through their entire visit. Anthony politely declined an invitation to dine at the vicarage.

Miss Wade expected him to be able to find someone to replace her by December 1, but even if he could, he did not want to.

The museum and the reconstruction of the villa here in Hampshire were of immense importance, not only to scholars and historians, but also to show that an appreciation of history should not be limited to the upper classes, but should instead be the right of all British people.

He was determined to buy enough time to keep Miss Wade here until March at the very least, and preferably longer. If he had his way, she would stay until the entire villa was done, until the last mosaic pavement was repaired and the last fresco restored, until the last pearl crotalia and the last clay amphora were out of the ground, sketched, cataloged, and on display in his museum in London.

Anthony snapped the reins of his horse, urging Defiance into a gallop on the road home from the village as he once again contemplated the various means he could use to keep her in Hampshire for the next four or five years.

You cannot make me stay.

Oh, yes, by God, he could, though Miss Wade might be naive enough to assume otherwise. He had several options from which to choose.

Money would not do the trick. He had tried that, and had soon realized that additional money alone would not be enough to tempt her.

With all the power and influence at his disposal, he could force her to remain by any number of devilish means, but he was not tempted to such a course. He was an honorable gentleman, after all, not the horrid fellow she painted him to be.

No, Viola was right. Keeping Miss Wade in Hampshire would require tactics much smoother than force. By the time he had returned to Tremore Hall, he knew exactly what he was going to do.

Chapter 8

It was dark by the time Anthony reached the house. He gave orders to Haverstall, the house steward, to have the cook prepare a fresh meal for him and to have Richardson draw him a hot bath. He then inquired as to Miss Wade's whereabouts and was informed that she was in the library.

She was sitting at the far end of the long room, curled up in one of the two big leather chairs by the windows, a book in her hands, her feet tucked beneath her, and a pair of flat-heeled slippers on the floor beside her chair. A candelabra on a nearby table washed a soft glow over her corner of the room.

Anthony started toward her, his own boots making no sound on the thick Turkish carpet. He had never seen her at this hour of the evening, and it startled him that her hair was no longer pulled back in that hideous bun. Instead, it was gathered into a loose, thick braid that lay across her shoulder, honey-brown in the candlelight.

She was so absorbed in her book that she did not even look up as he came closer, a fact which began to irritate him when he stood right in front of her and she could not possibly fail to notice he was there.

Anthony waited several moments for her to acknowledge his presence, but she did not, and he grew tired of waiting. He had never been a patient man. He cleared his throat and spoke. "I would like to speak with you for a few moments. Please," he added, when she did not respond.

She turned a page. "Our compromise was that I would work at a reasonable pace for the remainder of my stay. Since it is now dusk, my working hours are over. Could we please postpone this until morning?"

Yesterday, she would have jumped to do his bidding, like any other person in his employ, and Anthony began to wonder if perhaps he was having a very strange dream, a dream in which Miss Wade was no longer Miss Wade. Overnight, she had transformed into an impudent, recalcitrant sort of creature, who resigned her post without so much as a by-your-leave, dared to dress him down and call him inconsiderate, and who decided for herself what hours she would and would not work when there was so much to be done.

I am not your slave.

He smothered an oath under his breath.

Miss Wade glanced up at the sound. "Did you say something?"

That question made him realize he was just standing here like an idiot, when his purpose was to initiate a conversation. But damn it all, she was not cooperating. His plan was to make her life here so appealing that she would want to stay. So far, he did not think he was succeeding.

He watched her return her attention to her book, and he tried again. "I do not want to discuss your work. What is there to discuss? It is always exemplary."

"Thank you," she said as she turned another page, "but if your intention is to flatter me into staying, I would rather you save your breath."

"Miss Wade, can you and I not make peace?" When she did not reply, he added, "After all, you are here for at least the next three months. Therefore—"

"Two months, three weeks, and three days," she could not resist correcting him. "And there is no at least about it."

He refused to be drawn into a petty argument. "And since we have a great deal of work to do, and the pace will become quite stressful, I would like the time that you remain here to be pleasant for both of us. I thought we might start with a bit of conversation."

She hesitated for a long moment, but she did not refuse. Instead, she closed her book and placed it on the table beside her chair. After pulling off her spectacles, she set them aside as well. Then she put her feet on the floor, clasped her hands together in her lap, lifted her face to look up at him, and gave him her undivided attention. The moment she did, he forgot whatever he had been about to say.

She had beautiful eyes. This was the first time he could recall seeing her without those gold-framed spectacles, and it rather startled him what a difference their absence made to her face. Though her eyes appeared dark in the candlelight, he remembered their color from this afternoon—an uncommon lavender shade. Now, without those glass lenses to distort his view, he could see that her eyes were also large, deeply set, and surrounded by thick brown lashes.

He had never thought there was anything attractive about her, but looking at her now, Anthony was forced to revise his opinion. At this moment, bathed in candlelight, with loose tendrils of hair around her face and those big, almond-shaped eyes looking up at him, she seemed softer than she ever had before. Not pretty, exactly, but not quite so plain, either.

"Your grace?"

Her voice brought his attention back to the reason he was here. He sat down in the chair opposite hers and struggled for something to say, something innocuous and pleasant. "What are you reading?"

"A biography of Cleopatra."

"Indeed?" He glanced at the slim red volume on the table. The gilded title stamped on its face glittered in the candlelight. "That particular account of her life is rather an indifferent one. If you really wish to make a study of Cleopatra, there is a much better biography of her somewhere about."

"What is wrong with this one?"

"There is no real historical value to it. It is completely personal."

"Yes, but that is what I wanted. I already know the history surrounding her. I wanted to know more about her as a woman."

"I see."

The ironic note in his voice did not escape her. She bit her lip and looked away. After a moment, she returned her gaze to his and said, "By all accounts, I mean . . . she was not beautiful, but she did have a certain . . . certain . . . well—"

"Sexual allure?" he supplied, rather enjoying the way her cheeks tinted a delicate pink at his words. God, Miss Wade was embarrassed. She was usually as placid as a millpond, but the past two days were making him wonder if beneath her unruffled exterior, there might be a woman after all.

She carried on valiantly, trying to sound quite academic and intellectual on the subject. "That, of course, but she must have had more than that. Something undefinable. A magical, captivating quality."

"Is that what you wish to be, Miss Wade?" he asked. "Magical and captivating?"

She stiffened in her chair, suddenly as prickly as the outside of a chestnut. "Are you making fun of me?" she asked in her quiet voice.

The question startled him, for he'd had no intention at all of making fun. "No," he answered. "I was not. I was simply curious."

She did not seem to believe him, but she shrugged as if it did not matter and continued, "Caesar knew making Cleopatra his queen would not be a popular decision, but he had planned to do it anyway because he wanted her so much. He was murdered because of his passion for her."

"No," Anthony corrected, "Caesar was murdered because he was stupid. His passion for a woman was the catalyst of his death."

"Perhaps, but for all that, his feeling was no less powerful. Then take Marc Antony. At the battle of Actium, he gambled everything to win Cleopatra's kingdom back for her. Why?"

"Does it matter why? Marc Antony was as foolish as Caesar had been. Whatever his feelings, he should never have engaged in the battle. It was a futile attempt."

"Futile? He nearly won."

Before he could reply, a voice spoke from the other end of the room. "Begging your pardon, your grace, but Mr. Richardson says your bath is waiting, and your meal will be ready shortly."

Anthony glanced up to see a footman standing in the doorway. "I shall be along in a moment."

The footman gave a bow, then departed. Anthony returned his attention to the woman opposite him. "In war, Miss Wade, the fact that he nearly won counts for nothing. Marc Antony was a brilliant general, and he should have known he would lose at Actium. Octavian had marshaled all the forces of Rome against him. Reason dictated that he retreat."

"But what makes you think reason had anything to do with it?" she countered. "He loved her, and that power she had over him went beyond his reason."

He made a sound of impatience. "Trust a woman to bring emotion into an intellectual discussion."

"Trust a man to denigrate the power of love."

He folded his arms across his chest and leaned back in his chair. "Love should never conquer reason."

"But it so often does."

"With tragic results."

"For Marc Antony and Cleopatra, perhaps," she was forced to concede. "But not for everyone. Some people can be made quite happy by it."

"In the short term, perhaps."

He could tell his firm resolve in this discussion frustrated her. She lifted her gaze heavenward, clearly frustrated with him. "Oh, for heaven's sake," she cried, "have you never known anyone who was happy in love?"

A memory flashed through Anthony's mind of the night he'd found his father dead, four empty vials of laudanum beside him. "Yes, I have," he answered. "And the results were tragic."

He found he was no longer in the mood for conversation. Abruptly, he stood up and gave her a bow. "Forgive me, but I must have that bath or it will get cold. Good night."

He left her without another word.

First Viola, and all her uncharacteristically romantic talk of love. Now Miss Wade. Damn it all, love was not everything. Why did women always think that it was?

As much as Daphne had come to enjoy the lush, beautiful countryside of England, it did present its share of problems to excavation work, particularly in the reconstruction of frescoes. In the deserts of Africa, Palestine, and Mesopotamia, sand could be brushed away to reveal an intact, beautifully preserved wall painting, but in England and other damp climates, it was different.

It was bad enough that mud made unearthing the plaster pieces of a fresco a messy, difficult task. The damp soil in which the fragments had lain for sixteen hundred years tended to degrade the plaster itself, making Daphne's job of reassembling fresco pieces into a complete painting much more difficult. Matching the color and design details of hundreds of crumbling fragments could take days of exasperating work. Some days, she found, were more exasperating than others. This was one of those days.

She had already gone through the baskets of fresco pieces the men had uncovered so far and sorted them into groups by the images painted on them. Now, using a tiny trowel, she was fitting and cementing the pieces back together. Like the floor mosaic she had finished repairing the day before, this piece of the bedchamber wall was painted with an image of Venus. Reassembling it was a bit like putting together a child's picture puzzle, but the work was much more painstaking.

She was not accustomed to frescoes that crumbled so easily, and the task required all her attention, but she found her mind preferred to wander, taking her back to that very odd evening in the library a few evenings ago, when Anthony had tried to engage her in conversation.

Daphne remembered his words that he had known someone who was happy in love but with tragic results, and she wondered who he had been talking about. Himself, perhaps? That might explain his cynicism about marriage, she supposed, and his cold, logical approach to it. She forced such speculations out of her mind. She did not care whom he married.

Since that evening in the library, he had gone out of his way to thank her for each task she accomplished, added the word *please* to all his orders, and had an occasional chat with her about the weather and how the cooler temperatures this week must be making her work more pleasant. He sometimes mentioned the events of the day, such as England's current overabundance of governesses, or the dullness of London and its environs during the autumn and winter months. He even had maids come by the antika every hour or so to see if she might like a cup of tea or other refreshment. He often sent workmen in to ask if she needed their assistance.

As if such things would make her stay. Since more money had not tempted her, he was now trying to prove to her that he was a considerate employer.

She gave a disdainful sniff. He was not a considerate employer. He was selfish and toplofty and had no genuine consideration for the feelings of others. He was cold as well, so cold that he would deliberately, in calculated fashion, pick a wife he would never fall in love with.

Yet, despite all that, she had fancied herself in love with him. Why? Daphne paused in her work, staring into space, thinking it over. What was it about him that she had loved?

She thought of Cleopatra, and she realized that women were not the only ones who could possess a sort of magical appeal that captivated others. Anthony had it too.

She thought of all the times he had looked at her in a way that made her feel special, singled out for his attention, as if she were the only person in the world at that moment. But it was only for that moment, only when he wanted something he knew was especially difficult or unreasonable, then he could bring out a potent charm that made her want to please him, no matter how hard it might be to accomplish. Once that objective was obtained, he was gone, leaving her dazed and flattered and not realizing he had ordered, not requested, something that would take her hours and hours of hard work.

She knew now that all those times when he had looked straight at her in that special way, he had been looking through her without seeing her at all, his only intent to get what he wanted. And yet, the other day when he had been trying to persuade her to stay, she had felt a momentary temptation to agree, just because he had asked it of her.

Yes, he had an inexplicable alchemy that could

make a maid run off to the dairy for fresh butter at two o'clock in the morning without any resentment, that made Mrs. Bennington's breath come faster just because he was talking with her about the state of the roads, that made plain, ordinary Daphne Wade feel like the world's greatest beauty. But it was not real.

She took a deep breath and returned her attention to her work. She was wise to him now, and that magic wasn't going to work on her anymore.

Daphne picked up a flake of plaster about the size of her palm and began smearing wet cement onto the back of the piece with her trowel, but the pressure of such a task was too much for the delicate plaster fragment. It broke apart in her hands, falling between her gloved fingers into pieces and dust, her fourth one of the day, another priceless piece of history ruined.

"Oh, this English mud destroys everything!" she cried, and threw her trowel aside, thoroughly exasperated. It hit the stone floor with a clang. That sound was followed by a low whistle, and Daphne turned her head to find Anthony standing in the doorway of the antika.

"Careful where you throw things, Miss Wade," he said, and bent to pick up her trowel.

"Did I hit you?"

"No," he answered, "but it was a near miss."

Daphne watched him cross the room toward her. She could tell he had not yet started working on the dig with Mr. Bennington, for though he wore no waistcoat or neckcloth, his shirt was immaculate, without a speck of dirt to detract from its snowy whiteness. Daphne was relieved that at least he was wearing it.

She hastily looked away. "I am gratified you are not hurt," she said as he paused by her side.

"Why are you cursing the English mud?" He set her trowel down beside the bowl of cement on the table.

Daphne drew a deep breath and inhaled the sharp scent of lemon soap and, with it, the heavier scent of him. It flustered her, and she shifted her weight from one foot to the other. Did he have to stand so close? "It is nothing," she said and reached for the trowel. "I am feeling rather cross today, that is all."

"Cross? Now, I know I must be dreaming."

She scooped up a dollop of cement. "I do not know what you mean," she said and began to smear the adhesive on one of the small pieces of plaster she had shattered.

"I feel as if I have been lost these past few days in a bizarre sort of dream," he continued, and moved away from her side.

Daphne drew a deep breath of relief, but she could feel his eyes studying her as he circled the table to stand on the opposite side. "It seems you are not quite what I thought you to be," he said, "and I find that a bit disconcerting."

Daphne fitted two pieces of fresco together and did not reply. She lifted her gaze a notch as she waited for the cement to adhere, watching him roll up his sleeves. As the white linen rolled back from his tanned skin, she could see the stria of sinew and muscle in his forearms, and his long, strong fingers. Warmth began radiating out from her midsection, and an image of him without his shirt flashed through her mind. She fought to focus on what he was saying.

"I find that my preconceived ideas about you are falling away, Miss Wade. One by one."

She was human, she was not a machine, and she could not stop herself from asking, "What preconceived ideas are those?"

The moment the words were out of her mouth, she wanted to take them back. She did not want to hear him utter flattering, false opinions of her because he wanted her to stay and finish his project. She returned her gaze to the plaster pieces in her hands and tried to throw herself back onto solid ground. "Never mind. I do not need to know."

"I shall tell you anyway. I thought you were a meek and mild little miss, willing to run here and there and everywhere to do my bidding."

You also thought I was a stick bug. Daphne did not make that resentful addition aloud, though part of her wanted to make him feel guilt and remorse for what he had said about her when he had not even known she was listening. "You were wrong."

"So I was," he admitted. "I am discovering that you are neither mild nor meek. In fact, Miss Wade, I have discovered that you have a temper, for you have no compunction about throwing tools when you are cross. Nor have you been hesitant to speak your mind of late. You certainly expressed your opinion of me quite eloquently two days ago. All of this after five months of quiet compliancy baffles me, and I cannot help but wonder at the reason for this change in you."

Daphne's entire body tensed at those words, and she vowed he would never find out. It would be too mortifying. She drew a deep breath. "I cannot think what came over me the other day. I do not usually speak so harshly."

"I accept your apology."

Daphne's chin shot up, and she found that he was smiling at her. That alchemy at work. "That was not an apology," she said emphatically. "I never apologize when I am provoked into giving an honest opinion."

Anthony rested his palms on the table and leaned a bit closer to her. Laugh lines appeared at the corners of his eyes, though he did not smile. "Miss Wade, do you not know when you are being teased?"

"You are teasing me?"

"Most assuredly."

She did not want to be teased. It caught her off guard and made disliking him harder to do. He knew it, too. "Do you enjoy teasing people?"

"I am enjoying teasing you at this moment. I confess, I am finding it . . . intriguing. I might have to do it more often." He straightened away from the table and clasped his hands behind his back. "Dine with me tomorrow evening, Miss Wade."

"Is that a request or a command?"

"It is a request."

She looked away, feeling trapped. She did not want to have dinner with him. She did not want to become better acquainted. "I do not believe it would be proper."

"I shall ask Mr. and Mrs. Bennington as well." Though his face remained grave, the laugh lines were still there, and a glimmer of amusement flickered in the hazel depths of his eyes. "I will even say please, if that would persuade you."

Daphne did not want to be persuaded. Still, as he had pointed out a week ago, if they could at least be pleasant to one another, the next three months would be much easier for both of them. "For the sake of civility, I accept your invitation."

"Excellent. We shall break bread together, Miss Wade. If we continue in this fashion, we might even become friends."

Daphne stiffened. "I advise you not to place any wagers on that, your grace."

Chapter 9

Eviction of tenants was always a difficult matter. It was the one part of his position Anthony truly despised. Most peers left all decisions about such things in the hands of stewards, and he could have chosen to do the same, but to his mind, that was a cowardly way of handling one's responsibilities. He looked across the desk at his steward. "The man is ill. I refuse to believe there are no other options."

Mr. Cox, who had been Anthony's land steward for only six months, was not yet cognizant of his master's little eccentricities in dealing with the yearly tenant rents, but he did know the duke preferred honest opinions to tactful evasion, so he spoke plainly. "Your grace has already given him a year gratis. He has not paid his rent for last year, and because he is bedridden, he will be unable to bring in his harvest this year. By allowing him and his family to remain, you are setting a precedent—"

"Mr. Cox," Anthony cut him off with some impatience, "with the husband so ill he will not be able to bring his crop in and half a dozen children to feed, I am not going to turn them out of their house. There are other options."

Cox gave him the resigned look of a good steward. "What is it you wish me to do about this matter?"

"His wife is in health. Have Mrs. Pendergast find work for her and her eldest daughter in the laundry until her husband's on his feet again, and have some of the other tenants watch his younger children. That will suffice as their rent for last year."

"Your grace, the wages of a laundress could not possibly cover—"

"Those are my orders, Mr. Cox. Carry them out. A fortnight from now, if he is still in ill health, I want to see some of his fellow tenants bringing his crop in so it does not rot in the ground. Pay them in ale from the brewery. That should make them willing enough to help."

"Very good, sir." Cox rose from his chair and departed. Anthony was glad of it, for eviction decisions were finished for another year. He glanced at the window, frowning at the rain pouring down outside. Rain like this played merry hell with the excavations.

He thought of Miss Wade throwing her trowel and berating the English mud, and it made him want to laugh. It was so unlike her. Yet, as she had pointed out yesterday, he had been wrong to think her a milk-and-water miss. She was proving to be far more unexpected than that.

He walked to the window, leaned one shoulder against the window frame and looked out. He lowered his gaze to the huge expanse of lawn below, and what he saw confirmed his thoughts. Standing in the middle of the lawn, without even a macintosh and hat to protect her, was Miss Wade, her head tilted back and the rain washing over her.

What was she on about, standing outside in this sort of weather? Though August had been quite warm, September had brought autumn into the air, cooling the temperatures considerably. If she stayed out there in the rain much longer, she'd catch a chill.

Anthony turned away from the window and left his study. Several minutes later, clad in an oilskin cloak and carrying an opened umbrella like any sensible person out in the rain, he was striding across the lawn toward her.

She was in the same place he had seen her from the window, standing between a pair of flower-filled urns in front of the fountain with her head tilted back. She was not wearing her glasses and her eyes were closed. She stood motionless, hands outstretched, almost as if she were mesmerized by the feel of the rain on her face.

"What are you doing out here, Miss Wade?" he asked.

She opened her eyes at the sound of his voice and straightened to look at him. "Good morning. Did you come out here to join me?"

"God, no. I came to fetch you." He halted a foot in front of her, holding his umbrella over both of them, observing the smile on her face in puzzlement. What did anyone who was soaking wet on a cool autumn day have to smile about?

"Is something wrong?" she asked.

He felt compelled to point out the obvious. "You are standing out in the rain."

"Yes, I know," she agreed, and to Anthony's amazement, she began to laugh. "Isn't it wonderful?"

"I believe you have gone quite mad, Miss Wade. That is the only explanation for your unaccountable behavior of late." He put a hand on her arm, intending to lead her back to the house.

"No, no." She pulled away from him. "I've not gone mad, I assure you. I just want to stand out here a little bit longer."

"You are joking."

She shook her head and took a step back, out from under the protection of his umbrella. "I am perfectly serious," she told him as the rain poured down over her in rivulets. Her clothing was soaked and wet tendrils of hair that had escaped from her bun were plastered to her cheeks. "I love rain. Don't you?"

"No, I do not. And neither do you. Were you not cursing the English mud just yesterday?"

She laughed. "Well, yes. I hate the mud because it makes my job more difficult. I do love rain, though. I can see that does not make much sense to you."

"You are correct. If you do not come inside, you will catch cold."

He stepped forward, again trying to protect her with the umbrella and steer her toward the house, but she seemed determined to stay beneath the downpour. Shaking her head in refusal, she began walking backward away from him as he moved toward her. "No, really. Thank you for your concern, but I don't want to go inside. Not yet."

He was still frowning at her, for her smile faded and she stopped evading the protection of his umbrella. "You don't understand," she said. "I have lived in deserts most of my life, with only a few short months in Naples or Rome each year to provide a respite. Do you know what it is like to spend nine months in never-ending heat and drought?"

He shifted the umbrella to his left hand. "No," he answered. "I have never been to a desert."

"It is so hot in summer that the air shimmers over the horizon in waves, so hot it's hard to breathe. The heat makes your skin feel stretched so tight over your bones that it hurts." She closed her eyes and rubbed her wet cheeks with the tips of her fingers as if in remembrance of the hot desert sun. "And all you feel is your own sweat turning the dust on your face to caked mud. Your mouth is dry, and you keep licking your lips over and over, but it doesn't help. They are so chapped and dry."

Anthony lowered his gaze to her mouth, watching as she ran the tips of her fingers back and forth over her moist, parted lips. Though they may have been chapped in the desert, there was nothing but softness to them now.

Lust hit him with such unexpected force that he could not move.

"Sand blows all the time," she went on as he watched the tip of her finger slide down over her chin and along the column of her throat. His throat went as dry as her desert.

"The sand blows in every direction and rubs your skin like sandpaper. All your clothes have to be drab colors that hide the dirt. There's so little water, you can only bathe once a week, and it is never a full bath, just a tin pail of water, soap if the supply caravan has come through, and a sponge."

He tried to say something, anything, but he made the mistake of looking down, and the thought of any sort of reply vanished from his mind. For once, she was not wearing that apron of hers and her beige cotton dress was plastered to her form, molding to every curve of her body, the rain making the cotton fabric seem almost transparent. She seemed blissfully unaware of the view he had of her, the round fullness of her breasts beneath the cotton layers of her clothing, the deep dip of her waist, the flare of her hips, the fold of wet fabric between her thighs. And her legs. God. How long were they?

This was Miss Wade, he reminded himself. Not a goddess by any means. And yet, he could see for himself that she had a body like one. Never in a thousand years would he have dreamed that such a luscious shape was concealed beneath that horrid apron and drab cotton.

Anthony tore his gaze away from her rain-soaked form to stare instead at the stone image that graced the top of a fountain beyond her left shoulder. A satyr, he realized as the thick heaviness of lust surged through his body. How appropriate.

She worked for him, he reminded himself, and there were rules about that sort of thing. He returned his gaze to her face and tried to focus on what she was saying as he strove to regain his control.

"All my life, whenever I have had the chance, I go walking in the rain, because I love it so. The rain here in England is especially nice, because it is so gentle and misty and your gardens are beautiful. The first morning after I arrived here in March, I went for a walk around the estate, just breathing in the fragrance of wet grass and damp leaves. It was lovely." She let out her breath in a deep sigh. "Oh, you just don't know how it feels to be here when you have lived in dry, hot climates all your life."

Anthony could not form a coherent word of reply. In some vague, dim part of his consciousness, he could appreciate what she meant, and he could imagine how hard it would be for anyone, especially a woman, to live as she had. A flash of anger at her father went through him at the idea of any honorable man subjecting his daughter to such hardships. But for the most part, Anthony could not do much in the way of thinking. Standing in front of him was a woman he had never seen before, a woman whose body was a hidden treasure, a woman whose eyes were the exact shade of the larkspur still blooming in the stone urn beside her, a woman who thought sodden grass and leaves were fragrant. A woman whose innocent pleasure in getting soaked by a rainstorm was proving as erotic to him as any aphrodisiac could be.

With all the discipline he possessed, Anthony set his jaw and reminded himself of his position and hers. "Pray, is this going to become a habit with you?"

She blinked, whether from the water flowing over her face or the sudden hardness in his voice it was impossible to tell. "Is what going to become a habit?" she asked. "Standing in the rain?"

"Enjoying yourself instead of doing the work for which I am paying you, and paying dearly, I might add."

"What has put you into a fit of temper?" she asked with some asperity. Then, before he could answer, she held up her hand to halt any reply he might have made. "Never mind, I don't want to know."

"No," he said, his voice sounding oddly strangled to his own ears, "indeed, you do not."

"But since you asked about my work," she went on, "I *was* working. I was doing research on pottery fragments in the library, but the rain started, and I could not resist the opportunity—"

"To drown yourself, yes, I know," he interrupted, keeping his gaze fixed firmly on her face. Even that was not helping, however, for when he reached out and pushed a tendril of hair away from her face, he could not seem to pull his hand away. The skin of her cheek felt warm and satiny beneath his fingers. How? he wondered. How did a woman who had lived in deserts all her life have skin as soft and fine as this? He touched his fingers to her lips as she had done. How could her lips be so velvety as this?

She was looking at him, her eyes wide with shock, but in their depths, there was also something else, something that reflected what he was feeling. Yes, desire was in her eyes and in the rapid wisp of her breath against his fingers. It was in the way she stood so still, tense and poised like a deer about to flee. If he slid his hand down, he would feel her heart pounding as hard as his own.

His hand moved an inch in that direction before he yanked it back.

"Come inside," he said. "You are soaked through, and could very well catch a chill. I know this climate better than you do, and I will not have you becoming ill when we have a great deal of work to do."

To Anthony's relief, she did not argue. Holding the umbrella over both of them, he escorted her back to the house. Inside, he handed the dripping umbrella and the dripping Miss Wade over to an astonished Mrs. Pendergast. "A hot bath and a small glass of brandy for Miss Wade," he ordered.

Turning to Daphne, he said, "Next time you want to feel like you are washing away the desert, or whatever, please take a bath indoors. I hope we may still expect your presence at dinner tonight?"

"Of course," she said, managing to sound dignified despite the fact that she was forming pools of water on the white marble floor.

"Good. I will see you this evening." He turned away without another word and started back to his study. He reminded himself that Daphne Wade was a woman in his employ, a young, innocent woman. A woman he had barely noticed and had certainly never desired. Until now.

Now, he thought of her in soaking beige cotton, and he could not rid himself of the hot, smothering desire that coursed through his body, nor the image of the satyr's face mocking him for it.

Chapter 10

At first, Anthony's prediction that breaking bread together might make them friends did not seem likely to come true.

For one thing, the dining room seemed absurdly grand for any man having only three guests to dinner, even if he was a duke. The gold- and silver-patterned ceiling thirty feet above their heads, the long dining table and the chairs of crimson velvet, the columns of white marble, the gilt-edged mirrors and paintings of winged cherubs did not induce a comfortable and relaxed atmosphere, at least not to Daphne.

Second, there was the food. Two different kinds of soup from which to choose, one cold and one hot. Then three selections of fish, followed by two courses of four meats each, one an enormous joint of beef he carved himself. It was all beautifully presented, and what she sampled was delicious, but to Daphne, it seemed an extraordinary waste, since only four people could not consume even a tenth of it.

She was accustomed to dining at a dust-covered folding table in a tent, or at a modest Italian pensione, where she, her father, and any other British men involved in the current excavation discussed Roman history and antiquities over every meal.

Third, there was her host. His conversation with all three of them was amiable, and Mr. and Mrs. Bennington were able to return his pleasantries with ease, but she could not. His manner, particularly toward her, was all consideration and regard.

Daphne knew that Anthony's assiduous attention was just another part of his campaign to keep her in Hampshire. She also knew how charming he could be, but that charm was seldom directed at her and never in a social situation. She had no idea how to respond, especially since she knew what he truly thought of her.

Aside from his concern for her enjoyment of the meal, he also had the curious notion to make a study of her person. Whenever she looked up from her food, she found him watching her, with a strange sort of intensity she could not define.

She did not look any different than usual. She had taken off her glasses and donned the only nice dress she had, a mauvish-gray muslin frock that must be at least half a dozen years out of fashion, and she had no illusions that either of those trifling changes would cause Anthony to deem her anything worth staring at. She could only think his disconcerting scrutiny was a result of her morning walk in the rain. He had accused her of having lost her mind, after all.

By the time the desserts arrived, she could not help remarking on it. "Mrs. Bennington," she said, looking at the older woman across the table, "his grace studies me most intently this evening, do you not think so? He examines me as if I were an artifact."

"Heavens, dear!" Mrs. Bennington exclaimed, a hint of reproof behind her little laugh as she glanced uneasily toward the duke and back again to her. "You should not describe yourself in such a way. Artifact, indeed."

Anthony picked up his glass of wine and leaned back in his chair at the head of the table. His lashes lowered as his gaze raked over her with the leisure of a well-fed lion. "But Mrs. Bennington, I might describe her that way myself, for artifacts are rare and mysterious things, intriguing and difficult to interpret. One so often draws erroneous conclusions about them."

Daphne's hand tightened around the serviette in her lap. What was he saying? she thought wildly. That she was not an unnoticeable stick insect after all? She forced herself to unclench her fist and pick up her wine glass. "You believe I am a mystery, your grace?"

"I do, Miss Wade."

"I cannot think why." She took a sip of claret and set her glass back down. "I assure you, I am no great mystery at all."

"Miss Wade, I believe the duke has a point," put in Mr. Bennington from her other side. "Why, Mrs. Bennington and I have often discussed that very thing ever since your resignation."

"I know you were surprised, but—"

"Surprised?" Mrs. Bennington interjected. "Bless us, it was astonishing. Not that we blame you, of course, for wishing to go to Lady Hammond. Such a treat for you, dear, and no question you deserve it. But we had no idea you were such a great friend of the viscountess. So you see, his grace is quite correct that you are mysterious. Close as an oyster."

Daphne did not know what to say. She had never thought of herself as either mysterious or secretive.

"So you see?" the older woman went on when she did not reply. "Even now, you tell us nothing. If you were a bit more forthcoming with others, it would not go amiss, dear. One never knows what you think and feel."

"Can't expect the young dandies in London to be able to read your mind, you know," Mr. Bennington added with a chuckle.

"Not dandies, dear," his wife corrected. "That term is quite out of date. Beaux, they are called nowadays."

"Since we have all agreed that Miss Wade is a mystery," Anthony put in, "shall we allow her to choose what our entertainment shall be, now that dinner is over? Then we may draw conclusions about her from what she chooses." He set aside his glass of wine, leaned forward in his chair, and looked at Daphne as if her opinion were of the gravest importance. "What shall it be, Miss Wade?"

"You must help me, your grace," she said, smiling sweetly at him. "You are so thoughtful and considerate that I am sure you have prepared several amusements for us. You must tell me what they are."

"A very deft and clever answer," he said, laughing. "It flatters me, buys you time, and tells none of us more about you. Very well, I shall give you choices. If you would like music, I can summon musicians for you. Or would you prefer poetry?"

"Do not choose poetry, Miss Wade, I beg of you," Mr. Bennington said. "I shall fall asleep."

"No, Mr. Bennington," Anthony admonished him. "Do not say such things. I should be happy to recite Byron or Shelley or Keats for Miss Wade myself if that is what she wants. Her wish is my command."

Daphne did not want to hear him talk that way, as if he meant such an outlandish thing. And she could not bear the idea of hearing him reciting romantic lines of Byron to her. She stood up and cast aside her serviette. "I believe I should like to see your conservatory, your grace, for Mrs. Bennington has told me it is quite the most breathtaking thing, and I have had no chance to see for myself if that is so."

"A walk in the hothouse it is," Anthony agreed, rising to his feet with the others. "Haverstall, send a footman ahead to have the conservatory lit."

"Very good, sir."

The house steward signaled for a footman as Anthony turned toward the door, offering his arm to Daphne. "Shall we go?"

She tucked her hand in the crook of his arm, and they left the dining room, Mr. and Mrs. Bennington behind them, a footman racing ahead to obey the duke's instructions.

They strolled down the long corridor toward the conservatory at a much slower pace than the footman. Neither of them spoke, but she could feel him watching her out of the corner of her eye. She stared straight ahead, compelled to give nothing away, but they had not quite reached their destination when she had to ask the obvious question. "What conclusions do you draw from my choice of entertainment?"

"That you are fond of flowers?"

Despite herself, she laughed at how pat his answer and how ruefully he said it. "You see, I am not so mysterious, am I?" she countered. "All women are fond of flowers."

"I like hearing you laugh."

Her insides took a tumble, and she almost stopped walking but recovered herself just in time. She did not reply, and they continued toward the conservatory without speaking.

He broke the silence between them just as they reached the conservatory. "I must confess, Miss

Wade, that taking a turn around the hothouse was not what I was hoping you would suggest."

"And what had you hoped for?"

"Twenty questions," he murmured as they walked inside the conservatory. "But only if I could ask them of you."

She pulled her spectacles from the pocket of her skirt and put them on. "Not in a thousand years," she said primly, and turned away for a look at the indoor garden around them.

Like all the other rooms at Tremore Hall, this one was enormous. At least fifty feet long, its ceiling was composed entirely of octagonal glass panes. Three of the walls were glass as well, braced every eight feet by stone columns. Arches curved overhead, attaching those columns to another set of identical ones that ran down the center rather like a Roman forum. The glass reflected light from sconces that lined the wall of the house. Additional light was provided by various candelabra set atop tall stone pillars placed throughout the room.

Mr. and Mrs. Bennington started strolling toward one side of the building, and Daphne moved to the center, Anthony beside her as she studied her surroundings. There were lemon trees, which she recognized at once, and there were also date palms and towering fig trees that reminded her of Palestine. There were three different fountains, several statues, and plenty of stone benches so one could sit and enjoy the serene environment. Flowers in brilliant colors bloomed everywhere. Some she recognized, some she had never seen before.

"Is it not as magnificent as I told you, Daphne?" called Mrs. Bennington from somewhere behind a grove of trees and palms.

"It is," she agreed, and paused in the center of the vast expanse, staring at the arches overhead and the many panes of glass above them. "I have never seen anything like this before," she added, and returned her attention to the man standing nearby. "I am awed, your grace. Truly awed."

He smiled at her, and she caught her breath. Like the sun coming out. "From you, who has seen so much of the world, that is the highest of compliments. Thank you."

Daphne took another look around, spinning in a slow circle, then she faced him again. "It is so very English, is it not?"

He laughed, and she looked at him in bewilderment, unable to figure out what he found so amusing.

"Miss Wade, you are surrounded by Greek statues, Italian lemon trees, bonsai in the custom of Nippon, and pineapples from the Sandwich Islands. How much less English can it be?"

Daphne couldn't help smiling back at him. "Well, it is very English. No one I ever knew in Italy had a lemon tree inside the house, and the date palms in Palestine are so scrawny compared with these. And what on earth is a bonsai?"

He pointed to a stone planter near her feet. She

gave a cry of delight and knelt down for a closer look. "Why, these are miniature apple trees, with apples on them!" Looking up at him, she asked, "Are they really apples?"

"See for yourself." Anthony knelt beside her, plucked off one of the cherry-size fruits, and pressed it to her mouth. She hesitated only a moment, then parted her lips. "Apples mean temptation, you know," he said as she took the fruit into her mouth.

Daphne almost swallowed the miniature apple whole at the touch of his fingers against her lips. He had touched her just this way earlier in the garden, and just as before, her whole body felt suddenly warm, as if a delightful wave of the Aegean Sea had washed over her. She wanted to stay here forever. She wanted to run away as fast as she could.

In the end, she did neither. She rose to her feet, striving to maintain her most impassive expression as she chewed and swallowed the fruit. "They are indeed apples," she finally said, keeping her voice devoid of any of the turbulent feeling rushing through her. "Just as I said. Very English."

She turned away and found that in front of her was a raised flower bed of the strangest-looking plants she had ever seen. Each was composed of a cluster of long, upright leaves, with one stem coming out of the center that was capped with some sort of fruit. "How very odd they look," she said to Anthony over one shoulder. "What are they?"

"Pineapples. They are given as a gesture of welcome. Have you ever eaten one?"

When she shook her head, he lifted his hand, and a footman appeared out of nowhere. "Cut a pineapple for Miss Wade," he said, and before she could protest, the servant snapped one of the strange, prickly fruits from its stalk. "Take it to the kitchens, please, and tell them to serve it to Miss Wade with her breakfast tomorrow."

"Yes, sir." The footman bowed and vanished with the pineapple as Anthony returned his attention to her.

"If you are fond of the taste," he said, "feel free to have one any time you like during the remainder of your stay."

She did not want Anthony to do things for her. That was never what she had wanted, and it was too late now to make a difference anyway. "Thank you," she murmured. "That is very kind of you, your grace."

"Contrary to certain reports, I have been known to be kind on occasion." Laugh lines appeared at the corners of his eyes, though he did not smile. "But I confess I am not being kind just now."

"Yes, I know, and it is not going to work."

He tried to look innocent. "What is not going to work?"

"This blatant attempt to trick me into staying with charm and—and other such tactics."

"I know you are far too intelligent to be fooled by charm or trickery, Miss Wade. Can we not just say I am using the only weapon I have?"

"Persuasion?"

"Temptation. If I can tempt you with the fruits of

my garden of Eden, you might stay." He gestured to a grove of figs nearby. "Would you care to see the passion fruit?"

Daphne followed him through the jungle of trees to a trellis on the other side that was tangled with a lush growth of vines. "This is called passion fruit?" she asked as they paused before the trellis. She studied the plant for a moment, then said, "I think something with such a name should look more extraordinary than this."

"The vine may be unremarkable, but when it blooms, the flower is lovely. It signifies devotion."

She turned toward him with a quizzical look. "Apples for temptation. Pineapples for welcome. Passionflower for devotion. Do all plants signify a sentiment, then?"

"Many of them do. Have you never read *Le Langage des Fleurs*?"

"The language of flowers," she murmured.

"You speak French?"

"Of course. In Morocco, most people do not understand English, so I learned French."

"How many languages do you speak, Miss Wade?"

"Heavens, I don't know. Let me see. French, Latin, Greek, Aramaic, Hebrew, Farsi, and Arabic," she listed, counting on her fingers. "So, in addition to English, that makes seven."

"Extraordinary," he said, looking at her in amazement. "I must confess, Latin and French were all I could manage, even with a slew of childhood tutors and a Cambridge education. Miss Wade, you have awed me."

Daphne felt a momentary glow of pleasure at the compliment, but she quickly snuffed it out. "I do not know this language of flowers. Do flowers truly have their own language?"

"They do. It has been put into a book, *Le Langage des Fleurs*, by Madame Charlotte de la Tour. It is quite the fashion to convey one's sentiments with flowers, and several other books have been written, expanding on her original text, enabling a bouquet to serve as an entire letter."

"What a beautiful way to express one's feelings. I should love to receive something like that."

He bent down and pulled a spray of tiny pink blossoms from a potted plant at the foot of the trellis, then straightened and presented it to her. She took it, too surprised to do otherwise.

"It has a lovely scent," she said, holding it to her nose. What is it?"

"Your namesake. *Daphne odora.*"

"What does it signify?" Looking up, she added, laughing, "Do not tell me something awful, for I should hate that."

"Never fear, for it is quite the opposite." He took the spray of flowers from her hand, and Daphne caught her breath as he reached behind her head and tucked the tiny bouquet into the bun at the nape of her neck. "It means, 'I would not have you otherwise.' "

She released her breath in a rush and turned

away. Desperate for something to say, she gestured to the trellis. "But passionflower means devotion, and that does not make sense to me. Should not a passionflower convey passion?"

"Ah, but the fruit is where the passion is, Miss Wade. Intoxicating and delicious. Like passion itself."

A rush of intense warmth came over her, and she turned away before he could see that she was actually blushing. "One day I shall have to try them," she said, and resumed walking.

He fell in step beside her. "They are not in season now, but if you stay, you can enjoy them for breakfast in a few months—"

"No, thank you." She heard the breathlessness in her own voice, and tried to cover it by teasing. "Your grace, this will not do," she told him with mock sternness. "I shall not be led astray by exotic breakfast bribes."

"Then I shall keep my dates and figs to myself."

"Yes, please, for I have had enough of those to last a lifetime. They tempt me not at all."

"I wish I knew what would tempt you, Miss Wade."

Daphne did not answer as they circled to the other side of the conservatory. Nothing he had could tempt her. Not now. Not ever.

Daphne drew in a sharp breath at that stern reminder to herself and caught a scent so delightful that she came to an abrupt halt and stared at the source, a tall, fat shrub with the most beautiful snow-white flowers she had ever seen. "Oh, my," she whispered, reaching out to touch the velvety petal of one blossom as she inhaled that exquisite fragrance. "It is like heaven just to stand here."

He looked at her, smiling. "You do like flowers, don't you? Especially scented ones."

She breathed in again. "What are these?"

"Gardenias."

"Mmm." She closed her eyes. "I have never smelled anything so divine in my life."

"Secret love."

"What?" she squeaked, feeling as if she had just been hit with a spray of icy water. She opened her eyes, but she could not look at the man beside her. "I—" She cleared her throat, staring straight ahead. "I beg your pardon?"

"Gardenias signify a confession of secret love."

She *would* like that sort of flower, she thought. With an exasperated sigh, she turned away and resumed walking toward the center of the conservatory, where the Benningtons were seated, waiting for them.

"Have I said something to vex you?" he asked beside her.

"Not at all." She forced a laugh. "It is just that sometimes I can be very, very foolish."

"You? I do not believe it. I have never seen you make a mistake of any kind, Miss Wade. I cannot imagine you the fool."

She is never ill. She never makes a mistake. She is a machine.

"I was in love once," she blurted out before she even knew what she was saying. "Everyone plays the fool in love."

"I suppose so."

There was a strange note in his voice she did not understand, and she looked over at him as he added, "I have not experienced that myself."

"You have never been in love?"

"Only in my dreams, Miss Wade."

His answer was so glib and offhand that she stopped walking and gave his back a rueful stare as he continued toward the Benningtons. "That makes two of us," she murmured under her breath as she pulled the spray of daphne flowers from her hair.

Chapter 11

Anthony had always been a disciplined man. Whether he was orating his views in the House of Lords, or discussing his estates with one of his stewards, or conducting any of the dozens of other matters inevitable to his position, he never allowed himself to be hampered by distractions of any sort, least of all a woman.

However, during the fortnight that followed Miss Wade's escapade in the rain and his dinner with her, Anthony found it hard to concentrate. Though he avoided her, the image of her remained fixed in his mind as if carved in stone, and desire returned to taunt him at the most inopportune and inexplicable moments.

He put his preoccupation down to shock—the

shock of discovering that for the last five months he'd had a woman living in his home who had the body of a goddess, and he hadn't even noticed.

Anthony watched as half a dozen workmen lowered the huge slab of tessellated floor onto the hypocaust of the villa, but he was not paying any attention to what they were doing. Beside him, he could hear Mr. Bennington barking orders to the men, but the words were lost on him.

He had not even noticed.

Not until a rainstorm and a soaking-wet dress had awakened him to the truth. All through their dinner together that evening, he had been unable to stop staring at her, knowing the luscious curves beneath the plain, pinkish-gray thing she had worn to that meal. Now it seemed as obvious as an elephant in the drawing room, but the beauty of Daphne Wade's body had completely escaped him for over five months. He had always been able to appreciate a sight like that. How could he have missed it?

Perhaps it was because she was in his employ. He had never allowed himself the indulgence of noticing any of the women who worked for him, especially one who made no effort to make herself noticed.

Or perhaps he had been working too hard. The pressure of fulfilling his obligation to the Antiquarian Society was wearing on him. He had not enjoyed the pleasures of a woman's body since the London season.

Anthony shifted his weight restlessly from one foot to the other, and he wondered if her legs were as long as they had seemed beneath the drenched cotton fabric, or if that had only been his imagination.

"Your grace?"

"Hmm?" Anthony jerked himself out of his reverie to find Mr. Bennington looking at him.

The older man's bushy eyebrows bunched together in a frown. "Are you well?" he asked. "You have been quite preoccupied of late, your grace, if I may be so bold as to say it."

Anthony drew a deep breath and raked a hand through his hair. "I am perfectly well, Mr. Bennington," he answered. "Carry on."

He knew he could not allow himself to be distracted by any lusty speculations. His museum, his excavation—those were what mattered right now, and he would not let momentary desire for any woman have control of him. Even if she did have the body of a goddess.

He turned away and started to the stables, thinking to take Defiance out to the downs at the southeast section of the estate and let the gelding go at a dead run until both of them were exhausted.

He had barely taken half a dozen steps toward the stables before Anthony veered away from his destination and he found his steps carrying him to the antika instead. He had been avoiding her for two weeks and allowing his own imagination to torment him. Perhaps that was causing this annoying preoccupation with her. One more look, and he would be cured. Just one more look at her without that damnable apron to get in the way, and he would be satisfied on the subject and able to forget it.

She was in the antika, but his secret purpose in

seeking her out was defeated at once. The apron had returned, effectively shielding the shape of the woman beneath it, and Anthony took some comfort in that. No other man in the world would have been able to discern the full breasts and shapely hips beneath that loose-fitting, box-shaped monstrosity of a garment. It was a perfect suit of armor, he thought, as he paused in the doorway. Or chastity belt.

It was, of course, quite suited to the work she did, but why she was wearing it now was a mystery, for she was not working. Instead, she was standing close to the center of the room, reading a letter.

"If you begin to avoid working during the day as well as the evenings, Miss Wade, I shall have made a very bad bargain," he said as he entered the room. He watched her look up, and the almost frantic expression on her usually impassive face brought him to an abrupt halt several feet away from her. "What's amiss?" he asked.

"I have here a letter from your sister."

"And how is a letter from Viola making you look as if Doomsday is upon us?"

"I had written to her explaining that I am remaining here until December first."

"And?"

"She says that though London is rather dull in December, she has heard that the Marquess of Covington intends to give a ball at his home there on December 31, in honor of his grandmother's seventy-fifth birthday, and she will be sure I am included in the invitation."

"And?"

She turned away without replying and walked to the window. "I had forgotten all about dancing when I agreed to stay two more months," she muttered as if to herself. "What was I thinking? I could always say no to the Covington ball, I suppose, but I cannot say no to every ball."

"Miss Wade, I am all at sea. Why should a ball be cause for such distress? I thought you wanted the amusements of good society."

She looked at him as if he were the densest of creatures. "I don't know how to dance!"

"Ah." His gaze followed her as she paced to the other side of the room. "You have quite a problem. Moving in society will be difficult enough when you have not been raised in it. Dancing, I am afraid, is de rigeur for all young ladies."

She groaned.

"You could always stay here," he could not resist pointing out.

"Of course that is what you would say. You are quite pleased about my distress, I am sure. Which is why Lady Hammond's suggestion is so preposterous."

"Suggestion? What suggestion?"

Daphne held up the letter in her hand and began to read from it. " 'If we are to see you begin moving in society, you must learn to dance, dear Daphne. I realize that attending dance lessons with the little girls on Saturday mornings at the assembly rooms in Wychwood might be a bit awkward for you. Please consider my well-meant advice and ask my brother for assistance. Though he does not often go to balls nowadays, he is an excellent dancer. I am certain he would not be so ungracious that he would refuse to teach you the waltz and a few quadrilles.' " She looked up, making a sound of disbelief rather like a sneezing kitten. "As if you would agree to teach me anything."

Anthony saw nothing silly about it at all. In fact, he thought the suggestion an excellent one and quite in keeping with his own intentions. Here was a way to keep Daphne at Tremore Hall a bit longer, a way that was fair and beneficial to both of them. He began to smile.

She pounced on his pleased expression at once. "You see?" she said, pointing at him with the letter in an accusing fashion. "My ignorance of these matters and the possible consequence of my being a social failure no doubt fill you with overwhelming glee. I am sure you are looking forward to watching me make the most complete fool of myself on a ballroom floor, thinking disgrace will force me back here to finish your artifacts."

"Do not think so ill of me as that. I would like you to finish your work here because you choose to do so, not because you were forced to it."

She folded the letter and put it in the pocket of her apron. "I do not believe you."

"With the amount of power and influence I possess, if I wanted to force you to remain here until my villa was completely finished, I could do so, baron's granddaughter or no. I have many faults, Miss Wade, but taking pleasure in someone's social embarrassments is not among them. You have already expressed your dislike of me quite frankly. Do not go on to impugn my honor as a gentleman."

She looked away, then back again. "I did not mean to insult you. However I cannot help but question your motives."

No one had questioned Anthony's motives since he had become a duke at the age of twelve, and he seldom felt the need to explain them. In this case, however, he knew it was important that he do so.

"I mean what I say, Miss Wade. You intend to leave, and I intend to do all I can to persuade you to stay, but I am a man of honor. If I cannot succeed in my objective by fair and honest means, I would prefer to fail, even if my museum is delayed indefinitely as a result." As he spoke, Anthony saw a perfect opportunity to further that objective, and he went on, "In light of your distrust, I should like to prove it to you."

"How?"

"Contrary to your low opinion of me, I have no desire to see you disgraced, and I should be happy to adopt Viola's suggestion and teach you to dance." Before she could get over her astonishment enough to reply, he added, "In exchange for more of your time here, of course."

"Hmm. I don't suppose you could simply offer to do this without expecting something in return, could you?"

"No. But you must admit I am not making any attempt to deceive you."

"How honorable of you." She looked up at him,

her arms folded, her head tilted to one side. "How many dances?" she asked in a brisk, no-nonsense fashion. "How much time?"

Anthony felt as if he were negotiating the terms of a business venture. So he was, really. "Country dance is complicated, and a young lady of fashion needs to know many figures. I will give you dancing lessons each evening, teaching you the waltz, and the most common figures of country dance, if you stay until March first."

"I will stay until December fifteenth."

"Two weeks? That is not nearly enough to be a fair offer. I am not particularly fond of dancing, and two weeks is not worth my while. Twelve might be."

She tapped the letter against her arm, studying him, and he could tell that her desire to make a good show in London was at war with her enmity for him, an enmity which he still found baffling, but which he was determined to rectify if it would persuade her to stay longer. He waited for her answer.

To his surprise, the fear of social failure was not enough to tempt her for long. She shook her head in refusal. "I will offer you three weeks. December twenty-first."

"February first."

"It hardly does me any good to take dancing lessons from you so that I may attend a ball, only to miss that ball because of the lessons. Three weeks."

Anthony would take whatever he could get. "You are a hard bargainer, Miss Wade, but I will accede to your terms. December twenty-first, it is.

We shall meet at eight o'clock tonight in the ballroom. I shall arrange for musicians and tell Mrs. Bennington."

"Mrs. Bennington? Does she have to be there?"

He looked at her in puzzlement. "Why should she not be? She is your chaperone."

"Only in the most general sense. It is not as if you and I have never been alone." She gestured to her surroundings. "We are alone now." She shifted her weight, glanced away, looked back at him again. "I would rather not have an audience."

Anthony was becoming curious. Surely Miss Wade could not have some sort of romantic purpose in view. After all, she did not even like him. Now that he had seen her in the rain, he rather wished she did. But he set aside his baser nature and said, "You would still have an audience. We will need musicians."

Her cheeks tinged pink. "I understand that musicians will be needed. That cannot be helped, I suppose. But Mrs. Bennington is a different matter."

Anthony could not make this out at all. In the face of his obvious bewilderment, she went on, "It is just that whatever I undertake, I seek to do it as well as possible."

Anthony knew her work was usually flawless, and he understood at once what she meant. "What you are saying is that you do not wish to do anything in front of people unless you can do it faultlessly?"

"Well . . . yes."

"Miss Wade, you are far too severe upon yourself. No one can do every single thing without flaw."

"Yes, I know, but . . ." She paused, bit her lip and looked away. After a moment, she drew a deep breath, and let it out on a sigh. "The truth is, I have a horrible fear of being laughed at," she confessed in a small voice, returning her gaze to his. "Until I become at least somewhat proficient at dancing, I should prefer not to have an audience."

Anthony looked at her—the smoothness of her countenance that never gave anything away, the discretion in her that never revealed a secret, this need to do things perfectly. He felt another flash of anger. What sort of upbringing had she had, that she should reach the age of four and twenty without any ability to like herself and laugh at her foibles? He could almost understand Sir Henry taking her out into the wilds of Africa because of his work, but not the emotional neglect such a life had inflicted on her. The more he learned about her, the more tarnished Anthony's respect for her father became. "I will see you make mistakes," he pointed out, his voice gentle.

"That is different. I do not care what you think."

He gave a shout of laughter. "Now that I can well believe. Very well, Miss Wade, we shall keep your lessons to ourselves. There are plenty of places in a house this size where a duke, his pupil, and a quartet of violinists can hide. I will find one."

"Thank you." She nodded, and moved as if to walk past him and depart, but Anthony spoke again, bringing her to a halt. "In addition to dancing, could I tempt you to stay longer with lessons in etiquette?"

"No, thank you." She took two steps sideways, then walked past him.

He turned, his gaze following her. "Why not?"

Daphne paused and looked at him over one shoulder. "I have already found four books on matters of etiquette in your library."

Anthony laughed, watching as she walked out of the room. He was beginning to enjoy this battle with Miss Wade. He had lost on his attempt to buy more time with lessons in etiquette, but if he paid close attention, other opportunities would present themselves. If he kept his wits about him, his museum just might be opened on schedule after all.

Chapter 12

After dinner that evening, while she was working in the library, a footman came in search of her. "Miss Wade?" he asked from the doorway.

Daphne looked up from the Romano-British tablet she was translating. "Yes, Oldham?"

"His grace sent me for you."

It must be time for her dance lesson. She glanced at the clock on the mantel, which showed the time as quarter to eight, but perhaps the clock was slow. She set her book aside and followed the footman out of the library. He picked up a lit candelabra he had placed on a table outside the door and proceeded to lead her up a set of stairs to the top floor, and all the way across the house to the north wing. Anthony had found a place that was indeed far away from any sort of audience.

During the nearly six months she had been at Tremore Hall, Daphne's life had been limited to a small part of the immense ducal house and she had given herself little time to explore the rest. As a result, she was completely lost by the time she and the footman reached a door at the end of a long corridor. Oldham opened the door for her to enter and stepped aside.

Anthony was waiting for her, standing beside the fireplace in an empty room. He bowed to her as she came in, and he nodded to Oldham to depart. By the light of the fire as well as the four lit wall sconces in the corners, she could tell this room had not been used for a long time. The floor was covered with a layer of dust, and the heavy draperies of robin's-egg blue that covered the windows seemed as if they had not been taken down for a good shaking in years. The only object in the entire room was an intricately carved wooden box on the mantelpiece.

"I have never been in this part of the house," she said as she looked around. "What is this place?"

"This is the children's wing."

"But it is so far from the other rooms."

He gave her a look she could not explain, a bit of both cynicism and humor. "I do not think Tremore Hall was originally built with children in mind. The fashion has long been to keep children well out of the way."

"A poor fashion, in my opinion." She looked around. "Was this your room as a boy?"

"Yes."

She tried to imagine him as a child, but it was not easy. She looked at the wall and the purple chalk marks on the cream-colored paint. She smiled and traced a line with her finger. "A map of the Roman empire?"

"Well, an attempt at one. Not perfect, but good enough for Parliament, as my mother was wont to say."

He had never mentioned his parents. "What was your mother like?"

Anthony looked past her as if remembering. "She was one of the most extraordinary people I have ever known, and yet I doubt I could explain why in any satisfactory way. She was always busy with the many duties of a duchess—and those duties can be overwhelming—but she made time for my sister and myself every day, going over our lessons with tutors, making sure the cook prepared our favorite desserts, thoughtful little things like that. Viola and I both adored her. I was only nine when she died, but I remember that everyone who knew her felt the same." He looked at her. "So, are you ready to begin learning to dance?"

"Yes, of course." She glanced around again, puzzled. "What about musicians?"

He pointed to the wooden box on the mantel beside him. "Given our conversation this morning, and your desire to avoid an audience, I thought perhaps you would prefer this to a group of violinists."

A musical box. Daphne walked slowly over to his side, staring at the carved walnut object on the mantel. She wanted so much to hate him for what he had said about her, why was he making it so hard?

She ran her finger along the polished silver trim of the box. “I had a musical bird when I was a little girl,” she said, “but when Papa and I left Crete it would not sing anymore. Too much sand and dust in Mesopotamia, I think.” Turning her head, she looked at him and found he was watching her. “Thank you, your grace. This was very considerate of you.”

Anthony looked away. “Not at all,” he said, and cleared his throat almost as if he were embarrassed. “I suppose we should begin. The first thing you need to know—”

He broke off as he turned toward her. His gaze made a slow perusal from the neckline of her dress, over her apron, down to the sturdy brown boots on her feet, and she was sure he was likening her to a brown mantis, or making some other equally unflattering comparison. But when he spoke, his words were not at all what she expected.

“Take it off.”

“I beg your pardon?”

“The apron, Miss Wade. Remove it, I beg of you.” When she did not move, he stepped closer and brought his hands to her sides. Before she could stop him, he was pulling at the ties that held the front and back of the apron together. Shocked, Daphne started to move away, but his grip tightened on the strings, preventing her escape.

“Do not move,” he ordered as he pulled at the first two bows, untying them. “I am ridding you of this, for I vow it is the ugliest thing I have ever seen."

"I believe *please* was supposed to become part of your vocabulary," she shot back. "And my apron may be ugly, but is also a very practical garment."

"It is atrocious." He bent down slightly to unfasten the second set of ties, then the third. "You are a woman, Miss Wade. Why should you wish to hide the fact behind a suit of canvas armor?"

There was more than irritation in the question. There was genuine bewilderment as well. When he straightened, the candlelight caught on gold lights in his brown hair and softened the lean planes of his cheekbones. For an instant, she remembered the man she had thought him to be—a man she had fashioned out of her imagination, a man who was not only a sort of prince, but also a kind and thoughtful man. Now she saw something in his face, something that reminded her of that day in the rain, and she suddenly realized what it was. He was looking at her, and he was not seeing a stick insect. He was not seeing a person in his employ, not a servant, not a machine. He was seeing a woman.

Daphne felt her countenance freeze into the safe, placid lines she had always used as a mask to hide her feelings from him, a mask she had thought would protect her from heartbreak, but it had not protected her at all. Heartbreak had already come and gone, there was nothing to hide now, so why did she care how he looked at her? She shouldn't. But she did.

He lifted his hands to her shoulders to undo the

last two sets of ties, then he took a step back, pulling the two pieces of canvas away with him. He held them up, eyeing them with distaste. "I believe I shall burn this thing."

"You will not! I wear that to protect my clothes."

"If you had clothes worth protecting, I could see your point."

She ignored that. "It belongs to me, and you have no right to destroy anything of mine."

"Miss Wade, I do not ever want to see this garment again unless you are working. Please," he added as he tossed the two pieces of her now dismantled apron toward a corner of the room.

She was not fooled into thinking that word made it a request, but she did not argue. She hoped they could just get on with the business at hand, but he did not seem inclined to do so. Instead, he reached out and jerked off her spectacles.

Daphne gave a cry of outraged protest, but of course, he ignored it. He folded the glasses and put them in the pocket of his jacket, then took another look at her face. "Much better."

"Give them back."

"Miss Wade," he interrupted, "you have beautiful eyes. To distort them behind a pair of thick glass lenses is a shame at any time. When you are with a gentleman, it is unpardonable."

How many times had she wished he would notice something, anything, about her? She was fully aware that any compliments he gave her now were empty ones. He wanted her time, and if compliments would get him more of it, he would tell her she was as alluring and captivating as Cleopatra had ever been. Daphne held out her hand. "Give me back my spectacles."

"Do not the rules of *please* and *thank you* apply to you as well as to me? I just paid you a compliment, Miss Wade."

"Thank you. I want my spectacles back, if you please."

"You are not going to be wearing them to Covington's ball. I promise I shall give them back to you when we are finished here." He lifted his hands to her neck.

Daphne gasped as his fingertips brushed against her skin, too startled to continue arguing with him. "Now what are you doing?" She reached up to pull his hands away, but her efforts were futile.

"That bun is almost as hideous as the apron," he answered as he began removing pins from her hair, the pads of his thumbs brushing against the sides of her neck. "Since we are alone and there is no one here to stop me, I am ridding you of it. I have wanted to do this for days."

As her hair came down, Daphne felt her sense of control unraveling. She could have pulled away, but that would imply that she was affected by what he was doing, and she forced herself to remain still. "And you always get what you want, of course."

"Not always. If I did, you would be staying. Hold these."

Daphne looked down and took the pins from him. She could not believe she was letting him do this, but the feel of his hands in her hair was so delicious, she could not bring herself to pull away. No man had ever touched her so intimately before. "How do you know how to dress a woman's hair?" she asked, trying to distract herself from those dangerous feelings.

"I don't." He raked his hands upward through her hair, twisting her tresses into a pile atop her head. Holding her hair in place with one hand, he took a pin from her with the other and pushed it into place. "I am making this up as I go along."

"But if it isn't pinned right, it could come tumbling back down."

He looked at her between his upraised arms and gave her a wicked grin. "God, I hope so."

Her heart slammed against her ribs, and she spoke again. "I cannot imagine why you are concerning yourself with something as trivial as my hair."

"To a man, a woman's hair is never trivial. Imagining a woman with her hair down, imagining how it looks loose around her shoulders, how it feels in his hands or spread across his pillows, can become a man's obsession." He paused to look at her, curling a loose tendril of hair at her ear around his finger, his knuckles brushing her cheek. "I know it has been mine on occasion."

Waves of heat flooded through her body at his words and his touch as the image of her hair spread across his pillows flashed across her mind, followed immediately by horror at the very thought of such a thing. She reminded herself of his contempt and her pain, throwing the chilling water of reality on the hot, inexplicable hunger flaring inside her, a hunger she could see reflected in the intensity of his gaze.

Daphne forced herself not to look away. "The outside of a woman is your first priority, then?" she asked as if they were discussing the weather. "Are all men concerned only with the package rather than the goods within?"

He took another pin from her hand and continued his task. "In thinking about women, men are not very deep."

She gave what she hoped was a disdainful sniff. "You do not seem to have a very high opinion of the character of your own sex."

"Men have no character when it comes to women. Love turns us into complete idiots or dishonorable villains. Usually both."

"Why do you always speak of love in such a derogatory manner?"

"Do I?" He paused again, and his lips compressed briefly into a thin line. "That is an irony, for the truth is that I am in utter awe of love. It scares the bloody hell out of me. That is why I have never allowed myself to fall into that state."

This was a man who walked the earth as if he owned it—all of it. She could not imagine him afraid of anything. "Why does love frighten you?"

"Forgive me for my choice of language," he said, his gaze skating away from hers. "It is not proper for a man to curse in front of a woman," he went on as he resumed his task, "and I apologize. Discussions of this sort bring out the worst in me."

"You did not answer my question. Why should love be a frightening thing?"

"You should know the answer to that," he countered, plucking a hairpin from her grasp and pushing it into place. "It frightens you."

"It does not."

"Oh, yes it does."

"Don't be absurd. Love does not frighten me."

"Really?" He lowered one hand to grasp her chin in his fingers. He lifted her face, forcing her to meet his gaze. "Why do you insist on donning that apron, never removing your spectacles, wearing dresses in the most drab colors imaginable, and fashioning your hair in the most unflattering style invented by womankind? You are hiding from something."

Daphne realized he had neatly turned the tables on her, putting her on the defensive without revealing anything of himself, and she wished she had never asked him the question. She jerked her chin out of his grasp and lowered her gaze to his perfectly tied cravat. "I am a sensible person. I dress to suit what I do."

"How convenient, if one wishes to fade away and become unnoticeable."

Like a stick insect on a twig.

Repeating those words in her mind was like a kick in the stomach. Her mind flashed through all the times her feelings for him had compelled her to withdraw into herself, to be so afraid of her own emotions and his certain rejection of what she felt that she had tried to become invisible. Repeating the pattern of her whole life. Knowing she would always be leaving for the next project, the next set of acquaintances, the next good-bye.

No wonder she had been so hurt. His opinion might have been unkind, but it had the ring of truth. True or no, she would die before admitting anything of the sort to him. "I am not afraid of love," she lied. "If I were, I certainly would not be considering the idea of a husband."

Anthony did not reply, and he did not look at her, but he was standing so close that even without her glasses, she could see every feature of his face in perfect focus. His brows were drawn together as if this task were the most important thing in the world to him. His eyes were narrowed in concentration, the dark lashes above and below nearly tangling together.

He shoved the last hairpin in place and lowered his arms. As he stepped back to survey his handiwork, Daphne felt that horrid ache of vulnerability. Fading into the wallpaper was so much safer than being noticed.

His lips tightened. If he said one horrid thing, just one, their bargain was off. His museum and her future could both go to the devil.

"Much better, Miss Wade." He broke off and took a deep breath. "You look . . . very pretty."

There was something in those words, or perhaps in the almost unsteady note of his voice as he said them, that caught at her heart, that made her want to believe he meant more by it than he really did, but she would not delude herself ever again to think he set any store by her. "Two compliments in one evening? I am astonished at your sudden propensity to flatter me."

"I never flatter anyone. I give my opinions honestly." He pulled her spectacles out of his pocket and held them out to her. "If you really wish to find a husband, Miss Wade, stop hiding your lights under a bushel. We shall then see if a husband is what you really want."

She took the pair of spectacles from his hand, and the moment she did, he took a step back from her. "We have gotten well away from your dance lesson."

The idea of dancing with him just now was unbearable to her dazed senses. She was already raw from his touch and his words and his razor-sharp perceptions of her deepest fears. "Perhaps we should postpone this until tomorrow night," she suggested.

To her surprise, he agreed. "Very well." He took another step back from her, bowed, and turned away. "In the morning, I shall wish to meet with you," he said over his shoulder, "and begin taking an inventory of those artifacts which you have ready for me to have taken to London. Please be in the antika at ten o'clock."

Daphne stared at his back as he walked away, still feeling the tingle of his touch against her neck, and he was halfway to the door before his words sank into her consciousness. "Tomorrow is Thursday, your grace," she called after him. "My day out, if you remember our bargain."

"I do." He paused in the doorway, turning to look at her. "We shall meet on Friday. Enjoy yourself, Miss Wade."

With that, he departed.

Daphne remained where she was, staring at the empty doorway, bemused. He was the most unpredictable man. One day, she was a stick insect, and the next, she had beautiful eyes. Just when she was starting to loathe him, he did something nice, and just when she was starting to like him, he did something to remind her of all the reasons she should hate him.

Daphne reached up to touch her neck, still tingling from the brush of his fingertips, and she was forced to admit that even though she no longer cared about having his good opinion, she could not find it in her heart to hate him.

Chapter 13

During the entire six months she had been at Tremore Hall, Daphne had seldom had opportunities to explore the house and its environs or go into the village. She had Sundays free, of course, and always rode into Wychwood for early service with the Benningtons, but she had never taken time away from her duties to visit the village shops or appreciate the beauty of Anthony's estate.

Now that she had Thursdays out as well as Sundays, Daphne decided to walk into the village for a bit of shopping. She wanted to spend a little of the thirty-two pounds she had earned since her arrival, her first step toward less work and more play.

She set a leisurely pace, enjoying the charming beauty of thatch-roofed cottages, ancient oaks, and the stunning reds and golds of autumn as she walked the road into Wychwood. She could not help comparing the scenery here in Hampshire to the date palms, sand, and scrub of North Africa, the red cliffs of Petra, and the hills of Crete, hills covered with the green of rosemary and the pink and white of dittany. Each place had its own attractive qualities, but Daphne found the English countryside more beautiful than anywhere else she had lived. She doubted she would get tired of the English weather, but if she ever did, all she would have to think of was Mesopotamia in a sandstorm, and rain would seem wonderful again.

Thinking of rain brought Anthony's face to mind, and her own realization last night that he had looked at her in a new way. Like a woman. She remembered the touch of his fingertips on her skin, and his words about how a woman's hair could be a man's obsession. That triggered again that hot, aching hunger in her body, just like the lovesick girl who had gazed at his naked chest through a spyglass. She could not really blame herself for that. After all, it was rather a stunning thing when a handsome man you had adored finally noticed you, even when it was too late. Even when it did not mean anything.

Perhaps he did believe she had beautiful eyes, perhaps he had come to see her as more than a machine, but Daphne knew he was far more concerned with his museum than with her. She pushed thoughts of Anthony firmly out of her mind and quickened her steps into the village.

Within Wychwood itself, there was a High Street lined with shops, and Daphne began walking down one side, content for now just to look in the shop windows she passed, but when she reached the shop at the corner, she found herself lingering for more than just a glance.

Daphne stared through the glass window of Mrs. Avery's Dressmaking Establishment, where several beautiful gowns were displayed to tempt young ladies passing by. One of them tempted her. It was of rose-pink silk with a beaded filigree design around the hem in cream and deeper pink. It had a neckline that barely skimmed the shoulders, and looked just as likely to fall down as not, and the sleeves were absurd puffs of silk with more beading of deeper pink. A pair of embroidered silk slippers to match were displayed beside it. Daphne had never seen anything so feminine and pretty and impractical in her life before.

She touched the glass, staring at the gown, and a wave of longing swept over her. She had never taken any interest in clothes before—there was little use for pink silk in the desert sands of Morocco or Petra—and her practical, thrifty nature had never allowed her to justify a pretty dress, especially one so frivolous as this evening gown. But her life was very different now, and she was not in the desert anymore.

Daphne imagined how it would feel to wear such a dress, and before she could even think of changing her mind, she pulled open the door and went inside the shop.

As she stepped inside, a tiny bell sounded, and

the half dozen or so women in the shop looked up. Daphne gave a smile of greeting that took in all of them, then she turned to have a closer look at the gown in the window.

The moment she did, she was lost. She wanted that dress, and she didn't care if she spent every shilling of her thirty-two pounds to acquire it. It looked as if it would fit her, but even if it did not, she would have one made up just like it.

The bell over the door sounded again, and Mrs. Bennington entered the shop. The other woman came to her side at once. "My dear Miss Wade, did you not hear me calling you? I spied you from down the street. Why, I had no idea you were coming into the village today. Why did you not tell me so at breakfast?"

"I did not know how I would spend my day out. By the time I decided, you and Mr. Bennington had already left."

"It is fortunate, then, that I have seen you, for the duke has been so kind as to allow my husband and myself to use one of his carriages today, and you will be able to ride back with us."

She gave Daphne's arm an affectionate little pat. "I am glad to see you spending more days out, my dear. Heaven knows, going to Enderby will be such a tonic for you, trapped as you have been in that dirty cottage—what does Mr. Bennington call it?"

"The antika."

"Yes, yes, the antika. Such an odd name."

"Good day, Mrs. Bennington." Another voice

entered the pause in conversation, and both of them turned to find a red-haired young lady of about seventeen standing only a few feet away.

"Miss Elizabeth, how lovely to see you. I hope you are well?"

"She is always well, ma'am," a slightly older girl said, coming up to their group. "And silly, too."

"So are you," Miss Elizabeth replied, then cast Mrs. Bennington a pointed glance and looked at Daphne, causing the older lady to give a cry of vexation.

"Oh, have the three of you not met? How remiss of me! Miss Wade, this is Miss Anne Fitzhugh," she said, gesturing to the older girl, "and Miss Elizabeth Fitzhugh. My dear young ladies, Miss Wade."

They dipped mutual curtsies.

"It is such a pleasure to meet you," said Miss Fitzhugh. "Why Mrs. Bennington has never introduced us after church services, I cannot think."

"I would, I would," the older woman assured with a laugh, "but Miss Wade always runs away before I have the opportunity."

They all gave her such a curious look that Daphne felt compelled to explain. "Mr. Bennington is uncovering artifacts so rapidly that I have been spending my Sunday afternoons in the duke's library, sketching as fast as I can."

"If I were staying at Tremore Hall, I should find any excuse not to leave either," Anne confessed, "just on the chance the duke himself might come by and actually speak to me."

"If he did," her sister put in, "you would faint dead away, I am sure."

"I would never do anything so undignified."

"Of course you would," Elizabeth answered, laughing.

"I would not!"

"That will be quite enough, my dears." A new voice spoke, and Daphne turned to another older woman who joined the group. "Do not quarrel."

When the woman moved to stand between Elizabeth and Anne, it became evident to Daphne that she was the mother of the two, and a very attractive-looking woman, with a face as yet unlined by age. Her hair was free of gray and was a darker red than her younger daughter.

After being introduced to Daphne, Lady Fitzhugh said, "It is a pleasure to meet you, Miss Wade, for I have heard nothing but praise about you from my husband."

"Sir Edward is very kind."

"He is fascinated by antiquities, as I am sure you are well aware. I believe he read every paper your father ever wrote, for he quite admired him."

"Papa says you draw very well," Elizabeth put in, "and know Latin and Greek, and have been to all sorts of wild places. Have you been to Abyssinia? That is where the Nile is, am I not right?"

"Yes," Daphne replied, smiling. "You are right, and yes, I have been there."

"You must come to tea on Sunday and tell us all about such places, for we know nothing of them. Anne and I are not very studious girls. Papa thinks we are frivolous, which of course is one of the reasons he so admires you, Miss Wade. He says you are a sensible person." She laughed, adding merrily, "From Papa, that is the highest of compliments."

Lady Fitzhugh put in, "We would enjoy having you to tea very much, Miss Wade, even though my daughter is inclined to jump straight to an invitation without considering the previous obligations of the person she invites."

"Oh," cried Elizabeth, "that is true. I had not thought of how your Sunday afternoons are not free. You would have to ask the duke for permission to come, and that is a difficulty, I am sure, for he is a bit intimidating. A duke has to be, I should think."

"Not at all, Miss Elizabeth!" Mrs. Bennington put in. "He may seem a bit so, but once you have spoken with him a few times, you find he is quite amiable. His tenants think him a good and just landlord, and Mr. Bennington regards him very highly. Why, he had Mr. Bennington, Miss Wade, and myself to dine with him two weeks ago, and he was all ease and amiability. Was he not, Miss Wade?"

"Yes, he was," Daphne admitted. *And far too charming for my peace of mind.* "Asking him for permission is not necessary, and thank you, Lady Fitzhugh, I should like to come very much."

"Excellent. Edward deems you to be a nice, steady young woman, and I vow you would be quite a favorable influence upon my daughters."

"I believe it would be the other way about,"

Daphne said, "for it has been expressed to me of late that I am far too severe and sensible, and it is your daughters who would provide the favorable influence."

"Then it is settled," Anne declared. "You must come to tea, and tell us all about the duke."

"Oh, yes!" cried Elizabeth. "Tremore shall make far more interesting conversation than Abyssinia! We have met him, of course, but Papa is so tiresome, for he refuses to take us with him to the hall when he calls on the duke. And you are of no help, Mrs. Bennington, for you tell us nothing of him."

"I know nothing," the older woman assured. "I almost never see his grace. Our suite of rooms is well away from the family quarters. The duke is a very private sort of man, and even Mr. Bennington tells me very little."

"Papa is the same, so I fear we must turn to you for information, Miss Wade, for you have surely seen more of the duke than we have. Of course, we attend the annual fête up at the hall, along with the rest of the county, so we see him there, and sometimes catch a glimpse of him riding by on that big, black gelding of his when we walk in the park at the hall, but that is all. He never gives parties or balls, and he never comes to the local assemblies. Oh, how I wish he would. Perhaps he might even engage me for a dance. How wonderful that would be!"

"Then you would be the one to swoon," Anne put in, "and embarrass us all."

"Now, Anne, that is enough idle chatter," Lady Fitzhugh broke in. "We came here with a purpose in view beyond your mooning over his grace. We must get you fitted for that new gown." She turned to Daphne. "Miss Wade, we look forward to seeing you on Sunday, and you as well, Mrs. Bennington."

As Lady Fitzhugh and her elder daughter left the group, the shop assistant stepped forward and asked the other three women how Mrs. Avery's establishment could be of service.

Elizabeth shook her head at the shop assistant and said, "I've spent all my pocket allowance already this month. I cannot purchase a thing."

"Nor I," Mrs. Bennington told the girl. "I only came in because of Miss Wade here."

"Then we can only hope you intend to purchase something, Miss Wade," Elizabeth said, "for both Mrs. Bennington and I are being so dull."

Daphne pointed to the pink silk concoction in the window. "I want that."

"Oh, yes!" Elizabeth cried. "It is a perfect color for you, and would look ever so nice. It appears to be about the right size and if it could be made to fit in time, you could wear it to the assembly rooms on Saturday."

"Oh, Miss Wade will be needing it for more than our little assemblies here," Mrs. Bennington said, moving her stout form out of the way so that the shop assistant could take the dress down from the window. "She is going to Chiswick shortly to spend the winter with Lady Hammond. And the season in London with her as well."

"London!" Elizabeth cried. "Can it be so? We are going to Town as well. We leave after Twelfth

Night, for Papa has business to attend, and we shall be staying through the season."

"I shall be leaving earlier than that," Daphne answered. "December twenty-first is the last day of my stay at Tremore Hall before I go to Lady Hammond." As she said it, Daphne felt an odd pang of what almost felt like homesickness, and she pushed it aside at once. Tremore Hall was not her home.

"Oh, how wonderful to be companion to a duke's sister!" Elizabeth said. "I should love that."

"Not companion, dear," Mrs. Bennington corrected. "Miss Wade is a friend of Lady Hammond."

"Even better. I shall dare to call on you there, Miss Wade. I saw the viscountess once at Brighton, when Papa took us there for a holiday to go sea bathing. She is beautiful, isn't she? As you are a friend of hers, you shall be moving in very high circles."

"I know, and I confess, I am a bit intimidated by it," Daphne admitted. "I have not been much in society."

"Nor have I, but we shall not be daunted, Miss Wade. We shall brave the season together and you shall introduce me to all your toplofty friends." A mischievous smile lit her face. "If we make fools of ourselves, we shall console each other."

"Nonsense!" Mrs. Bennington said. "Both of you will do very well."

Daphne saw the shop assistant was waiting patiently nearby with the pink gown in her hands, and she added, "Forgive me, but I cannot wait another moment to try on that lovely dress."

She left the other two women and followed the assistant to the back of the shop. She could not remember feeling more excited about something as simple as a piece of clothing.

The patterned hem of the skirt had barely settled at her ankles before she knew she had been right. She stared at herself in the glass as the shop assistant began doing the buttons up her back, and something came over her, something so intoxicating that she felt as if she were the most beautiful woman in the world. As the assistant began pinning where the dress needed adjustments, Daphne looked at herself, and for once, she did not see a plain, unnoticeable woman who wore glasses and faded into the background. She felt beautiful, and the feeling came from the inside out. How a froth of rose-pink silk could create that sort of strange, instant alchemy was a mystery, but she did not need to know how.

An impatient knock followed her thoughts. "Does it fit?" Elizabeth asked from the other side of the door. "Do show me."

Daphne padded over to the door in her stockinged feet, and Elizabeth's reaction when she opened the door was all she could have hoped for. "You look lovely!" the girl declared as she entered the small room and closed the door behind her. "I knew it would suit your coloring and your figure. You are going to take it, are you not?"

"I am."

"It does look ever so nice on you, miss," the assistant said, coming up behind her to take the gown in a bit at her waist. "The bodice needs a gusset under each arm, for it is a bit tight there, and the waist is too loose, but with that and a few other little adjustments, it will fit as if it had been made for you."

A voice behind Elizabeth called her name. She opened the door and looked back down the hallway to the shop. "Oh, that is Anne calling me," she said, and came back inside the fitting room. "I suppose she and Mama are ready to return home, so I must go."

Elizabeth grasped Daphne's hands and gave them a quick squeeze. "I cannot wait until you come to tea, and you shall tell us all about Abyssinia, and everywhere else you have been, but especially, you must tell us about the duke. He is so handsome, and so tall. Rather like a prince in a story, I think. And a duke is very nearly a prince, is he not?"

Before she could reply, Elizabeth was slipping out the door to join her sister. Daphne leaned out through the open doorway and watched her new young friend walk away down the corridor to the front of the shop. "Yes, I thought he was a prince once, too," she murmured under her breath. "But taken all in all, he is just a man."

She stepped back inside the dressing room and closed the door. The assistant began to unfasten the hooks down the back of the gown, but Daphne stopped her. "No, not yet. I want to wear it a minute longer."

The assistant met her gaze in the mirror with a

knowing smile, then stepped away, and Daphne returned her attention to her reflection in the glass, savoring again that feeling of exhilaration, a sensation as heady and potent as drinking champagne. Right now, at this moment, she felt like the most beautiful woman in the world, a far more delightful thing than dreaming of a fantasy prince. Daphne hugged herself, and she couldn't stop smiling. A pretty dress was a wonderful thing.

Chapter 14

Some peers were of the opinion that their rank made them gentlemen, but Anthony had always felt that being a true gentleman required honor as well as fortune of birth. He had offered to teach Miss Wade to dance in exchange for more of her time, and he had assured her that he would carry out that instruction to the best of his ability. He intended to keep strictly to his word, though she was beginning to test his honor in a very dangerous way.

He had told both her and himself he wanted that apron off of her because it was so damned ugly, but the truth was far less honorable. He wanted to look at her without it, envision again the figure he had discovered hiding beneath its stiff canvas protection that day in the rain.

He had been right about that thing. She wore it like a chastity belt, and with that body, she had good reason to need it. Standing so close to her last night, with his hands in her hair, it had taken everything he had not to lower his hands to far more intimate places. Her first dance lesson, and her tutor was imagining the oldest dance of all.

This morning, as he made his daily tour about the estate, just thinking of last night was enough to make him burn.

Anthony brought Defiance to a halt beside the lake, and the groom who rode with him paused a respectful distance away.

It was a glorious afternoon, pleasantly warm, though the chestnuts, elms, and oaks were showing the full glory of their autumn color. But he barely noticed. As his gelding took a drink, Anthony closed his eyes and allowed himself the indulgence of a bit of harmless imagining, in which a pair of long, shapely legs played a very significant role.

When he opened his eyes, Anthony found that Defiance had finished quenching his thirst. He pulled on the reins, starting to turn the horse around, intending to head toward the farm, but as he lifted his gaze above the water to the folly on top of the grass-covered knoll opposite, something caught his attention and he stopped again.

Sitting in front of the folly, shaded by a huge chestnut tree, was the woman who had been occupying his thoughts all morning. She was seated on a blanket spread across the grass, a large picnic basket on one side of her, and her discarded straw bonnet on the other.

Anthony gestured to the groom to follow him and spurred Defiance to a canter around the lake and up the hill toward the folly.

Like all the other garden ornaments of the estate, the folly had been designed by Capability Brown fifty years earlier for the ninth Duke of Tremore, Anthony's grandfather. It had been given the grand name Temple of Apollo, but it was simply a small, round structure of curved limestone blocks capped with a dome and surrounded by decorative columns and faux Roman statues.

She looked up at the sound of their approach. "What a lovely place this is!" she called out as both men halted their horses about ten yards from her and dismounted.

Anthony handed the reins of his gelding over to the groom. "Wait here," he ordered, and turned away to join Miss Wade.

"Thank you for the compliment to my estate," he said, walking over to where she sat and coming to a halt at the edge of the blanket. He bowed to her, then clasped his hands behind his back and turned his head slightly to look at the sketchbook on her lap. On the top sheet of drawing paper was a half-completed image in charcoal of the lake, gardens, and fountains below, with Tremore Hall in the distance. "I see you have come to sketch the view."

"Who could not?" She gestured to the basket beside her. "I also have a picnic. Would you care to join me?" She moved her hat out of the way for him to sit down beside her. "Your cook is generous with your larder, and I have far too much for one person."

He remained standing. "Are you certain you want me to do so? After all," he added softly, "you do not like me. Remember?"

"If you are still waiting for that apology, you can just go away," she answered with spirit. "If you are prepared to be nice, you may stay."

"Thank you." He bowed to her. "I shall endeavor to be as charming as my nature will allow."

She looked at him with doubt. "I do not know if that is enough, your grace."

Anthony gave a shout of laughter, but his humor vanished as she scooted over to make room for him on the blanket. The movement caused the hem of her skirt to ride up, revealing her bare feet. Very pretty feet they were, but his mind led him upward, thinking of delicate ankles, rounded calves and smooth, taut thighs.

"Are you all right?" she asked, staring up at him, her eyes wide behind the lenses of her spectacles.

All right? God, no. He was making himself insane.

Anthony drew a deep breath, feeling as if he were dragging himself out of quicksand. "Of course," he said, and moved quickly to join her on the blanket before she could notice what was so close to her eye level, grateful that she was still looking into his face. "I am perfectly well, thank you."

He pulled off his jacket and draped it as carelessly as he could manage across his hips as he stretched out his legs. He loosened his cravat, then leaned his weight back on his arms, noticing her brown leather boots placed neatly at one corner of the blanket, each one holding a rolled-up white stocking. He stared at them, trying to think of something to say. He took refuge from his own lust in the only thing he could think of—teasing her.

"So this is how you decided to spend your day out," he said, with mock disappointment. "You spurned my company for a picnic basket and a day of sketching?"

"I am afraid so," she said, mirroring his injured demeanor with a pretense of apology in her tone. "But you would have made me work."

"And you prefer to idle away your day in such frivolous pursuits as these?"

"It is worse than that," she told him gravely. "I also went into the village this morning and did a bit of shopping. I bought a set of gardenia-scented soaps and a box of chocolates."

"I had hoped you would choose to buy a new dress."

She leaned toward him in a confidential fashion. "I did that, too."

Surprised, Anthony glanced at the dun-colored cotton fabric of her skirt. But that made him think again of her legs, and he fixed his gaze on the lake and gardens spread out below them. "If you bought a new dress, then why in heaven's name are you not wearing it?"

She hit his shoulder with her pencil. "I bought an evening gown!" she cried, laughing. "And do not tease me about my clothes."

"An evening gown? Miss Wade, every moment I spend with you is filled with surprises. What color? Do not tell me any shade of brown, for if you do, I shall go to Mrs. Avery myself and order you a different frock, thereby ruining your reputation for the remainder of your life."

"It is not brown. It is pink. Rose-pink, and made of silk." Her breath escaped on a dreamy little sigh, and he turned his head again to look at her. On her face was an expression of pure bliss.

Like men everywhere, he did not understand how something as trivial as a mere garment could engender such joy in women, but he did appreciate the effect. A woman could be as beautiful as she felt herself to be, and it seemed as though even the efficient and sensible Miss Wade was not immune to the magic of a pink silk frock to help that feeling along. But then, the woman who sat beside him was not the same Miss Wade he had known a month ago. "You have relieved my mind."

He watched as she bent her head over her sketchbook again, and he caught the golden glint of sunlight in the intricately braided crown of her hair. "I also note that you have taken my advice."

"Advice?"

"About your hair."

She did not look at him, but he saw a tiny blush creep into her cheeks as she tucked a loose tendril behind her ear in a self-conscious gesture. "Ella helped me. She was a lady's maid once."

"Ella?"

"Third housemaid. Do you not know the names of your servants?"

Anthony shook his head. "Only the upper servants. I have seven estates, most of which I only visit for one week each year to tour the park and meet with the steward. Each has its share of staff, and I do not hire any of them myself. That falls within the purview of butlers and housekeepers. I could not remember all the names of my servants if I wanted to." He gave her a rueful look. "I suppose you are now going to reprove me and say that I should know all their names."

"Perhaps I was," she admitted, and gestured to the groom who was standing motionless about thirty feet away, ready and waiting to obey any command given him. "Do you know his name?"

"No, and I do not wish to," he said, feeling almost defensive and wondering how he got that way. "It would not be appropriate. A man of my rank only speaks with upper servants unless absolutely necessary. He is a groom."

"He is a man."

"He is not a man, not to me. He is a groom. If I knew his name, if I knew anything about him, he would become a person to me, and that begins to narrow the gap between my rank and his. Over time, I might even begin to regard him as a friend."

"And that would be a bad thing?"

"It is not a question of whether it is good or bad. It is not acceptable."

"What a convenient way to prevent anyone from

getting close to you," she murmured, and resumed her sketching. "You can always pull rank."

"I do not think how I treat my servants is your concern."

"No," she shot back without looking up. "It is yours."

"Are we quarreling again, Miss Wade?" He drew a deep breath and raked a hand through his hair. "How is it that you and I seem to be doing that so much of late?"

"Because I no longer allow you to treat me like a nameless servant, perhaps?"

"Have I been doing that?"

She looked over at him, her face as unreadable as those of the marble statues behind them. "Yes."

She bent her head, returning her attention to the drawing in her lap and he studied her profile, wondering for the hundredth time what went on beneath that placid exterior. He wanted to know, suddenly, what she was thinking, what she was feeling, for she was a mystery he wanted to solve.

That wisp of hair had fallen forward again. He reached up, tucking it back, feeling both the hard, gold line of her spectacles and the velvety softness of her ear against his fingers. She froze to rigid stillness as he ran the tip of his finger down the column of her throat to the thin ochre braid that trimmed her plain white collar. Slowly, he moved closer, then curled his hand around the back of her neck. "I do not think of you as a servant."

She gave a little start and leaned sideways, away

from him. "What do grooms do, exactly?" she asked, her voice almost desperate as she reverted to the safe topic of servants. "I fear I know little about horses. I am an accomplished rider when it comes to camels, but I have never ridden a horse."

He could have continued his tantalizing explorations, but he allowed her to escape them. He lowered his hand and sat back. "Camels?"

"Yes, indeed." She nodded several times, tightened her grip around her pencil, and continued to draw the view. "Camels are rather difficult animals. Contrary, hard to ride, and they spit."

"I cannot imagine any camel getting the better of you, Miss Wade." He glanced at her bare toes peeping out from beneath the hem of her skirt, and he felt desire flicker dangerously within his body. "I know I can never seem to do so."

"Good," she said in a prim voice. "I prefer it that way."

"Yes, I am certain you do." Anthony forced his gaze away from her feet. "Would you care to learn to ride?"

She continued to sketch without looking at him. "And in return for riding lessons, how much time would I have to give you?"

At this moment, time was not what he really wanted to bargain for, but something far more intriguing and not at all honorable. "A month?"

She shook her head, laughing. "Thank you, but no."

"Riding on the Row is quite the thing to do," he said in an attempt to intrigue her.

It worked. She looked at him. "The Row? What is that?"

"Rotten Row is a track of sand in Hyde Park where the fashionable people gather from twelve o'clock to two o'clock for riding."

"Rotten Row. What a name!"

"Being seen riding on the Row is an excellent way for young ladies to impress country gentlemen. Riding is yet another of the season's many opportunities to meet prospective husbands. So you see, you should learn how to ride."

She pressed her pencil against her lips, her expression wary as she considered the matter. "I do not believe a month is a fair exchange," she finally said. "I already know how to ride a camel."

"I am open to negotiation. What would you believe to be fair?"

"As I told you, camels are difficult animals. I shouldn't think more than a day of practice on a trained horse would be needed."

An image flashed across his mind of Miss Wade astride a camel, her legs encased in trousers. He shoved that tantalizing image aside and made a calculated guess. "And when you rode camels, did you also master a sidesaddle?"

That got to her. She blinked behind her spectacles. "I had not thought of that."

"I told you before, I will not lie to you." As he said the words, he admitted to himself that some fashionable young ladies, through ignorance or preference, did not ride horseback, but he was not going to offer Miss Wade that additional piece of information. After all, he reasoned, an omission was not a lie. "There is no question that a sidesaddle is considered de rigueur for young ladies."

"All right, then. In exchange for riding lessons, including the proper use of a sidesaddle, I will give you two days."

"Two days? A week."

Those lavender-blue eyes narrowed a bit. "Two days, until December twenty-third."

He pretended to think it over, though he knew he had no choice. "Very well," he agreed, and moved to sit opposite her, stretching out his legs beside her hip, and gestured to the basket. "So, are you going to allow me to sample these picnic viands of yours?"

"Of course." She set aside her sketchbook and her pencil, then folded her legs beneath her, tucking her feet under her hips and out of his view, which was probably a good thing.

She placed the picnic basket between them and opened it. Anthony leaned back on his hands and watched as she laid out their meal of roast chicken, apples, cheese, bread and butter. "No wine?" he asked. "Miss Wade, a picnic should always have wine."

"Not necessarily." She pulled a bottle of cider and a glass out of the basket. She pushed up the metal clip of the bottle that held the stopper in place. "If our picnic were in Palestine," she added, as she poured cider into the glass, "you would not have wine."

"Nor cider."

"True." She held out the half-empty cider bottle to him.

He stared at the bottle in her hand, but he did not move to take it. "I wish we were in Palestine," he said abruptly.

"Do you? Why?"

"I should like to see it, along with all the other places you have been. Egypt, Syria, Morocco." Even saying the names stirred something inside him, a longing he had often felt but never acknowledged, and he surprised himself by confessing, "God, how I envy you."

She stared at him, seeming just as surprised as he by his admission. "You envy me?"

"Yes." He leaned forward and took the bottle from her hand. "You have ridden camels, you have lived in tents amid Roman ruins, and you have had the opportunity to be part of excavations throughout the Mediterranean crescent. What a romantic, adventurous life. Is it so hard to believe that I would envy you?"

"Well, yes," she said with a half laugh, and gestured to the lush scenery all around them. "You are a duke. You have all that life can offer."

"So it would seem." He took a swallow of cider, then set the bottle on the short grass at the edge of the blanket. He leaned back again on his hands, staring up at the monument to idleness that stood behind her. "There is one thing you have that I lack, the one thing I long for more than anything else because it the one thing I can never have."

"What is that?"

"Freedom."

She shook her head, uncomprehending as she pulled the loaf of bread toward her and reached for a knife from the basket. "You have money and power. If one has those, one can do anything."

"Perhaps it seems that way, but it is not true. I may have the means to do whatever I please, but I do not have the opportunity."

"I do not understand."

He met her gaze. "My father died when I was twelve, and I became the Duke of Tremore. My uncle served as my guardian and fulfilled my actual duties until I was sixteen, but from the day my father died, I established the power of my position. I made all the decisions, and it was I who told my uncle what was to be done, not the other way around."

"At the age of twelve? But you were a boy."

"I had known all my life that I would be the duke, and that someday I would be required to step into that position. Even at twelve I was old enough to appreciate power and what it means. I could, perhaps, have taken the easy road and done all manner of enjoyable things, such as travel, but I knew my estates were the core of my life, and I felt they deserved my full attention. I never took the Grand Tour. I have never been out of Britain in my life." He gave her a slight smile. "So I am forced to be an armchair traveler. I will never see Rome or any of the many other fascinating places of the world."

"But why do you not go now?" she asked as she

began to slice bread. "You could afford to go anywhere on earth if you wished to do so, and surely a few months away would not go amiss."

"I can never seem to find the time. Being a duke is an enormous job, Miss Wade. The tasks and duties are demanding and endless."

"And you say I am too severe and sensible!"

He conceded the point with a nod. "Perhaps I was speaking as much to myself as to you, for my excavation is the only indulgence I allow myself."

She stopped slicing bread. "I see now why the excavation is so important to you," she said softly. "It is your Grand Tour."

"Yes."

Daphne set the slices of bread aside and returned half a loaf to the basket. She then pulled out a wedge of cheese. "Tell me more about what it is like to be a duke," she said as she began to pare off slices of Cheddar.

"It is not a romantic adventure," he said. "It can feel like a prison. It can also feel like heaven. Most of the time, it is tedious and trivial and deadly dull. It has compensations, good ones—wealth, power, and prestige."

"And influence. To think of all the good things one can do with money. If you could see the poverty I have seen—"

"I should hate it and be angered by it, for waste and futility always anger me, and there would be nothing I could do to truly alleviate it. If I gave all my money away, the world would still be just as full of poor people, sad to say."

"Yes," she agreed. "I suppose it would."

"I do what I can. There are charities, and they are one of the greatest responsibilities I have. Politics, too, of course. And tenants. Then there is the constant scrutiny and the never-ending struggle for privacy."

"When I was in the village today, I met Sir Edward's wife and daughters, and they were talking with Mrs. Bennington about you. They said you were a very private man."

His insides tightened, for they had probably discussed him at length. His father's illness and death were always a favorite topic of gossip and speculation. "I have no doubt they told you quite a bit more than that, Miss Wade."

"Not very much, and in what they did tell me, there was no spite or malice, if that is what you imply."

Anthony gave a humorless laugh. "It was probably a short conversation, then." He glanced at her and found that she had stopped slicing cheese. She was watching him with that solemn face, no different than usual, and yet, he could feel censure in her silence, censure and a hint of sadness. "I do not like gossip, Miss Wade," he felt compelled to say. "I do not like my life, my family, and every move I make to be the subject of discussion. I take a great deal of trouble to give gossips little to talk about."

"Yet you have accused me of being secretive and mysterious and giving nothing away. Perhaps, despite the difference in our rank and position, we are not so very different after all."

She spoke as if she were surprised by her own words. "Yes," he admitted, just as surprised as she. "I suppose we are."

"As to gossip about you, you might be relieved to know that all of it was kindly meant. You were described as a very handsome man, as well as a good and kind landlord. The main criticisms leveled at you were given by Sir Edward's daughters and were limited to three. You are somewhat intimidating, you do not give enough parties for the local gentry, and you never attend the assemblies in Wychwood. They agreed that if you ever spoke with one of them during their strolls in your park or if you ever asked either of them to dance at an assembly, their reaction would be to faint dead away."

"I am gratified that I make young ladies swoon. Another of a duke's many duties."

"Do you not find their adoration to be a compliment?"

There was reproof behind that cool, soft voice, and he felt defensive again. "They do not even know me. My rank, my wealth, and perhaps my appearance allow them to build my life into some sort of fantasy, a fantasy in which they believe they should like to take part."

Daphne bit her lip as if she were holding back a sharp reply. She looked away and said, "It might be a fantasy, but it is a harmless one."

Anthony sensed that was not what she had wanted to say, and he would have given a great deal to hear the words she held back. He waited, but she said nothing more.

He stared into the distance, down into the brilliant autumn scenery of the land he owned. "You are right. I admit it freely. Their attentions are harmless, and a true compliment to me." He looked over at the woman beside him. "I should do well to remember that."

"Yes," she replied, looking back at him. "You should."

He gave her a wry smile. "Why is it that when I am with you, Miss Wade, I can never feel myself to be quite as arrogant a fellow as you have declared me to be? Quite the opposite, in fact, for with you I often feel the humbling effects of having been put in my place."

"I had no idea that my comments should have such an impact upon you."

"They do, for I am coming to have a high regard for your opinion. Please do not interpret my lack of enthusiasm for the attentions of Sir Edward's daughters to mean I am a callous man. But there are times when the duties of my position can be a great burden. As the daughters of a knight, the Miss Fitzhughs have no true comprehension how great a burden that position can be."

"I understand what you mean," she said, lowering her head to stare at the knife in her hand. "But one could also look upon such a life as a great comfort."

"I do not take my position for granted, I assure you. I fully understand and appreciate how fortune of birth has given me all the physical comforts of life, as well as the ability to indulge in all manner of luxuries."

"It is far more than that," she replied, sudden passion in her voice. "You have a place in the world, your grace, and you know what it is. That is a very comforting thing."

She did not move, but her sudden intensity startled him. In the past, he had taken her impassivity to mean she was not a person of deep feeling. Now, after a month of closer inspection, he was beginning to understand that the opposite was closer to the truth. Her fingers were curled around the knife in her hand so tightly that her knuckles were white. There was a great deal of passion there. It all lay beneath the surface.

"You have no idea how it feels to not quite belong anywhere," she went on with an odd little catch in her voice. "To have no roots that tie you to a place and give you purpose. It is I who envy you."

"It is understandable to feel rootless when you have had no home of your own." He could see her hand start to shake, and he tipped her chin up, wanting to see her eyes, even if it was a view through her spectacles. "You shall find your place one day, Miss Wade. Everyone does, eventually."

"I hope so, your grace."

He ran the tips of his fingers across her lower lip. "Tell me," he said before he could stop himself, "how does a woman who has lived most of her life in the desert manage to have skin as soft as velvet?"

Her mouth opened against his fingertips. "I—" She stopped, drew a deep breath, let it out in a puff of air against his fingers. "I worked under a tent, always."

"Did you?" He traced the outline of her mouth. So, so soft.

"Yes, and wore a hat, and a veil, too, much of the time."

Her sang-froid was admirable. Only a slight, momentary quiver in her jaw told him she was at all affected by what he was doing. All that passion just under the surface. What would happen if it were ever allowed to come out?

"Do you know," he mused, running his fingertip along the line of her jaw, "almost no one calls me by my name? Your grace, or Tremore, but only Viola calls me Anthony. Even amongst my friends, and there are few I trust enough to call them friends, my rank is always an inevitable barrier. Even they do not call me by my name."

He touched the tiny mole at the corner of her jaw, and her hand moved as if to push his hand away, but stilled in the air, hesitant.

What would it take, he wondered, for her to let down her guard? He had always prided himself on his own self-control, but she was a master at it. "If we were friends, Miss Wade, would you call me Anthony?"

She turned her face away. "I do not think that would be appropriate. I would . . . I would rather not."

He moved closer. If he kissed her, the dam might break, something might snap, all that passion might come out. He cupped her cheek to turn her face toward him.

"Do you want us to be friends, your grace?" she asked.

"I do. Believe me, I do." He could feel her desire and her apprehension in the rigid tendons of her neck beneath her ear, in the shallowness of her breathing. He bent his head.

"Do friends take such advantage as this?" she asked, her words more effective at stopping him than a slap across the face.

Anthony froze, his lips an inch from hers, his fingertips against her neck. He pulled back a bit and studied her profile in the dappled sunlight that filtered between the leaves of the chestnut tree. For the first time since he was a boy, he felt the agony of uncertainty.

He had no personal experience with virgins. He'd been sixteen when he had chosen his first mistress. In the thirteen years that had passed since then, he had provided himself with quite a few female companions. He also enjoyed the pleasures of London demireps on occasions when he went to Town. But of all the women he had intimately touched in his life, not one had been a virgin.

Desire had nothing to do with experience, and he felt Daphne's desire as much as his own, but she was in his employ, and at this moment, she seemed so very vulnerable, almost fragile. If he pushed, he could win a kiss, at least. But honor, which dictated everything in Anthony's life, dictated his decision now.

He sucked in a deep breath, summoning the iron will that had made his reason the master of his emotions since he was a child, and let her go.

He told himself the entire incident was innocuous. There was no harm in simply touching a woman. No harm at all. Nonetheless, he moved a safer distance away from her, and they finished their meal in silence on opposite corners of the blanket.

Chapter 15

Daphne did not know quite what to expect from her first real dance lesson, but she had thought it would begin with dancing. She was proven wrong at once.

"You want me to what?" she asked, staring at Anthony in astonishment.

"Walk." He took her arm and ushered her through the doorway to the long corridor outside his childhood room.

"Silly of me," she murmured, "but I thought I was going to learn to dance."

"You will, but first I want to study you as you walk."

That was the last thing Daphne wanted, but when he clasped his hands behind him and started down the long corridor, she fell in step beside him. "To dance well, Miss Wade," he added, "you must walk well. Dancing, especially the sedate steps of a quadrille, is little more than walking to music."

They had barely taken a dozen steps before Anthony came to a stop. Daphne paused beside him. "Why did you stop?" she asked.

Instead of answering, he turned toward her and pressed one palm against her diaphragm and the other against the base of her spine. She sucked in a deep, startled gasp at the contact, but he did not appear to notice, for he pressed his palms into her body with the pragmatic comment, "Remember to keep your back straight. Tonight you are not the antiquarian bending over a table of bronze tools or scanning the ground for pieces of clay pots. You are a young lady of fashion out for a leisurely stroll."

He let his hands fall away, but the warmth of his touch lingered as he continued walking down the corridor, and she felt anything but the proper young lady. She resumed walking as well, but her heart was pounding in her chest as if she had been running.

She was not used to being touched, she told herself. That was all. He had touched her several times now, and the unbelievable pleasure of it always took her by surprise. Just the memory of the odd, melting sensation he could evoke when his fingertips grazed her cheek or he laid his palm against her back set her nerves on edge, for she did not want to feel that way. Not about him.

They strolled up and down the long length of the

room countless times, their conversation minimal but for an occasional word of correction from him. Chin up, shoulders back, slow down.

She did not look at him, and in her peripheral vision, he was a blur along the edge of her glasses, but she could feel him watching her. When it seemed as if they had traveled the length of the corridor a thousand times, he stopped her.

"Excellent, Miss Wade," he said, as they returned to the room where they had begun. "You have a certain natural grace. No doubt you will dance well. But I advise you to wear stays. It will aid you in maintaining perfect posture. Besides, if you do not wear them, I fear you will shock your partner when he puts his hand on your waist for a waltz."

He walked to the fireplace, reached for the musical box on the mantel, and began to wind the key. "Just do not fall into the silly habit some women have of lacing them too tightly, or you will faint on the ballroom floor."

"Is it proper for you to be mentioning my undergarments?" she countered with as much dignity as she could command.

He paused in his task and met her gaze. "I believe I was mentioning your lack of one," he said gravely, but one corner of his mouth lifted in a teasing half smile. She had seen that smile a few times, and she was actually coming to like it. She found herself smiling back.

He set the box back on the mantel, and the music began to play.

"The waltz is a very simple dance," he said as he

returned to stand in front of her. He took her right hand in his left, and put his other hand on her waist. Daphne felt herself tensing at once.

"Relax, Miss Wade."

"I am quite relaxed," she lied.

"Are you? Your body tells me something different." He loosened their clasped hands until their fingers were barely laced together, then he rocked their hands in a slow, circular motion. "Do not make yourself uneasy. I am not going to make any further attempts to ravish you. At least," he amended, "not at this moment. Relax."

Daphne wanted to do so, but the idea of being ravished by him now or at any other moment made her feel strange, as if she had taken a second glass of wine at dinner. She remembered their picnic that afternoon, and how he had almost kissed her. Now, she was acutely aware of his hand against her waist, and she had to fight the impulse to shy away. All of a sudden, the room felt too warm for dancing.

"When you waltz," Anthony went on, not seeming to notice the blush in her cheeks, "the first thing to remember is proper distance. You stand about one foot from your partner, just as we are now. Put your hand on my shoulder."

She did, her hand hesitating an inch away for a moment before coming to rest on the crisp wool of his dark green jacket. Against her palm, she could feel the hard muscles of his shoulder. The sight of him without his shirt flashed across her mind to torture her again. She knew every chiseled contour of his chest, for she had not only drawn each of them in charcoal, but etched them on her mind. Heat pooled in her midsection, and she forced herself to focus on what he was saying.

"The second thing to remember about dancing is that I lead and you follow. Your body goes where mine tells it to go."

"I think I would prefer it the other way round."

"Would you?" he murmured. "An interesting notion, Miss Wade. Perhaps one day, I will let you." He lifted her hand in his, the palm of his other hand warm against her side. "The waltz is a dance with very simple steps and a cadence of one-two-three. Like this."

He started to move, pulling her with him, but she looked down at their feet, and he brought her to a halt at once. "The third thing to remember is to look at me, Miss Wade, not at the floor."

"But what if I tread on your feet?"

"I am certain I shall survive it. Do not worry about making mistakes. After all, it is only me who is watching, and you do not care what I think." He began moving again, and she moved with him as he counted in time with the pinging melody of the musical box. "One-two-three," he said, leading her in a swirling pattern around the ballroom floor. "One-two-three."

She felt quite clumsy, pulled around the room this way, but even with all the times she stumbled over his feet and brought them to a halt, he did not express a hint of impatience. He simply made her try again. And again.

"You are doing very well, truly," he assured her

as he rewound the musical box for their third waltz. "I knew you would dance well."

"You are a good teacher," she confessed as he returned to where she stood in the center of the room. "I just wish I did not feel so horribly awkward."

"That requires practice." He lifted her hand in his again, and they began to move in the steps of the dance, with Anthony reminding her to look at him every time she began to lower her chin as they danced.

"I keep thinking the only way to prevent myself from treading on your feet is to look down," she confessed. "But despite my efforts, I fear your feet will be black and blue before this evening is over."

"Then you should be very appreciative of the sacrifice I am making on your behalf."

She looked at him with mock sympathy. "Poor man. How you must be suffering. Although it could be worse, I daresay. I could be very stout."

His hand tightened at her waist. "That would be a shame," he murmured, his gaze meeting hers, "but you would still have those incredible eyes."

Her heart slammed against her ribs and she nearly stumbled again. "You dance well yourself," she said, veering the subject away from herself. She did not want him to pay her compliments, for she could not believe they were sincere. "Why do you dislike it?"

"In truth, it is not dancing itself I dislike. It is the consequences of it I abhor, so I have come to dislike it."

"What do you mean? What consequences?"

"The same consequence that impels me to avoid young ladies who swoon. Being a wealthy duke who is also a bachelor makes me the object of intense scrutiny at a ball. Every move I make is observed, dissected, and published in the society papers for all to read. If I engage a lady for a dance, the matrons begin circulating rumors about us all around the ballroom before the dance is over. If I enjoy her company enough to dance with her a second time, I am madly in love, and by the third dance, the wedding is a foregone conclusion."

"That would be maddening."

"It is worse for the poor young lady in question, for the gossip is never favorable toward her. No matter her beauty, sweetness of temper, and suitability, no woman with whom I am linked can compare with the daughter of whichever matron is doing the talking."

She laughed. "I suppose that is inevitable."

"Yes, which is why I rarely dance."

"Well, since no one is here to observe and gossip, you should be able to enjoy yourself tonight."

"I am." He intertwined their fingers more tightly. "I am enjoying myself very much indeed."

Before Daphne could think of a reply, the music began to slow, grinding down until it stopped, and Anthony brought her to a halt as well. His right hand slid away from her waist, but he retained her other hand in his grasp. "Not a single misstep," he pointed out.

"You are right," she said in some surprise. "I forgot to worry about making a mistake."

"Exactly so." He gestured to the side of the room. "After a dance is over, I escort you back to your place." He suited the action to the word, leading her to one side of the room as if they were truly at a ball. He let her go, took a step back from her and bowed. She suspected an answering bow was required of her, and she crossed one ankle behind the other and dipped a short curtsy.

"No, no, Miss Wade," he said, smiling. "You must give a deeper bow than that to me. I am a duke, after all. A knee almost to the floor is expected."

She dropped down again in a deeper curtsy. "You are just loving this, aren't you?"

"Well, yes," he admitted, as she straightened again. He looked at her mouth and his smile vanished. "After all, you did chastise me quite severely today for taking advantage of our friendship, and I must take my revenge where I can."

She had not felt severe at all. Her words that afternoon had been a desperate, last-ditch defense, for she had actually thought he intended to kiss her. Worse, she had hoped he would. "I did no such thing."

"I do not want another quarrel with you, so I will not start one. Although I feel compelled to point out that a young lady should never, ever contradict a duke."

"There are ever so many rules, are there not?" she said, forcing a lightness into her voice. "I have read all your etiquette books, and I still feel quite intimidated. Is there anything else I should know?"

"Yes." He took a step closer to her. "As I told

you before, a young lady of fashion would never wear her spectacles to a ball." He reached out, and ignoring her sound of protest, he removed the pair of eyeglasses from her face. "Try to wear these as little as possible. Accustom yourself to going without them if you can."

"I read that a young lady is expected to acknowledge her acquaintances. How am I to do that if I cannot see them?"

She reached for the pair of eyeglasses, but he stretched his arm out and back, keeping them out of her reach. She stood up on the tips of her toes, but even then, it did no good, for he was so much taller than she. Daphne knew she could not risk jumping up to grab the pair, for they might get broken. She lowered her heels back to the floor, put her hands on her hips and frowned at him. "Are we going to have another argument about this?"

"No." Anthony folded the pair of spectacles and put them in the pocket of his jacket. "Because I am not giving them back until our lesson is over. This time, I want you to dance without wearing them."

"But I can't see anything."

He pulled her close. "Can you see me?"

She looked into his eyes, eyes with all the deep, rich colors of English moss—green and brown and gold. "Yes, but—"

"Good, for your partner is the one you should be looking at." He stepped back, once again trying to lead her to the center of the room, but she pulled her hand out of his grasp and did not move.

She hated not having her eyeglasses on. Outside of about a fifteen-foot radius, everything was blurry, and that always left her feeling very vulnerable. She bit her lip and glanced at his pocket, wondering.

Anthony read her intent at once and shook his head. "I advise you not to try."

She did it anyway, reaching for the pocket at his hip, but before she could get her fingers underneath the flap, his hand closed over her wrist. "I warned you," he said as he pushed her hand outward, away from his pocket, "and you ignored my warning. You should never ignore a duke. We hate that."

Daphne's heart began to thud in her chest. He let her go, but he did not move away. She knew she should step back, move away, leave the room. She stayed where she was, almost as if she were under some sort of spell. What would it be like if he kissed her?

It was not until he moved to close the remaining distance between them that she slid one foot backward, then another, then another. He followed, still keeping less than a few scant inches of distance between them. It was not until her back hit the wall behind her and Anthony brought his arms up on either side of her that she came to her senses. With a glance from side to side, she realized that he had very neatly trapped her.

"Go," he said, as if reading her thoughts. He flattened his palms against the wall. "Run, Miss Wade. If you can."

Daphne looked up into his face, and in the hazel depths of his eyes, she saw something relentless and challenging, but though she felt her insides quivering, it was not with fear.

"You could get your spectacles back quite easily if you wanted to, you know."

His voice was deceptively soft, and Daphne knew she should take his advice and run, but the intensity of his gaze was enough to keep her pinned to the wall. "How?"

"Women have so much power," he mused almost as if to himself. "I fail to understand why they so often choose not to wield it."

"What power?"

"A woman can get anything she wants out of a man, if she goes about it the right way. Some women know this instinctively. Most have not the slightest clue. You, Miss Wade, fall into the latter category." He leaned forward, and she could feel the heat of his body even though he was not touching her at all. "If you want that power, I could show you how to use it."

"If there is something for my social instruction that I need to know, tell it to me at once," she whispered. "Stop toying with me."

"I am toying with you because this is a game. I will not let you win, but I can teach you how to play."

Something in those words made her shiver with excitement. "I really do not know what you are talking about."

"The real question is, what do you want? Do you want to be a proper young lady, or do you want to be Cleopatra?"

"Both."

"Ah. That is an interesting answer, and brings with it an even more interesting question. Can a young lady be captivating and alluring, and still be proper, do you think?"

"Why not?"

"Why not, indeed." His lashes lowered until his eyes were half-closed. "If I do give you back your spectacles, what do I receive in return?"

"The satisfaction of doing the right thing?"

He laughed low in his throat. "Not good enough."

"What, then?" she asked. "What do you want?"

His gaze moved to her mouth, lingered there. "What are you offering?"

Daphne licked her lips, and she heard his sharp intake of breath. "Three days," she whispered. "You may have three more days."

"Three days? You are a miser, Miss Wade."

She had to stick to her guns. She had to be strong. "Three days. No more."

"A week."

"Three days."

"No, then. What else do you have to offer?"

He bent his head, moving closer, just a little bit closer. This time, she was going to let him kiss her, and she felt again that wild surge of excitement and anticipation, remembering all the times she had watched him through a spyglass, dreaming, wondering what his kiss felt like. It was certainly living up to her daydreams so far, for her knees were weak and her insides shaky, but she would die rather than give him an inkling of how she felt.

She flattened back against the wall behind her, trying to gain a bit more distance between them and catch her breath, but it did her no good. Her own past imaginings still rose up to taunt her, of all the times she had imagined his lips gently brushing hers, of a sweet word of affection or regard. Just the thought of those things was enough to hurt, but she still wanted him to kiss her. Heaven help her, she did. She was a fool.

Anthony lowered his head just a fraction more, and she reminded herself that this was a game, his game. Because of that, she was the one who would lose. Damn him for playing with her like this. Damn herself, for this time, she could not even summon the will to turn her face away.

"I shall give you back your spectacles, if—" He stopped, his lips only a few inches from her own. "If you kiss me."

From sheer desperation to escape him and the sensations he was evoking in her, Daphne raised up on her toes and pressed her lips to one corner of his mouth in a lightning-quick move. "There," she said, lowering her heels back to the floor. "Now give them back."

"No, no, I must object to your definition of a kiss. That was not a kiss. It was a peck on the cheek."

"I say it was a kiss."

"I say it was not, and I believe I know more about kissing than you do."

Daphne stiffened. "Do not laugh at me."

"Laugh?" He shook his head. "I am not laughing. Indeed, I am in no mood to laugh just now, especially not at you. I am attempting to hide the strain you are putting on me at this moment."

She gave a huff of disbelief. "Rot."

"It is true. I am exerting a great deal of gentlemanly effort to not capitulate and kiss you first."

"Gentlemanly? Trapping a young lady against a wall and attempting blackmail to kiss her is hardly gentlemanly."

"I am not even touching you. This is hardly blackmail, for you know full well I will give your spectacles back to you in the end. As for being trapped, you are in no such position. If you wish to leave, then go. I will not stop you."

"I—" She stopped, swallowed hard, and did not move. "I do not think this is a game at all."

"But it is. We are engaged in a power struggle, you and I. Do you not see how much power you could have over me?"

She felt so out of her depth with him. "The only thing I see is that if we are playing a game, it is by your rules."

"On the contrary, the rules are in your favor, for as a gentleman, I am not actually permitted to kiss you, and you can torment me forever with the unspoken promise of one."

She tilted her head, slanting a speculative look at him, and she wondered if that was really true, or if he was being deliberately provoking. He claimed that women had enormous power over men, but she had never felt any power over him. Quite the reverse, in fact. Turning the tables was too tempting to resist, and Daphne decided to test his claim.

She licked her lips again, and this time, it was she who moved closer. "You mean like this?" she whispered, concentrating on getting one thing out of this situation, knowing there was only one way to win this game of his. "Am I tormenting you?"

"You are a very quick study, Miss Wade." He was rigidly still.

"Was that a compliment to my intelligence, your grace? I am flattered."

"Right now, I must confess that your intelligence is the last thing I am thinking of. Shallow of me, but there it is. Are you going to kiss me or not?"

"There is no need." It was Daphne's turn to smile as she pulled back and held up her hand between them. The metal and glass of her spectacles glinted in the candlelight.

Never had anything pleased her more than the astonishment on his face. Before he could recover enough from the shock to retaliate by claiming his kiss, she ducked beneath his arm and moved well out of reach. Facing him, she put her eyeglasses back on, feeling the sweet satisfaction of having the upper hand for once. "I believe I have won this game, your grace."

With that, she turned around and departed.

"Only the first round, Miss Wade," he called after her, his laughter following her out the door. "Only the first round."

Chapter 16

As she had agreed, Daphne took tea that Sunday with the Benningtons at the home of Sir Edward and Lady Fitzhugh. As expected, talk about their most eminent neighbor was the order of the day.

Mrs. Bennington opened the topic. "Yesterday, I received an exciting piece of news regarding his grace. My very good friend, Margaret Treves, lives in London, and she has just written to tell me everyone is talking of the duke's visit there six weeks ago." She leaned forward in her chair, her plump cheeks flushing with the excitement of being the first to impart gossip. "He was said to have brought the ducal emeralds with him to Bond Street to be reset. That can only mean one thing, of course."

"Yes," Anne put in, "the society papers have been talking of it for weeks, speculating on who his choice might be. Most agree that Lady Sarah Monforth would be the most sensible."

The affirmation of what she had overheard in the music room caused Daphne to pinch the handle of her teacup so tightly that her fingers began to ache.

"Ah, yes, the Marquess of Monforth's eldest daughter," said Lady Fitzhugh. "Yes, she would be very suitable, though I would not have thought her to be quite his type."

"A beautiful woman is always a man's type," said Sir Edward, earning such a look from his wife that he said no more.

Daphne closed her eyes for a brief moment, remembering Viola's words that night in the music room.

You are the Duke of Tremore and should marry high for duty's sake, even if your choice is without love and affection.

Daphne had known for some time that he would marry Lady Sarah Monforth, and she felt a flash of anger with him. He was marrying that lady for duty's sake. He did not love her.

Daphne opened her eyes, shoved away her anger, and put her cup gently back in its saucer. It was not her business.

"Did your friend know any of the details?" Lady Fitzhugh asked Mrs. Bennington. "The duke should marry, for he is twenty-nine years now but has an engagement been announced?"

"No announcement, but alas, I know nothing more than that, Lady Fitzhugh."

"Well, he will choose someone suitable, I am sure."

"Oh, I hope not!" Elizabeth cried. "Someone unsuitable would be much more exciting."

"Elizabeth!" Lady Fitzhugh remonstrated sharply.

Her daughter was undeterred. "But Lady Sarah is said to be deadly dull."

"Elizabeth," Sir Edward put in, "it is not our practice to criticize his choice of wife."

"Well, I suppose you are right. My only wish is that he would attend our local assemblies. Our cousin Charlotte has told me that Lord and Lady Snowden, as well as their son and daughter, attend at least three or four of the assemblies in their village in Dorset each year. Why, oh, why can our dear duke not do the same? Papa sees him at agricultural shows and race meetings, but I have lived in Wychwood all my life and seldom see him except at the yearly fête."

"He does not seem to care much for local society," Mrs. Bennington agreed, "but that is hardly uncommon for a duke."

"True," Lady Fitzhugh said. "The old duke took a very great interest in local affairs, but not every peer shares that interest, you know. And if the current duke does not, it is both acceptable and understandable."

"But Mama," Elizabeth replied, "isn't it strange

that he is so rarely in residence here? He's never given a country-house party for any lords and ladies, nor even a hunting party, and that is odd, especially for the ducal estate, do you not think?"

"His obligations weigh heavy upon him, to be sure," Sir Edward put in, and shot a pointed glance at his daughter. "Perhaps when he comes back to Tremore Hall, his intent is to rest in privacy and solitude, not gad about the countryside."

Lady Fitzhugh sighed. "I hope he does intend to marry soon, for it would be most agreeable to have a duchess in residence. His mother was a beautiful woman, and so very kind. When she was alive, things were so lively up at the hall. All sorts of elegant and obliging people coming and going, and two fêtes a year instead of one. Such a generous woman. The old duke was shattered when she died. I still remember how he wept at her funeral like a child. The son stood there, so stoic and stiff-lipped, without a word. It was more heartbreaking than the father's tears, really."

Daphne bit her lip and looked down into her teacup. That would be like Anthony, she realized. He would be the sort to just stand there, grieving inside, refusing to show it. She understood. Like herself, he prided himself on control of his emotions.

"Poor man!" said Mrs. Bennington. "It is not surprising he does not spend much time here. Difficult memories, I daresay."

"Very difficult," agreed Anne. "I should feel the same. Can you imagine anything more horrible than having your mother die and your father go mad?"

Shocked, Daphne stared at the girl, unable to quite believe what she had heard.

"Anne!" Lady Fitzhugh said sternly. "The old duke had just lost his wife, poor man, and it was grief made him so strange, nothing more. He did not go mad."

"Some of the servants at the hall say he did talk to himself," Mrs. Bennington said. "He used to roam the corridors at night and call for the duchess. He'd talk to the servants about her as if she were still alive. They say the old duke took a horsewhip to a groom who dared to say to his face that the duchess was dead. The son finally had to lock his father up somewhere in the house. Only time the boy ever wept, so they say. After that, it was he who ran the estates, and he was only a child."

Oh, God. Daphne thought of the boy he had been and how that boy must have had the courage of a lion. She thought of the man, of his need for privacy and his hatred of gossip. She stared down at the teacup in her hand, and something inside her snapped. She set her teacup back into its saucer with a clang. "I do not think we should talk about such things!" she cried. "He has lost both his parents. A man's pain and grief should be private, not bandied about in this fashion."

Lady Fitzhugh turned to her and laid a hand on her shoulder. "You are quite right to chastise us, my dear. We shall not speak of it again."

Daphne did not reply. The conversation veered tactfully to other topics, but she paid little attention. She thought of her own father, who had grieved his wife's death with great pain, but whose work and child had been solace enough to see him through. Anthony's father had given in to his grief and had lost his grip on reality, leaving his children to fend for themselves.

Love should never conquer reason.

Now she understood what he had meant about the tragic consequences of love and why he thought it a terrible and frightening thing. *Oh, Anthony.*

"Miss Wade," Elizabeth asked, breaking into her thoughts, "you must tell us all about your travels."

Daphne took a deep breath, grateful for the change of subject. "What would you like to know, Miss Elizabeth?"

"Heaps of things. Do the Africans really tear out the hearts of Europeans and eat them?"

"No," she answered, trying to smile. "But the lions do."

During the three weeks that followed, her dance lessons with Anthony were confined to the strict form of a proper young lady and gentleman, their bodies the correct distance apart as they waltzed. Daphne discovered that Anthony was right. If she kept her head up and talked with him, she did not stumble nearly as much, even if their conversations were mundane enough to be heard by the strictest chaperone. She could not help making the rueful observation that bargains over kisses were much more intriguing. But when he left for his estate in Surrey on matters of business, she appreciated that mundane conversation with Anthony was far more entertaining than his absence.

While he was away, Daphne's thoughts returned again and again to tea at the Fitzhughs'. Sometimes, when she was working in the library, she would find an excuse to stop for a stroll through the long gallery, looking at the family portraits in a new light now that she knew more about the people in them. She lingered longest over the ones of Anthony as a boy, thinking of how he had been forced to lock his father away, her heart aching for him.

She had plenty of work to occupy her time, and her days got busier, but her evenings got lonelier the longer he was away. Foolish, she knew, to miss a man who had once declared her to be a machine. Yet, in an odd way, they had become friends, and as the week passed, as she pieced mosaics, pottery, and frescoes, Daphne found herself looking out the windows of the antika every time she heard the sound of wheels, hoping it was his carriage passing by on its way to the house.

During her nights, there were times when she lay in bed, thinking of him, even touching her lips now and again with the tips of her fingers just as he had done, hearing his low voice proposing bargains for kisses, and she found it hard to sleep—so hard that there were actually moments when she thought of changing her mind. But every time she did, Daphne pulled the covers over her head with a groan and berated herself for such nonsense. He was getting married, and staying here was only a recipe for heartache and disaster.

One week after his departure, Daphne's thoughts were so preoccupied with him that she could not linger in bed, and she got up and dressed even though it was barely dawn. Work was better than lying here torturing herself, unable to go back to sleep. The sooner Christmas arrived, the better, she thought, nibbling on a scone from the kitchens as she walked down to the antika on a cold October morning.

When Daphne entered the antika, she heard someone moving about in the second storage room, and when she entered that room, she found Mr. Bennington had arrived before her. She was surprised to see him, for they never began work at this hour. He paused as she entered the room, and he was clearly just as surprised as she.

"Good day to you, Miss Wade." He pulled off his hat and bowed, but Daphne noticed at once that there was some constraint in his greeting and his manner. "I did not think you would be up and about at the crack of dawn."

"I woke early." She frowned, glancing in puzzlement at one of the shelves behind him, a shelf that yesterday had been empty and was now filled with half a dozen bushel baskets of fresco pieces. The ground was now frozen, and she thought she already had all the fresco remnants. "Where did all of those come from?" she asked in surprise, gesturing to the row of baskets behind him.

Mr. Bennington shifted his weight, looking very

uncomfortable. "Oh, these were uncovered weeks ago. His grace had them stored in a room at the hall, but he asked me to bring them down this morning. He wants me to take them to town this morning, along with all the rest you and I have done while he's been away."

Daphne's heart gave a foolish leap at those words. "The duke is back?"

"Yes. Arrived late last night."

She bit her lip and looked away, far happier at that news than she should be. After a moment, she returned her attention to the architect, her emotions well in hand. "But why is his grace having you take these down to London? Does he not wish me to repair and sketch them?"

Why, the man actually blushed. "I believe his grace intends these to be part of a private collection at his London house. He intends to hire someone at a later date to restore them in London. They are not for the museum, which is the truly important work, and you have far too much to do as it is."

Daphne understood at once. She bit down on her lip and tried not to laugh. "I am relieved to hear that I will not need to bother with them," she answered, trying to look convincingly grateful. "You are right that the museum work is far more important than his grace's private collections. On that note, I believe I shall get started with my duties."

She left him to his stock-taking and returned to the workroom. She began a sketch of the assembled fresco of Orpheus that was on her worktable against the wall, and she smiled to herself. Mr. Bennington was behaving so much like her father. Sometimes, men were so silly.

The architect had barely departed from the antika and headed to the house for breakfast before Daphne returned to the storage room to have a peek at the mysterious fresco pieces. She pulled a plaster fragment out of one of the baskets, and it was enough to confirm her suspicions. It was one of the erotic ones.

The assembled wall painting would probably contain nothing that she hadn't seen before, and yet Daphne began assembling fragments on an empty space of shelf beside the basket with a curiosity that was anything but intellectual.

After a few minutes, she had enough of the wall painting assembled to see the main image. As far as Roman frescoes went, this image of a naked couple engaged in the act of lovemaking was not anything out of the common way. The woman was on top, her legs spread wide over the man's hips, his hand cupping her breast. A commonplace pose, but Daphne stared at the painting, feeling warmth spreading through her body, the warmth she felt every single time she had wondered what Anthony's kiss felt like, every time she had studied his naked chest through a spyglass, every time he had touched her.

I shall give you back your spectacles if you kiss me.

But she hadn't kissed him. The sense of satisfaction she had felt that evening at having outwitted him had long since departed. Now, as she stared at the image on the shelf in front of her, she knew she should have just done it. Just wrapped her arms around his neck and kissed him. She could have satisfied her curiosity on the subject of Anthony's kiss once and for all, and she hadn't done it. Three weeks of dancing lessons, night after night they had been alone together, and he had been so proper and distant, so gentlemanlike, never hinting by word or deed that he even remembered wanting her to kiss him.

She was leaving in only a few weeks, and she knew she would probably never have another chance to kiss a man like him. She felt an unabashed sense of regret, and she vowed that if the chance ever came again, she was not going to let it slip away.

She stared at the painting, thinking of Anthony, and she lifted her hand to touch her mouth with the tips of her fingers, just as she had done countless times during the past few weeks. She closed her eyes and imagined far more. A kiss, a touch, his hand on her breast.

The sound of the door opening made her jump, and all her pleasurable speculations vanished as she turned around. Through the storage room doorway, she could see Anthony as he walked into the antika. He caught sight of her, and came to a halt. After a moment, he shut the front door and came toward her.

Careless of her not to have shut the storage room door, she realized, knowing there was no way to hide the pieces now.

"Good morning," she said as he entered the storage room, trying to look nonchalant. "I heard you had returned."

"Last evening." He crossed the room, and Daphne's stomach felt as if it were full of butterflies by the time he halted in front of her.

She cleared her throat and hoped she wasn't blushing, hoped her body shielded the fresco from his view. "Did you have a nice journey?"

He leaned sideways, and one side of his mouth curved in that one-sided smile of his. "You were not supposed to see these," he commented as he straightened and looked at her. "Mr. Bennington was very particular about that."

"Yes, I am sure he was," she answered, looking straight into Anthony's chin. "But I am a professional antiquarian."

"I believe Mr. Bennington was thinking of you as a young lady, not as an antiquarian."

"I have seen dozens of them before." God help her, the words came out in a whisper. All she could think about were the man standing in front of her and the sensual image behind her and how much she wished he would touch her.

"Excellent," he replied, and before she knew what was happening, he had turned her around to face the fresco. "I would appreciate your opinion on this one, Miss Wade."

Daphne stared at the image, unable to even pretend an intellectual interest when there was this deep, hot hunger inside her that made her skin tingle and her knees feel weak. She was acutely aware of his body behind her.

"What do you think of the artist's skill?" he asked over her shoulder. "Is this of purely historical value, or does it have artistic merit as well?"

Her cheeks burned. She tried to move away, but he put his hands on her shoulders to keep her there. "Come, Miss Wade, give me your opinion. Do we see gods depicted here or just an ordinary man and woman?" He leaned closer to her. "Give me some instruction on the academic aspects. For myself, I find it quite erotic, but I know you could not be moved by anything more than an intellectual interest."

Those words thrown on her already seething emotions ignited like brandy thrown on a fire. "Why should you think me unmoved by the sensuality of this painting?" she cried. She tried to turn around, but his grip on her shoulders kept her where she was. "Do you think I am so cold as that? Do you think that I have no desire in me? Do you think I am not a woman of feeling?"

"You cannot blame me for wondering," he said softly beside her ear. "You hide your feelings very well, Miss Wade."

She drew a deep, shaky breath and wrapped her arms around her ribs. "But I have them. I have the same hungers and desires as any other woman. How could you think I do not?"

"Perhaps because you would not kiss me," he murmured, his lips brushing her ear and making her shiver. "I was hoping—very strongly hoping, I might add—that you would, but alas, you did not. And as I told you, I am a gentleman and not really permitted to kiss you."

When she did not reply, he straightened away from her and his hands slid away from her shoulders. "You have diverted me from our discussion, Miss Wade," he said, and reached around her, his arm touching hers as he pointed to the fresco. "Do you suppose this red color of the background comes from red ochre or cochineal?"

She stared at his hand as his fingertips brushed the upper right corner of the background. "Ochre," she whispered. "Am I tormenting you with the promise of a kiss?"

"Most assuredly. But you were quite right to remind me that friends are what we ought to be. It was the proper thing for a young lady to do."

She looked at the plaster pieces on the table, at the man and the woman lying there. She did not feel very proper. "I suppose it was," she agreed, her voice just above a whisper, "but what do you suppose Cleopatra would have done?"

There was a long pause. After what seemed an eternity, he bent his head close to her ear. "Why, Miss Wade," he murmured, "have the tables turned? Are you asking me to kiss you now?"

"No, I am not asking."

"I rather thought you were. I must have been mistaken." He leaned forward enough that his body brushed hers as he touched the fresco again, as he traced the line of the woman's hip with his finger. "This particular image is remarkably fine, I think. Would you not agree?"

"I did not realize a woman had to ask a man to kiss her." She held her breath, watching the movement of his finger back and forth across the painted woman's body, waiting in an agony of uncertainty.

"Not unless the man has already thrown propriety to the winds, made an attempt to steal a kiss, and has been rejected. Then it is up to the woman to make the next move." His arm fell to his side, and he took a step back away from her. "If a kiss from me is what you desire, Miss Wade, all you need do is make your wishes clear."

It wasn't as if she were in love with him anymore. She no longer cared what he thought. She had no doubt he'd kissed dozens of women, and he would know how to do it properly. She would so hate her very first kiss to be disappointing.

She knew this was a game between them now, and he was giving her an opening. Daphne took it.

She drew in a deep breath and turned around to face him. She curled her fingers around the edge of the shelf behind her, raised her chin and looked him in the eye. "I should like it very much if you would kiss me."

She sounded so prim about it, which was a hypocrisy, since there was nothing prim about the way she felt. She gripped the edges of the shelf, her body tense with anticipation, a hungry sort of waiting. She watched him smile, those laugh lines forming at the edges of his eyes, but she knew he was not laughing at her. He just looked pleased.

"That is clear enough." He stepped closer to her, and her heart began to thud in her chest like a Somali drum as he pulled off her spectacles and leaned sideways to set them on the shelf behind her.

His hand touched her cheek, he brought his mouth closer to hers, and she felt a queer, weightless sensation in her stomach as if she had just dived off a cliff. His lips pressed to hers.

Pleasure unfolded inside her like a butterfly opening its wings to fly. Never in her imagination had she experienced anything so piercing and sweet as this.

Her body came keenly alive at this moment, all her senses heightened and focused on him and herself and the touch of his mouth until nothing else mattered. Everything else in the world receded into insignificance.

She breathed in the scent of lemon soap and the taste of him. She felt her hands relaxing their tight grip on the shelf. She brought them up between them, not to push him away, but to feel the hard muscles of his chest against her palms through the linen of his shirt, the rise and fall of his breathing, the beating of his heart.

His palm cupped her chin. There was a callous on his middle finger. She could feel it as his fingers splayed across her cheekbone. His free arm wrapped around her waist, lifting her onto her toes, pulling her closer. He parted her lips with his own, a lush, full openness that tasted her, that enabled her to taste him. Oh, how could anything as simple as this bring so much pleasure?

Daphne wrapped her arms around his neck, clinging to him as an ache spread through every part of her, a sensation never felt before, yet oddly familiar. Yes, her body seemed to say, this is what poets write and artists paint, this rush of joy and this need, this warmth of his body so close to her own and the exquisite tension that came with it.

She slid her hands up into his hair, and she pressed against him. Her leg curled around his, wanting to bring him even closer. It was as if her entire body knew just what to do, even if her mind did not. She rubbed her ankle up and down along the back of his calf and heard a sound, the mixture of his stifled groan and hers.

With an abruptness that startled her, he turned his face away, breaking the kiss, his breathing uneven. His arm around her relaxed and fell away. Taking her cue from him, she uncurled her leg from around his, and sank back down until her feet were flat against the floor.

Still touching her face, he bent his head to rest his forehead close to hers. "You see," he said, his breathing ragged as he looked into her eyes, "how much power you have when you choose to wield it?"

She did see. It awed her, it excited her—that she, who had been hauled across half the globe by her wandering father, who had convinced herself she had no influence over anything in her life, who had placed herself in the position of worshiping a man who had never even noticed her—she had power, power over the very man she had once worshiped.

Suddenly, plain, ordinary, Daphne Wade felt as captivating and alluring as Cleopatra, and a joy she had never felt before blossomed inside her. "Thank you," she whispered, "for making my first kiss one of the most extraordinary moments of my life."

"That is high praise indeed, but I think that I should let you go while I still can." His hand slid away from her face. He took several steps back and clasped his hands behind him. "For your very first kiss, I am honored that you chose me, Daphne," he said quietly.

Then his serious expression changed. She saw a glint of amusement come into his eyes, and he slanted her a wicked look. "In exchange for giving you one of the most extraordinary moments of your life, may I have another month?"

Chapter 17

Kisses for time. Anthony thought it one of the most intriguing suggestions he had ever made to a woman, but Daphne seemed unimpressed. "It is just like you to think up something like that," she said, laughing as she walked away from him. "It is one where you win both ways."

That was so true, he could not help laughing with her, but during the three weeks that followed, he found it to be no laughing matter. For he could not prevent his thoughts from returning to that kiss a dozen times a day. The exquisite tease of her ankle caressing the back of his leg, her arms coming up around his neck in a wave of delicate gardenia scent, the soft feel of her mouth and the heat of her body. Most of all, he remembered her face afterward, the astonished, genuine pleasure in her smile, pleasure that his kiss had given her, pleasure she had not been able to hide from him.

He'd been right. All that passion was within her. It simmered just under the surface. He had been driven to unleash it, and that was coming back to taunt him now, for he wanted to unleash it again.

In the afternoons, they sorted artifacts and debated which ones were worthy of his museum and which were not. Every night he held her in his arms and danced with her. He asked her endless questions about places she had been—demanding vivid details of the pyramids, the Coliseum, and the marketplaces of Marrakesh and Tangier. He argued with her, he teased her, he flirted with her, but during all the time they spent together during the three weeks that followed that kiss, not once did he make an attempt to kiss her again.

Kissing would be the prelude to all the delicious imaginings in his mind, imaginings that would compromise his honor and her innocence. He was a gentleman, he reminded himself again and again, something that had never been this hard to remember. Over seventeen years of fulfilling the obligations and duties of his position, a lifetime of obeying the strictures of society, an upbringing of self-imposed discipline, all served him well now. No matter what his rank and title, a true gentleman did not corrupt an innocent woman, especially one in his employ. It was not quite so low as shagging one's servant girls, but low enough that Anthony was always able to stop himself from kissing her. But he wanted to. God, how he wanted to.

The implications of his suggestion to her tantalized him unmercifully. In his mind, he came up with endless ways to pleasure her in exchange for time, ways that crept into his thoughts during the day and invaded his dreams at night.

She learned to waltz well enough that he began showing her some of the basic movements and figures of country dance. Not an easy task, since even the simplest country dance required at least four people. Explaining and demonstrating moves such as a *moulinet* or *interchassé* without other couples present was close to impossible, but he made the effort anyway. Holding hands was the greatest intimacy of country dance, and from his point of view, it was much safer than the waltz.

The presence of others would be a much more effective deterrent than his own determination, of course, and she was proficient enough now at dancing that it probably would not embarrass her to have an audience. But he did not suggest it to her, for God help him, he did not want to give up the tormenting delight of being alone with her. He was becoming addicted to it, addicted to the game of testing his desire for her against his resolve. A very dangerous game.

He knew he was playing with fire, but it was risk that made a game exciting. Resolve untested was moot, and three weeks after that kiss in the antika, he found himself pushing his resolve to the limit, for he put the cylinder for a waltz in the musical box.

"We are waltzing tonight?" Daphne asked as a now-familiar tune began to play. "We have not done that for a long time."

Anthony lifted her hand in his. "You must practice it on occasion." He pulled her closer and put his other hand on her waist. "Besides, I would rather waltz with you than parade about the room in the stiff, stylized moves of a quadrille."

"Would you?"

"Yes, even though my partner is very cruel to me."

"I am cruel?" she repeated, smiling at the teasing tone of his voice. "How can you say so?"

"You know how important my museum is to me, yet you refuse to give me any time in exchange for that kiss a few weeks ago, a kiss I know you enjoyed." He saw a hint of blush come into her cheeks, and he wondered how he could ever have thought her plain. She was the most enticing thing he had ever seen. He raised the stakes higher. "Perhaps we should reopen our negotiations about that."

"Oh, no, no." She shook her head, smiling at him, for she enjoyed their game as much as he did. "You are not getting another month."

"I would settle for two weeks."

"How conceited of you!" she cried, laughing, pushing playfully at his shoulder with the heel of her hand. "Do be serious in your negotiations or do not bother with them at all."

He pulled her a bit closer than was proper for a waltz. "What would you consider a serious offer?"

Daphne pretended to think it over. "That kiss

was two minutes long at most. I shall be happy to give you two minutes of time in return for it."

Anthony looked at her in mock dismay. "Two minutes? Is that all I am worth? Daphne, I am insulted. I believe my kiss should be valued more highly than that to a young lady who is soon to take her place in the fashionable world. I am a duke, after all."

Her beautiful eyes sparkled with mischief. "It might be worth more, if I could have bragging rights. But I could hardly go about telling London society how well you kiss, could I? It would ruin my reputation."

He grinned, liking this flirtatious side of her. "But it would do wonders for mine," he answered. "I rather like the idea of all the women in London knowing my prowess in that regard."

"And you say you do not enjoy all the attention you receive."

He pulled her another inch closer. "Ah, but Daphne, being considered a good lover is far more gratifying to a man than any other sort of gossip that might be said about him."

He thought he heard her catch her breath, but he could not be certain. Her reply, when it came, was cool and prim, but it was belied by the tease in her eyes. "They will not hear about your skill at kissing from me, your grace."

"You do not kiss and tell?"

"No." Her lashes lowered, then lifted as she met his gaze. "Besides, if you wish me to stay longer, you need to offer me far more tempting bait than a mere kiss."

He could. Ideas flashed across his mind of all the places he could kiss her—the velvety skin of her earlobes and the silken strands of her hair, the insides of her wrists and the round curves of her cheeks.

His imagination went wild. Her full breasts, rosy nipples hard and aroused by his mouth. The dent at the base of her spine and the dip of her navel. Curls of golden brown and the sweet, hot cleft at the apex of her thighs.

"A mere kiss," he said, his voice sounding strangled to his own ears, "can be far more tempting than you realize."

Somehow, they had stopped dancing again. Some way, he had brought them to a standstill without even realizing it. Somewhere in the far distance, he could hear the music slowly come to a halt.

He was going to kiss her again. He was going to let desire have the upper hand again, if only for a few stolen moments. He could keep his wits.

Just one kiss. Just one. He bent his head.

"The music stopped." She pulled back and turned away, then took one step toward the musical box on the mantel.

He would not let her take another. He wrapped an arm around her waist and hauled her hard against him. Both of them froze, her back pressed to his chest.

He closed his eyes, inhaling the scent of gardenia. Her hair felt soft, so soft, beneath his jaw. He could feel her breath quickening beneath his arm and the press of her buttocks against the tops of his thighs. The underside of her breast was warm against his thumb. All he had to do was lift his hand a little higher.

He leaned back a bit instead and opened his eyes. His throat went dry as he stared at the exposed skin along the back of her neck. Her hair was fashioned into intricate twists and puffs at the back of her head that Ella must have created for her. Tiny pewter combs somehow held it all in place, and it gleamed in the candlelight like amber. He wanted to take it down, slide his fingers through the heavy mass of it. Instead, he lowered his head to kiss the back of her neck. The tendons there were as tight as harp strings.

"Are you certain another kiss would not tempt you?" he asked and tilted his head to press his lips to the column of her throat.

"Not another month," she whispered over her shoulder. "The kiss wasn't *that* good."

He laughed softly, blowing warm breath into her ear. "Only the most extraordinary moment of your life," he whispered back. "I cannot recall any woman ever giving me a higher compliment than that one, Daphne."

He flicked his tongue against her earlobe, and she gave a shivery little gasp, but she still tried to spar with him. "I said . . . it was . . . was one of the most extraordinary moments. One of m-many. I have had others, you know."

"Have you?"

"Besides, I think two minutes was . . . gen . . . generous of me. I believe you should find kissing me to be its own reward."

Reward? He was rock-hard against the base of her spine, and he was shaking with the effort of holding back. This was torture, not a reward. Nonetheless, at this moment, if she were to demand a month back in exchange for letting him stand here and hold her like this, he would agree. God, yes. In a heartbeat.

He moved his hand, cupping her breast in the V of his thumb and forefinger. That startled her, and she turned around in his embrace, her hands coming up between them in a defensive move, flattening against his chest as if to push him away.

He could not let her. Not yet. "Is it my reward?" he asked, sliding his arms around her waist. He lowered his head. "Show me."

His lips grazed hers, parted over hers. As he kissed her, he moved his fingers up and down her spine in lazy, circular caresses, but Daphne did not move. She did not kiss him back. Instead, she remained rigid and still, her lips pressed tight together.

Now that he had given in to this temptation, the last thing Anthony wanted was resistence, and he knew he needed to entice her if he were to savor this delight a little longer. He brought his hands to her face and caressed her cheeks with the tips of his fingers as he ran his tongue lightly over her lips, back and forth, again and again, coaxing her to yield.

Her lips trembled, softened, the first response to the feather-light caress of his tongue against her mouth, but she was not ready to give in. He opened his mouth against her closed one. "Daphne, Daphne, kiss me back. I will even say please."

"I—" She broke off, but just the sound parted her lips against his, and he took advantage of it, deepening the kiss, sliding his tongue into her mouth as he felt her rigid pose softening. He lowered his hands to her waist and leaned his body into hers, stepping forward, pushing her back, one step and then another, until she was against the wall. Her fingers curled into his shirt, grasping folds of fabric, pulling him. Her mouth opened wider against his, her tongue meeting his. Silent permission. He grasped her wrists and laced his fingers with hers, pulling their joined hands downward, breathing in the essence of her, as bit by bit, she relaxed in his hold and her body yielded to his.

He let go of her hands, wrapping one arm around her waist and sliding his free hand up along her ribs. Thank God she had not taken his advice about the stays; the last thing he wanted right now was that sort of impediment. His hand moved higher to embrace the full, round shape of her breast, her nipple hard against his palm. Only two layers of fabric between sanity and madness.

I will stop, he promised her silently. *I will.*

He tore his lips from hers and trailed kisses along her jaw as his hand shaped and caressed her breast. Her soft curves burned him wherever her body was pressed against his. Her hips moved, arching against his weight, and shudders of pleasure fissured through his body.

All he wanted was to pull her down onto this hard, dusty floor and feel her hips move like that beneath him, feel those long legs wrap around his body. He wanted her to say his name, over and over while he made love to her. He would not let it go that far, he could not, but he wanted just a few more tastes of her before he let her go.

He tore his lips from hers and buried his face against the warm skin of her throat, kissing her skin, savoring the tiny gasps of pleasure she made as he shaped her breast against his palm. When he closed his thumb and finger over her nipple, teasing with a slow, coaxing motion, her gasps became tiny moans, the sweetest, softest sounds he had ever heard. Each one shattered a piece of his resolve, reminding him that he was going to stop. But not yet.

He trailed kisses up her throat, along her jaw and over her chin to her mouth. He recaptured her lips, and this time they parted at once, all her token resistence gone now. She wanted him as much as he wanted her. Before he could even think of stopping, she wrapped her arms around his neck, clinging to him. Her tongue entered his mouth and drove any stupid notions of honor from his mind.

He felt his wits slipping as he slid his hands down her ribs and around behind her to cup her buttocks. He lifted her off the ground, pulling her up until her hips met his. Her legs parted within the confines of her skirt, and the insides of her thighs squeezed his hips. She rocked against him, each instinctive move bringing exquisite pleasure, to her as well; all his senses knew that. He could hear her soft sounds against his mouth, taste her tongue against his own, feel each exquisite lash of her hips. He allowed himself only a few more seconds of heavenly torture, then he tore his lips from hers with a groan. It was time to stop.

Anthony smothered an oath against her neck. Hard and aching, he let her go, and took a step back from her, then another, tearing himself away as he tried to extinguish the unslaked lust that was raging through him like a house fire. Neither of them spoke. He stopped half a dozen feet away from her, where she was out of his reach.

She had no experience with what it all meant, but he did. He knew he could not stand here one moment longer, or he would act on it. Ruin for her, dishonor for him.

While he still had some vestige of sanity, Anthony turned away and left her, putting as much space between them as he could. But even with the entire length and two floors of the house between them, he could not escape her. The fragrance of gardenia still clung to his clothes, and much to his valet's bewilderment, he insisted on sleeping in his shirt. Even he did not know quite why, for the scent of her tortured him with erotic dreams all night long. When he woke in the morning, she still filled his senses, and he knew it would take miles to put a safe distance between them.

The following morning at breakfast, she learned he was gone. London, Mr. Bennington told her, with four cartloads of antiquities, every piece they had that was ready for the museum. No, he had not said when he would return. There was a letter beside Daphne's plate, but it was not a farewell note, for the seal did not bear Anthony's coronet. It was a letter from Viola.

Daphne stared down at the unopened letter in her hands without seeing it. Anthony had left because of what had happened last night, or rather, what had almost happened. He had not even said good-bye to her.

Kissing can be far more tempting than you realize.

Tempting, indeed. For both of them.

Daphne told herself it would not do to torture herself with thoughts about last night, and she opened the letter from Viola. Another letter was enclosed with it. She read the one from the viscountess first.

Daphne,

I am delighted to hear that Anthony is teaching you to dance. That skill will be so vital to your enjoyment of London, and I am glad to hear you find my brother very charming. I have always found him so, but since I am his sister, I am perhaps slightly biased in his favor, for he has always been fiercely protective of me.

My dear Daphne, I am afraid I have a confession to make to you. I have been a horribly meddlesome friend. Without your permission, I did a bit of investigating, and I have discovered information regarding the marriage of your mother and father. I have enclosed the letter I received from the vicar of a small parish church at Gretna Green in Scotland. That gentleman confirms that a marriage was recorded between Sir Henry Wade, G.C.B., and a Miss Jane Durand, daughter of Lord Durand, on February 24, 1805. Since you are twenty-four years of age, this date is a logical one.

If indeed your mother's name prior to her marriage was Jane Durand, it is my opinion that there is sufficient evidence in this matter to claim your connection. I pray you will forgive me for my interference, but please believe it was done with the kindest of intentions. You deserve the support and security of your family, and I hope you will find this to be good news.

In the interim, I shall expect your arrival just after Boxing Day. My felicitations to Mr. and Mrs. Bennington.

Your friend,
Viola

"Does the viscountess have any news of happenings at Chiswick and London?" asked Mrs. Bennington.

Daphne stared down at the letter in her hands without replying. The baron did not want her, and she had no intention of pressing a claim on him for money or support. She knew she had a great deal of pride, and that pride was perhaps foolish, but she would not go begging to relations who did not want her, not unless she had no other options. First, she would go to London, enjoy her season there, then find a post as a governess as she had planned.

Putting on her mask of cool serenity, she folded the pair of letters and looked up. "No news, I am afraid," she answered Mrs. Bennington and folded the letter. "Her ladyship gives her felicitations to you both." She put the letter in her pocket and turned to Mr. Bennington. "Did his grace say what he wanted done while he was away?"

"He mentioned those four mosaic pavements I brought you yesterday, and there are one or two wall paintings still to do. Of course, there is always plenty of broken pottery and the catalog as well. Enough to keep you busy until you leave, I daresay."

Daphne heard the truculence in his voice, and that cheered her a bit. "More than enough," she agreed. "You excavated far too efficiently before the frost."

"You do an excellent job, Miss Wade. As much respect as I had for your father's work, when his grace first introduced you to me, I was skeptical that you could be an adequate replacement. But now I know you are irreplaceable. The duke will not be able to find anyone as good as you. I shall miss you, my dear."

"Do not speak of it," his wife declared, "for it is too distressing." She turned to Daphne. "I do keep hoping you will change your mind and stay here."

Daphne felt the sting of tears. She smiled at them with affection. "You have both been very kind to me. I shall miss you as well. But do not talk as if I am leaving today. I am here six weeks yet."

"I know," Mr. Bennington said, pushing back his chair. "But come spring, it won't be the same without you. I must go. His grace wanted all that tesselated flooring put in place before he returns. There's much to do."

The architect departed. His wife turned to Daphne and said, "I had another letter from my friend, Mrs. Treves, and she said speculations on the identity of the future duchess are being bandied about London by everyone. A man of his position could not consider marrying any young lady lower than an earl's daughter, of course, and I doubt anyone higher than a viscount is in Town at present. Too early. So if his grace has gone to London again so soon, I doubt it could be to see Lady Sarah. It must be purely business. Or perhaps he has gone to see his sister?"

Mrs. Bennington looked at her as if expecting confirmation, but Daphne shoved back her chair and rose. "Lady Hammond did not mention the matter. If you will excuse me."

She walked away, leaving Mrs. Bennington staring after her. "My dear Daphne, are you ill?"

"No," she called back over shoulder as she left the breakfast room. "It is just that I have so much work to do."

She did not care who Anthony married, she told herself as she walked out of the house down to the antika. She would forget about what happened last night.

A mosaic of Europa lay waiting on her worktable. She stared at it, but the image of Europa blurred, and Daphne saw a different image—a fresco of a naked woman and a naked man. She saw Anthony tracing the woman's hip with his fingertips.

Last night, he had touched her like that. Tongues of heat curled inside her body at the memory of his touch. She remembered every moment—the solid heaviness of his body behind hers as he had held her in an embrace, his low voice murmuring in her ear, his kiss, the hardness of him pressed against her.

Seeing erotic wall paintings was one thing, but it was a whole different thing to feel his hands on her, his mouth on hers, that indescribable pleasure and aching anticipation for more.

He was marrying someone else. How could he have touched her that way if he was marrying someone else?

Men have no character when it comes to women.

Anthony's words came back to mock her, and she realized that just because a man desired a woman, it could mean nothing more than that. He had been flirting with her for weeks, and she had flirted back. Both of them had enjoyed it. He had kissed her, and she had kissed him back. Both of them had wanted more of it. They had gotten it.

Love and desire were not the same thing. He might desire her, but he was not in love with her. She desired him as well, for even now, she longed for his touch, but she was not in love with him any longer. Last night, it had been desire, not love, that had taken her closer to bliss than she had ever been. Love had broken her heart. She would do well to remember the difference.

Chapter 18

Anthony immersed himself in work. The usual duties and matters of business, meetings with other members of the Antiquarian Society who happened to be in Town at the moment, and the museum project itself kept him busy from early morning until late at night. All in an attempt to keep his mind occupied, away from thoughts of lavender-blue eyes and lust.

But as he stood in the domed center room of the building that would house the finest collections of Romano-British artifacts in the world, every fresco, every mosaic pavement, every wine amphora reminded him of what he was trying to escape.

What was it about the woman that made him unable to get her out of his mind? There had been a time when he had barely noticed her. There had been a time when he had never even thought about her unless she was standing right in front of him, stammering her way through explanations of a Latin translation he questioned or describing the nuances of meaning in a particular mosaic. She had obeyed every order he had given her without a word of protest. No matter how demanding or even unreasonable his expectations, she had always exceeded them. She had behaved, in fact, like any other person in his employ: subservient, unquestioning, and excellent at the work for which she was paid.

Then she had up and resigned her post, bursting out with the ridiculous reason that she did not like him and did not want to work for him any longer. At that moment, after five months in his household, she had transformed right before his eyes into someone he had never met before, someone who made short shrift of his position, his title, and himself, someone who had always been there, he imagined, hidden behind an impersonal, efficient mask for the sake of her wage. When the first opportunity to leave had come her way, she had taken it. He had been forced to use all his ingenuity to keep her in his employ as long as he had.

And why? Because she did not *like* him. But she had liked him well enough when he'd held her in his arms. She had liked him well enough to kiss him and enjoy it as much as he had.

Anthony knew he was liking her. Far too much. He desired her more than he had ever desired a woman before, a feeling so unexpected, given his initial impression of her. He had been wrong about her, and now she invaded his mind every time he let his guard down. Honor be damned. Why hadn't he bedded her when he'd had the opportunity? At least then his fantasies of making love to her would cease to be an obsession that continually took his mind from his work. He stared at the fresco that lay on the display table before him, his gaze fixed on a bowl of grapes, the faded color of the fruit more like lavender than purple. He slammed his fist down on the table. "Devil take it!"

"You called my name?" a male voice drawled from the doorway.

Anthony recognized that voice even before he looked up. "Dylan Moore," he said, drawing a deep breath, grateful for the distraction, as he tore his gaze from the wall painting on the table to the man entering the room.

"You call this a museum, Tremore?" Dylan said, glancing around. "It looks more like a mausoleum to me. All these stone walls and statues. Ye gods, it even has a sarcophagus."

"I see that you have still not cut your hair," Anthony commented, straightening away from the table. "How long is this latest rebellion against the fashionable world going to last?"

His friend grinned. "I've not quite decided. My valet is in histrionics about it daily. I fear he shall drug me senseless one night and take a scissors to it. But I am determined to bring back the fashion of longer hair for men. Deuce take it, Tremore, the London beaux need someone to hold them in check."

Dylan was no beau. When first introduced to England's most famous composer, most people could not manage anything beyond a mumbled how-do-you-do, for his appearance was always a bit shocking. It was designed to be.

He was almost as tall as Anthony. His thick black hair hung in waves to his shoulders and was always disheveled, as if he had scarcely risen from his bed. His eyes were black as well, so black the pupils were invisible, so black that Lady Jersey had once declared him a modern Mephistopheles. It was a comparison that suited him perfectly. His brows had a mocking curve, and his mouth a sulky one. He had the charm of angels and the luck of the demon after whom Lady Jersey had named him.

His fancy tickled by her comparison, he heightened his Mephistophelean image by always dressing in black, no matter the occasion, an affectation that amused him endlessly. His ankle-length black cloak with its gold silk lining was familiar to everyone in society, and so was his behavior, which grew more outrageous with each passing year. Dylan was wild, disreputable, and invited to every fashionable party. He also composed some of the most exquisite music Anthony had ever heard. They had been friends since Cambridge.

"So what has you invoking the devil, Tremore? Work, I would guess, since that is all you ever seem to do." Dylan, never able to stand still for long, began to wander around the room, looking at the exhibits. "Or perhaps it is the idea of putting the ducal emeralds around some young lovely's neck that has you cursing?"

"Can nothing in my life be private?" Anthony asked with an exasperated sigh. "How far have the speculations gone?"

"A fresh list of likely future duchesses was presented in one of the society papers only a week ago. What did you expect, dear fellow? That you would take your emeralds to Bond Street and no one would notice?"

"Foolish of me, I know."

"Very," Dylan agreed, pausing to look at him between a pair of tall marble statues. He lifted one eyebrow. "Well, out with it, man. Am I to know the identity of the lady fair?"

"Lady Sarah Monforth."

His friend made a sound of disbelief, rolled his eyes, and moved around the statues to pause at a table of bronze and iron weapons. "You jest with me, Tremore. Tell me the truth."

"Indeed, I am in earnest. However, she is in Paris until Candlemas, and I have not yet proposed, so I ask you to keep my confidence."

"I am too dismayed to do otherwise. Why on earth would you, of all men, choose to chain yourself to a nitwit?"

"It is a highly desirable alliance."

"No doubt. Her name was first on the list." Dylan picked up a bronze knife and studied it for a moment, then placed it back on the table. "Knowing that you abhor the marriage state as much as I, my guess is that you do this strictly for the heir?"

Anthony was becoming irritated. He did not need the meddling of his friends in his affairs. "Do you have a point?"

Dylan looked up and met his gaze. "You will have to bed her," he said, sounding appalled. "Lady Sarah is one of those beautiful women who haven't a whit of sensuality."

"Spoken like a true hedonist. I am making a sensible marriage."

Dylan's laughter ricocheted around the domed ceiling overhead. "God, Tremore, I wish I could be you. You are so controlled, so disciplined, so determined that all shall be as you will it. I suppose you have already informed God that you will require at least three sons to ensure the Tremore line?"

Anthony was accustomed to Dylan's caustic wit, and he refused to be provoked. "It is good to see you, my friend."

"And you as well, I confess it. We always manage a great deal of amusement whenever you are in town. What shall we do this time? We could go to Seven Dials and smoke opium. I did that a few days ago, and it was an indescribable experience. I shall be inspired to compose five new concertos because of it."

Anthony knew Dylan probably had smoked opium in Seven Dials. It provided just the sort of danger Dylan craved. He was always doing things like that.

"Or perhaps we should invade the brothels,

Tremore, since you have not been so wildly irrational as to fall in love with an actress or elope with the daughter of a chimneysweep since I last saw you. After all, you shall soon marry a woman as erotic as this creature here." He gestured to the marble statue beside him. "So, shall we go a-whoring tonight?"

For a moment, Anthony was tempted. Perhaps an interlude with a London courtesan was just what he needed to rid himself of the tense, hungry need that raged through his body. After all, if he were skirt-smitten, a demirep could cure him in less than half an hour. "A delicious idea, Moore," he admitted to his friend, "but I cannot. I have another engagement."

"Do not be tiresome. I have been attempting to work on a new opera, and I have not had a woman for at least a week."

Anthony's hand touched the edge of the fresco laid out on the table and he lowered his face for a closer examination of the fruit bowl. He closed his eyes and caught a hint of gardenia scent. His fancy, he knew. "That long?" he asked, straightening away from the table.

"What is this other engagement you have? Monforth and his family are in residence in Hertfordshire, I believe, not here in London." He paused as if considering possibilities, then he smiled. "Ah, the lovely Marguerite, I assume?"

Those words brought Anthony to his senses, for he realized he had not seen his mistress for over eight months. God, he hadn't even thought about her.

"I am not seeing Marguerite," he said, thinking perhaps he should, for that might return some semblance of order to his distracted mind, but it could not be tonight. "I am having members of the Antiquarian Society to dinner. We have business to discuss regarding the museum. Would you care to join us? I am certain they have never seen anything like you before. I will let you come if you promise not to do anything outrageous such as recite naughty limericks at table."

Dylan shuddered. "Sit around drinking port with a group of dry, old archaeologists, and try to behave myself? I think not. I would rather be flogged in a public square or drink insipid lemonade with giggling girls at Almack's."

"You cannot. They banished you. Lady Amelia, two seasons ago. Remember?"

"Ah, yes, Lady Amelia. I had forgotten that."

It was Dylan's refusal to marry Lady Amelia Snowden after kissing her during a waltz in front of over a hundred people that had compelled Lady Jersey and the other grand dames of Almack's to forbid him from entering that veritable institution for his entire lifetime. Dylan was not wont to weep over it.

"It was only because Lady Amelia slapped your face at once that her reputation was saved," Anthony pointed out. "That kiss would have ruined her otherwise."

"I told her to slap me. There was nothing for it. Everyone was staring at us." Dylan straightened away from the statue and began walking toward the door, the edge of his cloak churning up glimpses of gold silk behind his boot heels. "If you will not come out and chase petticoats with me, I must fend for myself. I believe I shall go to the theater tonight. Abigail Williams is playing in *The Rivals*. I shall jump down from my box and carry her off the stage."

"Really, Moore," Anthony called after his friend, "do you not think you are taking this mad artist charade a bit too far?"

"Is it a charade?" Dylan asked, pausing in the doorway to look at him with an odd smile. "I often wonder. Call on me, Tremore, when you wish to do something amusing."

Anthony watched his friend vanish through the doorway, and he shook his head. Dylan was a talented, brilliant man, but he seemed to be getting wilder with each passing month. He had not been the same since he'd taken that fall in Hyde Park three years before.

Anthony pushed thoughts of Dylan out of his mind and looked down once again at the fresco in front of him. He traced his finger along a serpentine crack amid the faded grapes, a thin, hairline crack repaired with precise and painstaking skill.

He would never want anything enough that its loss would drive him beyond reason. Never.

He jerked his hand back from the wall painting. When he left London, he would go to Hertfordshire and see Sarah. It was time to make their engagement official.

* * *

"No, no," Elizabeth said, laughing as she grasped Daphne's shoulders and turned her around. "You moved the wrong way."

"So I did," Daphne admitted, laughing. "Oh, dear, I shall never be proficient at this quadrille business," she confessed as she resumed the dance, concentrating on the figures Anthony had taught her. The music was provided by three violins in the corner instead of a tiny musical box, Elizabeth was her partner instead of Anthony, and the other couples were not imaginary. Twenty-two young girls having their lessons were moving with them in the steps of a country dance.

Though she had once been horrified by the thought of learning a new skill in front of people, her lessons with Anthony had given her enough confidence that at least now she could laugh at herself when she made a mistake. When she had mentioned to Elizabeth her lack of experience with country dancing three weeks ago, and her desire to practice, the girl had insisted they spend her next few Thursday mornings at the assembly rooms.

"Do not become discouraged, Daphne," Lady Fitzhugh called to her from her chair beside the wall, when Daphne once again turned the wrong way. "Dancing well takes practice. Anne and Elizabeth began receiving instruction in these very assembly rooms when they were just ten years old. You are doing quite nicely, dear."

"It's true, you know," Elizabeth said as they lined up with the other girls for a new dance. "By the time you join us in London, you will be quite fine. You dance better than you think."

Anthony had said the same, but moving in the same steps with other people present made her errors much more noticeable to her. Oddly enough, she did not care quite so much. Anthony had helped her gain a bit of self-confidence.

She did not want to think of Anthony, and she forced herself to say something. "Are you still leaving after Twelfth Night?" she asked as she clasped Elizabeth's hand and they turned in a *moulinet*.

"Yes, and I am so thrilled to be going. And to think you will be there when we arrive. Oh, Daphne, we will have such a wonderful time of it!"

Daphne tried to summon the same enthusiasm for London that Elizabeth had, but she could not manage it. As she moved about the floor with the others, she tried to concentrate on the steps, but her mind stubbornly clung to thoughts of her favorite dance partner.

He had been gone nearly a month, and there was still no word of when he would return. He might not come back until after she had gone. Any day might bring news of his engagement. She might never see him again. Three months ago, she would have been heartily glad to go. Now, she felt quite gloomy at the prospect.

She had tried to forget those passionate moments between them, but she could not forget. She had occupied herself with work, she had spent her Sunday afternoons and her Thursdays out with the Fitzhugh family, and Elizabeth had helped her to choose new gowns from Mrs. Avery to take with her to London. She had kept herself busy during all her waking hours, but Anthony stole into her thoughts every time she picked up an artifact, every time she came to the assembly rooms for lessons in dance, every time she walked in the rain.

Somehow, despite all her efforts to dislike him, she had been unable to sustain her animosity. Somehow, during the twelve weeks that had passed since she had first given him her resignation, her wounded pride had been healed. Somehow, a genuine camaraderie had sprung up between them as they had danced and flirted and laughed together. Somehow, he had made her feel beautiful and interesting as he had asked about her travels and touched her. Somehow, he had even become her friend. But having a friend who could set her afire with a kiss was a dangerous thing indeed. Especially when he was a duke and he intended to marry someone named Lady Sarah, a woman who was no doubt quite suited to being a duchess.

Anthony sat in his carriage by the roadside, staring at the rain-washed stone walls and lighted windows of Monforth House in the distance, but he did not order his coachman to go through the gates. He remained there for over an hour, listening to the droplets of sleet hitting the carriage roof on a gloomy, cold December afternoon.

He thought of Sarah, of her stunning beauty, her mercenary heart, and her understanding of the obligations and responsibilities that would come with being a duchess. She would be absolutely perfect for the role. Dylan was right, of course. There was not a hint of the sensual within her. Anthony had kissed her twice, and he knew that suggesting she do anything more venturesome than stare at the ceiling would send her for her vinaigrette and make her think him a barbaric husband. But that was why married men, as well as single ones, had mistresses.

He thought briefly of Marguerite. Not even once during the entire time he had been in Town had he gone to see her, and he could not understand why, for his body was raging with a hungry, almost desperate need.

He thought about his responsibilities. To marry well, to ensure that he had at least one son, to make the future as secure as possible for his descendants, were the primary duties of his life. He had postponed them as long as he could.

He thought about the additional power a marquess's daughter brought to his heirs, the additional connections both of them would gain from the alliance, and all the other reasons why marrying Sarah was a good idea. She would have him, there was no doubt of it. The vows would barely be uttered before she would have the Tremore emeralds around her neck and in her hair. She was exactly the sort of wife a duke had to have, and the sort of woman who would never demand anything of his soul.

He sat there as gray twilight began to settle over Monforth House, and he felt the burden of his rank more than he ever had before. He listened to the drumming of icy water on the roof, still not quite understanding why anyone would stand out in the pouring rain—even when it was August—and actually enjoy it.

It was dark. Anthony ordered his coachman to turn the carriage around and return to London, and he did not understand himself at all.

Chapter 19

Daphne vowed she was not going to count the days since Anthony had left, and she kept that vow. She did not look out the window every time she heard the rattle of wheels pass by the antika. She did not ask Mr. Bennington if there was any word of when his grace would return. She did not go to the north wing or walk in the conservatory.

None of that prevented her from missing him, missing verbal duels and midnight dances, bargains and kisses. She kept reminding herself that it did no good to miss him, for she was leaving. She kept repeating the words she had overheard him say about her, hoping that would be the antidote to missing him, but it did not work. Those words had ceased to evoke resentment.

Determined not to miss him, Daphne immersed herself in work. The storage rooms of the antika still had plenty of antiquities yet to be worked on, she attended two assemblies with the Fitzhugh ladies, and there was always plenty of reading to occupy the remainder of her free time—books on the peerage, publications of current fashions, a study of English politics, even a text from the local bookshop on what a young woman needed to know if she took up a post as governess. Daphne studiously avoided the society papers. She did not want to read speculations of Anthony and his future bride.

By Anthony's orders, his master of the stables taught her to ride a horse. Given her expertise with camels, it took only a few days for her to become comfortable with it, though she thought the sidesaddle a ridiculous device.

The holiday season came. Mr. and Mrs. Bennington went to their nephew's home in Wiltshire for Christmas, and Lady Fitzhugh invited Daphne to attend the holiday amusements at Long Meadows. She accepted, and wrote again to Viola, informing the viscountess of her decision to remain in Hampshire just a few more days. She had never experienced a true English Christmas, and going to the Fitzhughs' for the festivities appealed to her. She had become very fond of the Fitzhugh family during the last few months, and they had come to treat her almost as one of their own.

For her first English Christmas, Daphne ate foods as exotic to her as they were commonplace to her hosts. She was doubtful regarding the roast boar's head, but she loved the plum pudding, hard sauce, and wassail.

The Benningtons came back to Tremore Hall in time to give her their farewells and best wishes. Mr. Cox paid her the stipend of five hundred pounds. By January 5, there was no reason for her to remain in Hampshire. It was time to leave.

When Lady Fitzhugh heard Daphne was leaving for London the following day, intending to travel alone by post, she was horrified. She insisted Daphne celebrate Twelfth Night at Long Meadows, then journey to London a few days later in their carriage, for they were also departing for town, and could easily take her to Chiswick on the way. Daphne accepted their offer. The eve of Twelfth Night was when Anthony came home.

She was in the antika, occupied with finishing the restoration of one last artifact, a very rare piece of Samarian pottery. Putting the many broken shards of the large vase back together had taken all day and most of the evening. It was nearly midnight when she penciled in one last flourish on the sketch of that vase and wrote its catalog definition at the bottom of the page: *Globular vase. Group D: coarse pottery, Fig. 16.2. Samarian ware, with dark-red glaze and barbotine ornament; Hadrianic, second century. Villa of Druscus Aerelius, Wychwood, Hampshire. 1831.*

Daphne stared down at the sketch for a moment. This was the last artifact of Anthony's Roman villa that she would restore. She might see him in London, she might visit his museum, but this vase represented the end of her time at Tremore Hall, and she suddenly felt an overpowering sense of desolation. There were exciting possibilities in her future, but when she thought of Anthony, she could not summon that excitement.

The desperate infatuation she had once felt for him had long since disappeared, but another feeling had taken its place, a deeper feeling of respect and friendship. Desire was there, too—had always been there. Desire that still made her soft as butter when she thought of him without his shirt, of how strong his arms were when he had held her, of how intoxicating his kisses had been. It hurt to dwell on those feelings, hurt so deep it felt settled in her soul like a stone. Their time here together, working side by side, dancing, picnicking, bargaining over her time, had been special and wonderful, and the knowledge of her imminent departure seemed almost unbearable.

A tear blurred the lens of her spectacles and she hastily wiped it away with her handkerchief. She had vowed never to cry over him again, and she was going to keep that vow.

The fire in the grate had burned down to coals and ash, and Daphne realized how cold the antika had become. She flexed her hands several times, wincing at the ache in them from her day's work and the cold room. Then she rested her elbows on the table and pushed her fingers beneath her spectacles to rub her tired eyes. Her fingertips were icy and felt soothing against her closed eyelids. She yawned, knowing it was quite late. She should go back to the house and go to bed, for she was leaving for the Fitzhughs' first thing in the morning.

The door opened. Daphne looked up as an icy gust of wind blew out the candles on her worktable and stirred the listless coals in the fireplace to life. The fire flared just long enough for her to see who stood in the doorway before dying back once again to a faint red glow.

It was him. She could see his unmistakable silhouette in the doorway, his wide shoulders a black wall against the silvery winter moonlight behind him. Another shaft of moonlight slashed through the room in front of him, hitting the stone floor of the antika in a windowpane pattern at his feet.

"I saw you in here." He paused, expelling a harsh breath, then he added enigmatically, "Everywhere I went."

Daphne cleared her throat. "You have returned." Such an inane thing to say, but she could not seem to form the coherence of thought required to say anything more. She rose to her feet as he came inside, hugging herself against the frigid air that came with him.

He shut the door and flattened back against it, his body and his face still in darkness. "And you are still here," he said wearily. "I did not think you would be. December twenty-third was supposed to be your last day, was it not?"

He had not even intended to say good-bye. Daphne pulled all her emotions into a tight, hard knot of pride. "I am leaving for Long Meadows tomorrow. I will spend Twelfth Night there, then the

Fitzhughs shall take me to your sister's home in Chiswick on their way to town."

He made no reply, and as the silence grew, so did her emotions. Provoked by his silence, she said, "What, no temptations to make me stay, your grace? No talk of our friendship and my beautiful eyes?" Her voice cracked. "No farewell and good wishes for a faithful member of your staff?"

He shoved away from the door and started toward her, a shadow of black and gray. "God, Daphne, what do you think?" he demanded as he circled the table to stand behind her. "That I am made of stone?"

"Is that not what you think I am made of?" she countered and tried to step around the table, but he would not let her.

His hand came down on her shoulder, and the other touched the side of her face, brushing a tendril of hair back from her cheek. "No, not stone," he answered, pressing against her back. "I think you are like a truffle."

"Thank you for comparing me to a mushroom," she said, unfolding her arms and moving to step the other way.

He put his other hand on her other shoulder to keep her where she was, and his laughter blew warm breath against the side of her face. "Not the vegetable," he said, and kissed her cheek. "A chocolate truffle. A concoction of soft, sweet, delicious things hidden inside a hard, paperboard box." He lowered his hands to reach for hers. "A frozen truffle, I fear. Your hands feel like ice."

The heat of his body behind her was making her warm. She wanted to be cold.

"Let me warm you." He let go of her hands and turned her around. He reached up and took away her spectacles. Folding the pair, he put them in the pocket of her apron. He cupped her face in his hands, then he bent his head, and kissed her, but she turned her face away.

"I tried to stay away," he said, pressing quick kisses to her lips, her cheek, her forehead, her chin. "Because if I came back to say good-bye, I would not be able to stop myself from doing this. Daphne, you have been like a shadow beside me for six long weeks, and everywhere I went, I could see you. I am not made of stone. I am just a man, and God help me, I cannot stop wanting you. Do not torture me anymore." His tongue ran across the crease of her lips. "Kiss me back."

Her lips parted beneath his, and she closed her eyes, groaning into his mouth. So long. He had been away so long, and she had forgotten how it felt to have his mouth on hers.

She seized the folds of his cloak in her fists, pulling him closer. In response, he deepened the kiss, tasting her with his tongue. She wrapped one arm around his neck, and tangled the fingers of her other hand in the thick, short strands of his hair.

He broke the kiss, pulling back to look at her, his expression in the moonlight strangely resolute. "Say my name," he ordered, lowering his hands to tug at the ties of her apron. He pulled the bows apart two at a time. "Anthony."

"Stop giving me orders, duke," she said, rising up on her toes to recapture his mouth. "Don't ruin it."

He pulled the pieces of her apron away and tossed them over her head onto the table behind her. She heard a rocking sound, followed by a shattering crash, and she knew he had just smashed that priceless ancient vase to smithereens. Her last day's work wasted. She began to laugh against his mouth. "You broke it."

"What was it?" he asked, tearing away from her kiss to bury his face against the side of her neck.

"Samarian vase," she gasped, "made at Trier. Priceless."

He jerked at the ribbon of his cloak, and the heavy garment slid from his shoulders to land on the floor. "I shall mourn the loss tomorrow." He pressed kisses against her throat. "Say it."

Daphne ran her hands along his torso, savoring the hard muscles beneath his clothes, feeling the excitement of all their past bargains. "And if I do, what do you offer me in exchange, your grace?"

"What do you want?"

She thought of that fresco, of that man and woman, his hand on her breast, their bodies locked together, and she decided it was time for her to start being honest with herself about what she felt and what she wanted. "The same thing you do," she answered and reached for his cravat, but her inexperienced fingers could not loosen the tight, intricate knot.

"Let me do it." He made short work of the neckcloth, and it fluttered to the floor. He removed his waistcoat, then pulled off his shirt.

Daphne stared at him. No view through a spyglass, this. She reached out to touch his chest, and found that he was not cold beneath her hands. His muscles were hard like stone, but warm. He did not move, but she could feel his gaze on her face as she studied him in the silver light and traced with her fingers every line and shadowed contour she had so often drawn with her pencil. She flattened her palms against the chiseled muscles of his abdomen and leaned forward to press a kiss to his breastbone.

He stifled a groan and grasped her wrists. "Enough," he said. "Now, say it."

She did not want to. Oddly enough, it seemed too intimate, even as she kissed his naked chest, she did not want to say his name and evoke all the feelings of her lovesick former self. This moment was no fantasy view through a spyglass. This was real, and the feelings coursing through her body spoke of desire, not love, not even infatuation. Her body ached for him. She lifted her gaze to his. Wordless, she reached for his hand, held it in her own, touched it to her breast.

Anthony opened his hand over her, and she made a faint sound of surprise. Oh, the exquisite sweetness of it, spreading through her body like warm honey. He shaped and cradled her breast against his palm, and that warmth became a desperate longing that made her ache. She leaned into his hand, wanting more.

She did not get it. He pulled away, but before she could protest this abandonment, she felt his hands at her bodice, and he was undoing the buttons of her dress.

When they were unfastened, Anthony tugged the edges of her dress down her arms and pressed kisses to her neck just above the low neckline of her chemise. "My name," he said against her skin. "I will have you say it."

She knew they were about to engage in the most intimate thing a man and woman could do, but she could still not bring herself to say his name. She shook her head and put her hands on his hips, pulling him closer.

He brushed his fingertips back and forth over the bare skin at the tops of her breasts, and Daphne moaned, reaching behind her to grasp the edge of the table as her knees began to give way. He pulled back the edges of her gown, then unbuttoned her chemise, baring her breasts fully to the cool air, then covering them with the warmth of his hands.

Daphne could hear herself making inarticulate sounds as he shaped her breasts in his hands, each caress of his fingers making her burn with need, a need that made her arch closer to him. She rocked her hips against his thighs, and the contact sent shafts of pleasure through her body.

The contact seemed to spark something in him. He slid the gown and chemise back from her shoulders, then reached down, grasping folds of her skirt and petticoat in his fists and pulling them up around her waist. Cold caressed her bare legs above her stockings, and his hands burned against her bare buttocks as he lifted her onto the table.

She felt the shape of his phallus hard and aroused against the outside of her knee as his fingertips glided along the sensitive skin of her inner thigh.

"Yes, yes," she moaned instead of his name, leaning back, resting her weight on her hands, his featherlight touch making her hips jerk in response. The sanded surface of the table felt like satin beneath her. Her dress strained against her arms, the braid edging cutting sharply into her skin, but she did not care.

He bent down, unbuttoning more of her gown and tugging up the hem of her chemise. He kissed her belly, a hot, wet kiss over her navel, as his fingers moved farther down to touch her in a place she could not even name, each caress sending shards of indescribable pleasure through her. He knew it, too, knew what she wanted better than she did, for he was tormenting her with his relentless demand. "Say my name," he breathed against her skin. "Say it, Daphne. Say it."

He touched her with his thumb, and that tiny movement unlocked something inside her, released all the repressions and restraints she had imposed on herself ever since she had first met him. With the force of a river breaking through a dam, pure, indescribable pleasure rushed through her, and she could no longer stop herself from giving him what he wanted. "Anthony," she cried, "oh, please, oh, yes, yes."

He heard his name amid the almost incoherent rush of other sounds that came from her, pleas and sighs and moans that told him more clearly than any words what his touch was doing to her. God, she was sweet. So, so sweet.

Anthony caressed her until she climaxed a second time, then he moved between her thighs. If he held back any longer, he would explode. He tore at his trousers, undoing buttons with frantic haste, then he moved between her thighs, spreading them farther apart.

"Daphne," he said, sliding his hands behind her shoulders, pulling her to a sitting position. She slid to the edge of the table, and the feel of her, moist and inviting against the tip of his penis drove away any thought but the need to possess her. With one hard thrust, he entered her.

She cried out, and he knew he had hurt her. He stilled, but she wrapped her arms around his neck and tightened her legs around his hips, pulling him deeper into her, and he lost any semblance of sanity. He touched her breasts, kissed her face, and murmured words to arouse her without knowing what he was saying as he drove into her again and again, pushing himself to the edge of oblivion. When he climaxed, he went over that edge, falling into a white-hot heaven of pure sensation.

It was only afterward, when they were lying on the table, when he had one arm wrapped around her and the other beneath her head as a pillow, only when his cloak covered them both and his body was pressed to hers to protect her from the cold—it was only then that he came to his senses, reminding himself of the inevitable consequences of what he had just done.

Chapter 20

Daphne felt him get up, and she opened her eyes. The hint of dawn that came in through the windows enabled her to see him standing beside the table, his back to her.

She lifted herself onto an elbow and stared at his bare back. He was so close that she did not need her spectacles to see him clearly, so close that she could touch him. How wide his shoulders were, she thought, and how they tapered to hips narrower than hers. From her first sight of him at the excavation, she had known what an appealing sight a man could be without his shirt. Such strength, and yet he had held her so gently, touched her so exquisitely. Without the warmth of his body, the room was freezing cold, but just thinking about what had happened only a short while ago was enough to keep her warm. It was enough to make her smile.

With a huge yawn, she sat up, pushing aside his cloak to pull the sleeves of her dress back into place on her shoulders.

"I thought you were asleep," he said, without turning to look at her.

"No." She moved her legs astride his hips and wrapped her arms around his waist. She felt feminine, beautiful, and absurdly happy at this moment, content with the world and everything in it. How delightful that coupling with a man could do that to a woman. It was an extraordinary thing.

She laid her cheek against his back, and suddenly she realized how rigid he was in her embrace. She lifted her head with a frown. "Anthony?"

He pulled away from her, giving her the barest glance as he bent to pick up his shirt from the floor. "Are you—" He broke off as he straightened and pulled his shirt on. Then he faced her, cleared his throat, and looked away again. "I hurt you," he muttered, staring out the window into the dim gray light. "Forgive me. I did not mean to do that."

Was that what was making him so uncomfortable? It had hurt, but only a little, and only for a moment. "Oh, no," she hastened to reassure him, sliding down from the table. She laid a hand on his arm. "There was nothing to that. I am perfectly well, Anthony." She lowered her gaze to his chest, and the sight made her flustered and a bit shy, but venturesome, too.

"In fact, I feel quite wonderful," she confessed,

smiling, her hand straying to his chest. Her fingertips touched his warm skin where his shirt was not yet buttoned. She looked up at him, hoping he would take the hint.

He did not. His mouth tightened, and he bent down to retrieve his waistcoat from the floor.

She watched him for a moment. "Anthony, please do not distress yourself on my account. My discomfort was insignificant."

He barely glanced at her as he put on his waistcoat. "I am relieved to hear it."

She felt an uneasy disquiet setting in. She turned her back and began to straighten her clothes, buttoning her chemise, then her gown. Both of them were silent as they dressed. When they had finished, he rested his hands on her shoulders for a moment, and she stiffened beneath his touch. He moved away and bent down to pick up his cravat. She turned around, watching as he pulled up the high collar of his shirt, slid the cravat around his neck, and began to tie it.

"Anthony, what is wrong?"

He finished tying the neckcloth, then took her hand in his, lifted it to his lips and kissed it. "I take full responsibility for this," he told her, and let go of her hand. "You need not fear for your future."

She stared at him in bewilderment, for she was not in the least afraid. "My future?"

He picked up his coat from the floor. "We will be married after the banns have been properly posted. The ceremony will be here in the ducal chapel, if that is acceptable to you. If you prefer the parish church, simply tell me so."

Anthony was offering to marry her? She could not quite believe she had heard him right. He sounded so dispassionate, Daphne was not quite sure if she had just received a proposal of marriage or a comment on the weather. The delicious afterglow of their blissful experience was now completely gone.

He put on his coat, turned away from her and walked to the window. "Until the wedding, you must stay elsewhere," he said, staring out into the gray darkness. "Enderby will suffice. It would not do for you to be here. I will explain the situation to Viola. Due to the breadth of social difference between us, you will be the subject of gossip, and I regret that, but it cannot be helped."

He fell silent, standing with his back to her, the dawn light that outlined his profile hazy and indistinct to her eyes. She did not understand why he was talking of marriage now, but she remembered his words to his sister about never marrying for love, and she knew that one question had to be answered before she could even consider marrying him.

She took a deep breath. "Have you fallen in love with me, then, that you wish to marry me?"

He turned his head, but he did not quite look at her. "You must know by now that I have—that I have come to have—a strong, and very passionate desire for—attraction, I should say, to you."

"I see." Daphne did not know the proper etiquette of refusing a marriage proposal, since such an event had never come her way, but she felt she should at least be able to see him clearly when she did refuse. She leaned down and pulled her spectacles from the pocket of her apron, which still lay on the floor. She put the spectacles on, then walked to his side and laid a hand on his arm. "Desire, as wonderful as it is, Anthony, is not enough. I will not marry you."

"We have no choice now." He did not look at her. "I took that away from both of us just now."

"You talk as if I had no control over any of this. This was a mutual decision, Anthony, for my feelings are comparable with yours. I, too, have a strong and passionate desire for you, but that is all. Without love, I see no reason to marry you."

He turned to face her, and in his expression there was no hint of affection for her, only a resolute determination to have his way, an expression she was coming to know quite well. "You should realize by now that you do not have a choice in this. We must marry. There is nothing else to be done."

"The musts and shoulds of your life do not apply to me, your grace," she said, her voice as cool as his. "I understand that marriage is the accepted mode in situations such as this, but there are alternatives. No one knows of this but us. I shall go to London, just as I intended to do, and—"

"That is out of the question. You may very well be carrying my child. What of that?"

God in heaven, she had not even thought of a child. Her hand fluttered to her abdomen, and something sparked inside of her, a mixture of emotions. A wistful sort of hope and fear, and a sense of her own duty, and the courage not to have her destiny or that of her child dictated by circumstances.

"We do not know if there will be a child," she answered him. "Besides, you are an honorable man. I know you would take care of us and see that we are provided for. Illegitimate children of men such as yourself do not suffer any great setbacks in life, your grace."

"God, Daphne, what are you saying? That I make you my mistress?"

Before she could make any answer to Anthony's question, he answered it for her. "You cannot be my mistress. If that were possible, there are arrangements I could make for you, a house in the country, an income, but it is out of the question."

"You seem quite familiar with the appropriate arrangements for mistresses." A thought struck her, and she looked at him. "Do you have one now? A mistress, I mean?"

He stiffened, with all the hauteur and dignity that befitted a duke. "I did, yes, but I have not seen—"

"Does she . . ." Daphne choked on the question, a sick knot in the pit of her stomach. After a moment, she tried again. "Does she have any children that are . . . that might be . . ." She could not go on. Pressing a hand to her mouth, she turned her back on him.

"No," he answered her incomplete question. "Marguerite has no children, not even mine. Daphne, that is not important now. You are ruined but unwed, and that is my fault. I will not stain your reputation with the shame of an illegitimate child. As I said, we must marry."

She circled around to the other side of the table, putting it between them like a barrier before she turned to face him.

He did not follow her, but remained where he was. "You are the granddaughter of a baron, it seems, but Viola told me that you do not know his identity. If this is true, I will find him. We will establish your connection to him, and obtain his permission for the match. A mere formality, of course, given the circumstances, but necessary. I will negotiate the dowry and terms with him. Once we are wed, I will provide a quarterly allowance for your use. Five thousand pounds should be sufficient, but if you require more, you need only ask. As my wife, you will be entitled to my full support."

Daphne felt anger and frustration rising within her like the tide. He was talking as if she had no say in that. "Is not marrying me a bit extreme? I am somewhat ignorant of these matters, but I believe it is the usual custom for men in your position not to marry women for this sort of thing, but to pay them off."

He pushed aside the oak table between them so violently that it skidded across the stone floor and hit the wall. She did not move.

He took another step toward her, and the chair in his path followed the table. She still remained where she was, meeting his gaze as he halted, a few feet away.

"You insult my honor, Miss Wade, and your

own," he said, his voice low and furious, "if you assume that I would sink so low as to pay you off with a *douceur* as if you were some demirep or prostitute."

"It is you who makes me that, with all your talk of terms and settlements and quarterly allowances and no personal regard or respect for me behind them. Accepting your support for a child we might have is one thing. Marrying you is something else, a wholly unnecessary step, to my mind."

"You were a virgin, in heaven's name! If you believe that I would take the innocence of a young lady and not do right by her, you know nothing of my character as a man, of what my position as a peer means to me, or of my honor as a gentleman."

"And what of Lady Sarah?" she countered. "Were you not intending to marry her?"

"I suppose Viola told you. It hardly matters, as I have not declared any such intention to the lady, and now I cannot do so."

"You were not in love with her, yet you intended to marry her. You do not love me, yet you now wish to marry me. One wife is as good as another? With a mistress for additional variety, of course."

"Love, love," he said impatiently. "What is love? Define it for me, if you will. You are the one who had her heart broken, so you told me. Tell me about love."

"That was not love!" she cried. "That was infatuation! A foolish inclination not supported by anything but my own imagination, for you felt nothing for me at all. I knew it, but—"

"What?" His shocked question made her realize her deepest secret had just slipped out.

Somehow, she did not care. What other people thought of her no longer mattered. "Yes, Anthony," she admitted, looking him in the eye, unashamed of her feelings. At least they had been honest ones. "I was infatuated with *you*. God help me, I fell for you the moment I met you. Stupid of me, but there it is."

He was staring at her in utter astonishment, and somehow that only fueled her anger. "Unbelievable, isn't it? Me, of all women, wanting a duke. Me, a woman with no money, no connections, and no family—at least no family that wants to acknowledge her. Me, a plain, shy, serious woman who by all rights should become a spinster because she is as noticeable as a stick insect on a twig!"

She saw a flicker of something in his expression, and she went on, "Yes, I was standing outside the music room that night when you and your sister talked of me. I heard every word you said. Do you recall that conversation, your grace?"

Comprehension dawned in his face, comprehension and a hint of dismay. "I did say that," he murmured and began to walk toward her. "I admit, I had forgotten the entire incident. It meant so little at the time."

"So little to you, perhaps, but so much to me." She was too angry to care that it would serve no purpose to tell him these things now, angry with how he had turned what had just happened between them in to something that involved obligation and shame. "I believe I was also compared with a machine, a creature with no feminine appeal. I was pathetic, I believe that was the term you used—"

He stepped forward and grasped her shoulders to give her a little shake, as if she were getting hysterical, when in fact, she was quite calm.

"Listen to me, Daphne," he said. "I am grieved that you overheard me say something so thoughtless, but I did not know you. I mean, of course I knew you, but I did not really know—" He broke off. Lowering his hands to his sides, he took a deep breath and tried again. "It was true that I said it, but it was because I meant that you made yourself unnoticeable. That was all, and your tendency to do so was a subject, I might add, which we have discussed. Viola was talking of finding you a husband, and she asked my opinion—"

"You certainly gave it. You told your sister that finding me a husband was a hopeless business." She gave a humorless laugh. "Not so hopeless after all, since you are now feeling this absurd compulsion to marry me yourself. How odd life is!"

He stepped back, clasping his hands behind him and looking every inch the proper duke. "Please believe that I have nothing but regret for those words. What I said was cruel and thoughtless, and I realize you must have been deeply hurt, but I assure you that wounding your feelings was never my intent. Since then, as I have already stated, I have developed a strong attraction to you, strong enough that one could safely describe it as a sort of madness with me. A temporary madness, perhaps, but a madness nonetheless. I wanted you so badly, I—" He expelled a harsh breath and the ducal dignity faltered. "God, after what just happened, do I have to explain?"

"No. I believe it is safe to say you have changed your opinion of me. How soon before it changes again? How soon before your 'temporary madness,' as you put it, fades away, and I become a stick insect again?"

"I do not think of you that way!" he shouted. "Can a man not change his opinion? I have changed mine. When I look at you, I do not see a stick insect. I see—"

"You do not need to soothe my pride, your grace," she interrupted, unable to bear hearing compliments now. "It is not necessary. My heart was not broken by hearing your opinion of me. My pride was bruised, and that is all. I was not in love, I was infatuated, and I recovered from the experience."

"Damnation, Daphne, stop interrupting! I appreciate the wrong I have done you—in more ways than one, it seems—but that does not alter my obligation. We will be married as soon as the arrangements can be made, for I will not compound my wrong by abandoning my honor and my duty."

Daphne did not reply at once. She picked up the two halves of her apron and fastened them together at the neck, then slipped the garment over her head and began to fasten the ties. It was only after she had knotted the last one that she spoke.

"Once again, you seem to believe that this is all about you. Your duty, your good name, your heirs, your estate, your obligations, your feeling that what happened between us should be regarded as something sordid. Until we get married, of course, at which point, *your* honor will be satisfied. Most of all, this is about your sense of guilt."

She saw him flinch. Drawing a deep breath, she went on, "Unlike you, I do not feel guilty at all. I do not feel ruined. In fact, I was feeling quite delightful until you began talking of duty and shame ruined it all. I knew what I wanted, and I took it, as did you. You may feel that there is some dishonor in it, but your dishonor is not mine. What happened between us—"

Her voice caught for a moment. She swallowed hard, and went on, "It was a wonderful thing, truly the most exciting thing that has ever happened to me, and I will not turn it into something of which I should be ashamed. I will not marry you, because despite this mad attraction you seem to have for me now, you do not love me, nor even care for me in any sense that would result in a happy union. I will not be chained to any man in a loveless marriage by his temporary passion, nor his need to expunge his guilt."

"Love has nothing to do with this. This is about honor and duty."

"I will not be any man's duty." She walked over to her cloak, which lay draped over the cap of a Corinthian column. "I thank you for your offer, your grace, but I will not marry you. That is my final resolve. Your *duty* is now discharged."

Throwing her cloak over her shoulders, she left the antika, too angry to say one more word.

Anthony stared at the door that Daphne had just slammed behind her, feeling bewildered, ill-used, and rather angry himself. What did she expect of him? Did she think him a callous brute who would ruin her, then pay her off as if she were a streetwalker? That he could then abandon her as if he owed her nothing more, or that he could turn her into a courtesan? God, that wounded him, that she thought him capable of such an action.

But he had also wounded her. She had been infatuated with him, and his words must have hurt her deeply, but as he had just tried to explain, he had not known her then, not in any personal sense. He had hired her to do a job of work. He had been her employer, and he had treated her accordingly. And yes, his opinion of her as a woman then had not been flattering, but he would never have expressed it had he known her to be eavesdropping outside the door.

A stick insect. His words, true, but the way he thought of her now was so different. Could she not see that? She was no longer the unnoticeable subservient who did everything he asked, who took every word he said as if it were gospel, and who has always hovered by to obey his every order without question.

She had changed before his eyes, and somehow, she had become in his sight a woman as alluring and desirable as any he had ever known. Even now, when the consequences of what he had done were so grave, he wanted her again. Even now, when all the things he valued most—the future of his estates, the honor of his name, and the legitimacy of a possible heir—were in jeopardy, even now, he wanted her.

Yes, she had became a passion to him, a beautiful and vibrant woman. A woman he had hurt very badly.

These were not the most romantic circumstances under which to propose, and he had probably wounded her a second time by discussing their marriage in such blunt fashion. And having the subject of his mistress come out had not helped. He hadn't even had the chance to tell her he had written to Marguerite and ended the arrangement.

He supposed it had been rather arrogant of him to assume that she would accept him, but damn it all, he *was* a duke. It was not as if he were an attorney or a land agent. Only royal dukes, princes, and kings ranked higher than he, and it was not conceited of him to take her acceptance of his offer as a matter of course, especially under these circumstances.

Anthony walked over to the table by the wall. He pulled his cloak from beneath it and put it on, then left the antika.

Sunrise was breaking over the horizon, and Anthony paused for a moment outside the antika, staring at the crimson, pink, and gold horizon. Today was Epiphany. *Somehow that seems appropriate,* he thought wryly, as he began walking back to the house.

Marrying Daphne was simply the right and honorable thing to do, and he was going to have to figure out a way that would persuade her to accept. He had the feeling it was not going to be easy.

Chapter 21

Daphne had departed from Tremore Hall less than twenty minutes after she had left Anthony in the antika. He did not attempt to see her before she left, deciding it would be best to wait a fortnight before following her to Chiswick so that both of them could think over the situation in a calm and prudent fashion. For his part, he knew that he had not been particularly romantic in his proposal. In persuading Daphne to accept him, he would have to find a way to remedy that. Getting her alone would be an easy matter at Enderby, but when he arrived there, his sister turned his plans upside down.

He found Viola in the midst of packing to leave, surrounded by opened trunks scattered about the floor of her boudoir, with maids scurrying about her in a frenzy of activity, filling the trunks with gowns.

"Left?" he demanded of his sister. "What do you mean, she left?"

Viola shook her head but not at him. "No, no, Celeste, not the green silk, the green wool." She turned her attention to Anthony and gestured to a nearby chair of her sitting room. "Dear Daphne has gone on to London. Lady Fitzhugh was kind enough to offer to act as her chaperone under the circumstances."

Anthony frowned as he sat on the edge of a brocade chair, oblivious to the pile of gowns he crushed. "What circumstances?" He glanced around him. "Are you not packing for town?"

"I am going to Northumberland. Hammond has been in some sort of accident, and I must go to Hammond Park at once. I received an express from Dr. Chancellor last evening."

"What sort of accident?"

"He was shot."

"A hunting accident?"

"No." Viola bit her lip and looked away. After a moment, she returned her attention to Anthony. Looking him in the eye, she said, "He was in a duel. Over some woman."

"The blackguard!" Anthony slammed his fist into the padded arm of his chair. "By God, I will ruin him for this. How much more humiliation does he expect you to endure?"

His sister looked pained, and he expelled a harsh breath. Though Viola might have felt some distress at this news, he did not. Hammond had treated Viola damn badly, and a duel over some woman was the last straw. Anthony could spare little regret for the other man's injuries. "I am sorry, Viola, but Hammond is a rakehell if ever there was one."

"It hardly matters now, does it?" She shrugged and went on, "I was so glad to see Daphne, and we had a wonderful visit. Though she was disappointed that I cannot go to London after all, things have turned out quite well. She is going to stay with the Fitzhugh family for her season."

If Daphne was staying in London with the Fitzhughs, his task had just become much more difficult, for he would have no opportunity to be alone with her, not to mention that his task of making her see reason would be played out before the entire ton. The gossip would escalate to a frenzy of rumor and speculation. "Damn."

He could not help noticing his sister's surprised glance.

"You seem displeased by this news, Anthony. Why should you be? You knew she would be going to town." She began to smile. "Been hoping to persuade her back to your clay pots and mosaics, have you?"

Anthony shot her a sharp look. "Did Miss Wade not confide in you?"

"Confide in me? I do not know what you mean. What confidences should she be imparting to me? Has something happened?"

Most women would have been eager to impart

news of a duke's proposal, especially to his sister, yet Daphne had evidently not told Viola. As guarded about his private life as a man could be, Anthony was pleased by her discretion, but Viola had to know the truth sometime, and it was far better for his sister to hear it from him than from the society papers. He told her.

"You proposed to Daphne?" A wide smile lit her face as she jumped up from her chair and came to give him a smacking kiss on each cheek. "How delightful!"

"Not so very delightful," he replied as Viola returned to her seat. "She refused me."

"Did she? I cannot imagine why, for she is in—" Viola paused in whatever she had been about to say, and her brown eyes narrowed on him. "You did not ask her, did you? You told her. Do not deny it," she added as he started to speak. "I know you far too well, Anthony. You became all ducal and autocratic, and she told you to go to the devil." Much to his chagrin, Viola began to laugh. "Oh, I knew I liked that woman."

"I am gratified that you are enjoying this, but are you not supposed to be on my side?"

"No," she answered at once, her smile widening. "I am wholly on Daphne's. We women must band together in situations such as this." Before Anthony could reply, she went on, "But one thing does puzzle me. If she refused you, why are you here?"

He found Viola's amusement at his expense quite irritating. "If you think I am accepting no for an answer, you do not know me as well as you thought, dear sister."

"Quite right of you, I say, but Daphne has the right to expect to be courted, you know. You cannot just order her to marry you. A wedding is not like an excavation. Oh, how I wish I could stay and watch all of this play out."

"Yes, I am sure you do," he answered, unamused, "but the society papers will be able to provide you with the details, no doubt. By the way, there is something I need to ask you. Did Daphne ever tell you the name of her grandfather? I shall have to locate this baron and discuss settlements with him."

"Lord Durand. Estates in Durham, I believe, but I did discover that he is in town. I suggested that Daphne and I pay a call on him, but she did not wish to do so. She explained to me that Durand actually refused to acknowledge her. She wrote to him after her father's death, and he had an attorney respond that she was not his granddaughter and never would be. Her parents eloped, and evidently, Durand never accepted the match. Can you believe it? I almost wept when she told me. There she was in Tangier or wherever, all alone with no money, and the horrid man wrote to her that she could expect no help from him."

Anthony rose to his feet, rage flowing through his body like a flood, but when he spoke, his voice was hard, tight, and fully controlled. "Somehow," he told Viola, "I believe Durand will be much more amenable to acknowledging his connection after a visit from me."

"Yes," Viola said, looking at him with obvious pleasure. "I expect he will. But Anthony," she added gently, "I do not believe Durand is your problem. You still have to persuade Daphne to accept your suit."

That was not going to be a problem at all, Anthony vowed as he left Enderby for London. By God, Daphne would be his duchess, even if he had to court her under the unwavering scrutiny of all London society.

"Heavens above!"

The exclamation caused Daphne to pause in her sketch of Elizabeth and Anne, who were seated on the settee opposite her in the drawing room of the Fitchughs' London house. She turned to look at Lady Fitzhugh, who was sitting in the chair beside her own, staring at the card the maid had just handed to her. Her other hand fluttered to her heart as she leaned back on the settee. "The Duke of Tremore has come to call."

"What?" her daughters cried together.

"Well, that did not take long," Daphne murmured under her breath.

"This must be due to you, Daphne!" cried Elizabeth. "All our lives we have lived in Hampshire, yet the duke has never come to wait upon us."

"Indeed," her mother added, tapping the card against the fingertips of her other hand, "I have scarce conversed with his grace half a dozen times in the seventeen years since he ascended to the title, and we have never received such condescension as this." She tucked the card into the side pocket of her gown and straightened in her chair. "Show him in at once, Mary. It does not do to keep a duke waiting."

As the maid left the room, Daphne could not help but notice how Lady Fitzhugh and her daughters began to pat their hair and straighten their gowns in anticipation of the unexpected guest. Daphne did nothing of the sort, and she almost wished she had raked back her hair in that efficient, tight little bun he despised. When she caught Elizabeth gesturing to her in a friendly reminder to take off her spectacles, she ignored the girl and left them on.

When he entered the room, she rose and dipped him a curtsy along with the others, then took refuge behind her sketchbook as Lady Fitzhugh introduced her daughters and invited him to sit down.

Over the top of her sketchbook, she observed the faces of Anne and Elizabeth as they stared at Anthony, who was sitting to her right. Looking at them was a bit like looking at a mirror image of herself, for their expressions seemed to offer a precise reflection of her own initial impression of him. Overwhelmed, ridiculously nervous, and caught up in the heights of a giddy attraction. He was looking every inch the handsome, elegant duke today, with his blue coat and darker blue trousers, his striped blue and gold waistcoat, and his immaculate white linen, and it was clear by the admiring faces of the Fitzhugh daughters that they wanted to pinch themselves for even being in the same room with him.

He is no doubt accustomed to this sort of feminine reaction everywhere he goes, she thought, lowering her gaze and noting with dismay that she had involuntarily pressed her pencil across her sheet of drawing paper in a thick, dark slash, ruining her drawing of Elizabeth.

"Ring the bell for tea, Anne," Lady Fitzhugh ordered, but before her elder daughter could move to stand, Anthony protested.

"No, please, do not trouble yourself on my account," he said, "for I cannot stay long. I paid a visit to my sister just before she left for Northumberland, and I learned you had brought Miss Wade to town with you. I wished to pay my respects."

"That is very kind of you," his hostess replied, only the tiniest hint of surprise in her voice, though the fact that the duke had wished to pay a call upon them clearly surprised her very much indeed.

"I have come to town to make my museum ready for its opening, for that event is only a few short weeks away," he told her. "I do hope you will come?"

"Of course. We should be delighted."

Daphne stirred in her chair, wishing he would leave, knowing he was not here to make idle chitchat. She hoped he did not intend to make his intentions clear to Lady Fitzhugh and her daughter by asking for a private interview with her. That would be humiliating, especially for him, when she refused. But she soon discovered he was not going to be quite so blunt as that.

"I have been working at such a pace these last months," he said, "that I have had little time for society, but now that we are nearly finished, I hope to have the opportunity to enjoy the season in London. I shall be quite free to accept invitations."

His words were expressed with such emphasis that Daphne looked up, just in time to watch Lady Fitzhugh fall right into the trap. Before she could interrupt with something about the weather, Lady Fitzhugh said in a small voice, "Indeed, your grace? I plan to have a card party very soon, a small party of a half dozen of our friends, and far too modest for you, I am sure, but I would be delighted if you would come."

"I would enjoy that very much," he said with such a satisfied smile that Daphne wanted to throw her pencil at him.

Lady Fitzhugh seemed quite stunned, not only because she had been so bold as to issue a verbal invitation to a duke, but also because he had accepted. "I shall send an invitation round to you," she murmured.

"I shall be happy to receive it." He glanced over at Daphne, then returned his attention to his hostess. "Miss Wade has worked very hard on the sketches for my museum, and I regret that she has had so little time for amusements herself. She deserves to enjoy herself in town."

"We intend to help her do that, your grace," Elizabeth assured him, laughing.

Lady Fitzhugh shot her daughter a reproving look. "We are delighted to have Miss Wade with us."

Anthony turned his attention to Daphne. "This is your first visit to London, is it not, Miss Wade?"

"Yes," she answered, and stopped pretending to sketch. "I am looking forward to it, having spent so little time moving in society, buried in the country for so long."

"Ah, your words remind me of the purpose of my visit." He reached into the pocket of his coat and pulled out a small package wrapped in plain paper and tied with brown twine. He leaned forward in his chair and held the package out to Daphne. "This is yours, I believe."

She took it from him with a puzzled frown, noting by its shape and feel that it must be a book. "I did not realize I left a book behind me."

"Perhaps you did not," he replied, his oblique words puzzling her further.

She looked up and found that he was giving her that half smile that meant he was teasing. "I do not understand."

He did not enlighten her. Instead, he turned to Elizabeth and Anne. "It is a bit early yet in the season, but I hope you young ladies plan to attend some assemblies while you are in town?"

"Oh, yes," Anne assured him, a bit nervously.

"We shall be attending one at the Haydon Assembly Rooms three days hence, as a matter of fact."

"I am gratified to hear it. Ladies, please forgive me, but I must go. I fear I have trespassed on your time long enough."

"We are honored you did so, your grace," Lady Fitzhugh answered. She stood up, and her daughters and Daphne rose as well. "Please feel free to call upon us any time. Any time at all."

"I assure you that I shall avail myself of that pleasure as often as I can, Lady Fitzhugh," he said as he moved to stand. "Please tell your husband he may come to see the museum any time convenient. And I look forward to receiving your invitation. Please do not forget me."

Daphne could see all three of the other women practically melting on the floor, but she held back her frustrated sigh. So this was how he intended to get his way. By overwhelming her friends with charm, dazzling them with his condescension, and flattering them with his attentions. She realized with a sinking feeling that he was going to be nice. How awful.

"Lady Fitzhugh," he said. "Miss Fitzhugh, Miss Elizabeth, Miss Wade." His eyes lingered on her for a moment, and she stared back at him, appalled by this new campaign he intended to launch, but he did not appear to notice. "Ladies," he said with a bow, "it has been a pleasure."

After he had gone, no one spoke for several moments. Elizabeth, of course, was the first to do so. "What did he give you, Daphne?" she asked. "Did you forget a book in Hampshire?"

"Elizabeth," reproved her mother. "It is not our business."

Daphne owned scarcely a dozen books, having had to sell all of her father's, and she was certain she had not left behind even one of the precious few she did own. She untied the bow, pulled away the twine, and carefully tore off the wrapping paper. She was holding the book facedown, but the white linen cover alone confirmed her suspicion that it did not belong to her. "This is not mine," she said, frowning. "I have never seen this before."

She turned the volume over and read the gilded stamp on front. "*Le Langage des Fleurs*," she read aloud, with a tightening pang of pain around her heart, "by Charlotte de la Tour."

She stared at the golden fleur-de-lis below the title for a moment, then read the inscription he had written.

Miss Wade,

The words of Englishmen are known all over the world to be the most inarticulate of devices for communicating matters of true consequence, and they have certainly failed me. I must resort to another language to talk with you, and to that end, I give you this lexicon. Should you wish to send me any replies, may I venture to recommend DeCharteres? They are the most excellent florists in Town.

Your servant,
Tremore

Daphne bit her lip. That night in the conservatory. He remembered. She felt herself softening inside, felt a hint of pleasure like a ray of sunshine peeping between dark, stormy clouds, and she closed the book with a snap, striving to come to her senses. She had no intention of getting hurt again.

"If this is not your own book, it must be a gift!" Elizabeth pronounced. "Oh, Daphne, a gift from the duke. Why, you are so discreet! You never said a word to us."

Daphne looked up in dismay to find all three of them staring at her. "I do not know what you mean."

"Do you not?" Lady Fitzhugh asked softly, giving her such a knowing look that Daphne wanted to scream. "It is a very poetic sort of gift, is it not?"

"Indeed," Anne agreed with a sigh. "To be the recipient of a duke's attentions. How romantic."

"Is it romantic and poetic?" asked Elizabeth.

"Of course it is, silly goose!" Anne cried, laughing. "It is *Le Langage des Fleurs*!"

"Yes, yes, but I'm not a silly goose, and what does it mean?"

"The language of flowers," her mother explained. "You would know how to translate it, Elizabeth, if you had not railed so forcefully against your French lessons as a child. It is a book that explains the poetic meaning of particular plants."

"Lovers use it to send each other secret messages," Anne said with delight. "It has become quite the thing. So, Daphne, are you engaged to him yet?"

"Anne!" Lady Fitzhugh cried. "You do not need to confide in us, Daphne, my dear. It is not our affair, and we shall respect your privacy."

"But I am not engaged to him, nor shall I be!" She could tell by their faces they did not believe her, and she added, "There is nothing between us! Nothing at all!"

In her agitation, the book slipped from her fingers. As it fell to the floor, a small, flat posy of flowers tied with ribbon fell out, along with the two thin sheets of vellum in which they had been pressed. The posy and the papers floated down, surrounding the book on the floor.

"You see?" Anne cried. "A message already!"

Daphne picked up the bouquet, noting that though pressed flat, it was still fresh. He must have obtained the flowers on his way here, for they were not yet limp. One was a spike of tiny pink blossoms. Attached to it was a single flower of deep purple and pale yellow. She turned the stems in her fingers, studying it as the others came to surround her, also looking at her bouquet.

"The pink one is hyacinth," Anne told her. "The purple is columbine."

"Pink hyacinth signifies a game," Elizabeth pronounced, looking up from the book, now open in her hands. "And columbine means, 'I will win.' "

A game of flowers was clever, she had to admit, but it was so very much like him to proclaim victory before that game had even begun.

"This is so exciting!" Elizabeth cried. "The Duke of Tremore himself courting our Daphne."

"That is Daphne's personal correspondence," Lady Fitzhugh reminded her daughter in a severe tone, "and as confidential as any letter. You should be ashamed of yourself. Apologize to Daphne and give her back her book!"

"I am sorry, Daphne," Elizabeth said, chastened. She handed back the book. "This is a private matter between the duke and yourself."

"Not for long, dear sister," Anne said. "For if the Duke of Tremore is courting Daphne, every person in Town will know it within a few days. Everyone has been speculating about him choosing a wife ever since he took the emeralds to be reset. Oh, Daphne, if he has not offered for you, he must be intending to do so, for he would not have given you a gift, especially one like this. Oh, the papers will be filled with it, and with all of us."

"I am afraid that is true," Lady Fitzhugh said with a sigh of resignation that contrasted sharply with the delight of her daughters. "We had best prepare for the onslaught."

Daphne sank into a chair. "Onslaught?"

"Anne is right, dear Daphne. If the duke is courting you, then every move you make will be observed and commented upon, as will ours. We shall be inundated with visitors and discussed at length in the society papers."

"How lovely," Elizabeth said, laughing, "for we shall not lack for partners at the assemblies now! Daphne, do you think your duke could introduce us to his friends?"

"I despair of you, Elizabeth, I truly do!" Lady Fitzhugh said, sinking down in the chair beside Daphne's and laying a hand on her arm. "You must understand what this will mean, dear. You will be watched, and studied, and gossiped about. You must prepare yourself for that, for much of that gossip will not be favorable. Envy is a horrid emotion, and there will be a great quantity of it. Dukes are a rare commodity, and people can be full of avarice."

Daphne stared down at the book in her hands. She did not want this. She did not want him to be courtly and romantic, for if he did, she might fall for it. She might start to believe he truly cared for her, when it was only a façade to get his way and satisfy his honor. He did not love her, but she knew from the hurt in her heart that she was in great danger of falling back in love with him.

"I am not worried about gossip at all," she said, and stood up, hardening her heart against him. "For there is nothing to gossip about. There is no romance, there is no engagement, and I am not marrying him! The sooner everyone understands that, the better!"

Slapping the book in her hand against her palm, she walked out of the drawing room, leaving the others looking after her, astonished by her outburst.

A game such as this required two players, she told herself as she went up the stairs to her room. She decided she simply would not play his game. She would not play the fool for him twice. Sometimes, even a duke had to take no for an answer.

Chapter 22

Lady Fitzhugh's prediction that their house would be inundated with callers began to come true the very next afternoon. The first visitor Daphne received was Lord Durand.

She was not in the best mood for receiving any callers. She and Elizabeth had just arrived home after a walk to Montagu House, where she had been refused entry into that exclusive museum because she had not applied ahead of time in writing for a ticket to view the collections. The statement that she was the daughter of Sir Henry Wade, whose excavations made up part of those collections, had not impressed the curators enough for them to break their rules. So, when she arrived back at the house in Russell Square and found that Durand was waiting for her in the drawing room, her mood did not improve.

She halted at the bottom of the stairs, her hand tightening around the cap of the newel post. "Lord Durand?" she repeated, staring at Mary in shock as she handed the maid her bonnet and pelisse. "Why should he want to see me?"

The maid took them, and answered, "I don't know, miss, but Lady Fitzhugh said I should fetch you when you arrived."

Before Daphne could reply, Lady Fitzhugh emerged from the drawing room upstairs, evidently having heard their voices down below. She came down the stairs to them at once.

"Lord Durand is here," she whispered to Daphne. "He has been waiting for over half an hour." She laid a hand on Daphne's arm, and said gently, "He has informed us that he is your grandfather—your mother's father—and he has only recently been made aware of his connection with you. Daphne, is this true?"

"Yes," Daphne admitted, as she started up the stairs with her friend beside her. "But we have been estranged for years, and I have never met him in my life. Why should he wish to see me now?"

"He said he wishes to talk with you. He seems eager to meet you at last, and thinking it might perhaps be an awkward meeting for you, Sir Edward requested that he and I be present. The baron agreed. If you do not mind, of course."

"No, not at all. I suppose I cannot refuse to see

him, even though he has refused to see me."

"Has he?" Lady Fitzhugh frowned. "He seems quite eager to see you today. But in any case, I do not believe that would be your wisest course, dear. He has already acknowledged to Edward and myself his familial connection with you."

"Has he?" she asked as Lady Fitzhugh opened the door and entered the drawing room. Daphne followed.

Her first sight of the baron rather startled her, and she paused in the doorway. She had not expected him to be an attractive man at all. She had envisioned a sort of wizened, stooping old fellow with a pursed-up mouth and meanness in his expression. Instead, she found a tall, elegant-looking man, with silver hair and a countenance that, though lined with the marks of his age, was quite a handsome one. Which made his first words all the more appalling.

"My dear granddaughter," he cried, coming to take her hands in his. "It is so heartening to finally see you. Come, come, let me look at you." He gave her appearance scarcely more than a glance from head to toe, then tucked her arm over his and led her past Sir Edward, who stood beside the fireplace, to the settee opposite the chair where Lady Fitzhugh had seated herself. "Let us have a nice visit together."

Daphne pulled her arm out of his and chose the chair beside Lady Fitzhugh opposite the settee so that she could look directly at him, but before she could ask the only question to which she wanted an answer, the baron spoke.

"I am so happy for you, my dear child. Let me be the first to congratulate you."

She blinked. "I beg your pardon? For what am I to be congratulated?"

"On your engagement to his grace, the Duke of Tremore, of course."

Daphne was astonished. "I do not know what you mean. I am not engaged to the duke."

The baron did not seem at all taken aback by her words. "Of course, of course. I understand. The duke explained to me how impetuous his proposal had been, and how you expected him to court you in the proper way before allowing your engagement to be announced officially."

"Did he indeed?" she responded through clenched teeth.

"Yes, and I understand. You have every right to expect even a duke to woo you first."

"I have no intention of marrying him," she said, not knowing who was succeeding in irritating her more, Anthony or the baron. Just now, she had enough for both of them.

The baron winked at her. "Not many other young ladies would be so brave as to keep a duke dangling, but he seems fond enough of you that he is resigned to it. However, I must invoke a word of caution, my dear. Do not push him too far. He is a duke, after all."

Daphne had a feeling she was going to be hearing

that phrase quite often. "I am not marrying him," she said. "Pray do not speak of an engagement that does not exist."

"This desire for secrecy on your part seems a pointless business, for the duke made it clear to me that he would make no secret of his suit. You are my granddaughter, and as an honorable gentleman, I have an obligation to you. I am impelled to provide you with some counsel on this courtship, though of course, I already gave the duke my permission and my blessing."

She was getting very tired of honorable gentlemen. "I do not wish to be your obligation, sir."

Before he could reply, she rushed on to the only subject she wished to discuss. "Why did you hush up my mother's elopement to my father, and how did you keep it a secret?"

The baron glanced at Sir Edward and Lady Fitzhugh. He frowned, as if annoyed at this abrupt change in the conversation to uncomfortable questions, but he answered her. "My daughter was very young, only seventeen. I did not approve of the match, for the obvious difference in their station made it clear to me that such a marriage would be unsuitable. When they eloped, I chose to avoid the inevitable scandal, and told people I had sent Jane to relatives living in Italy because she wanted to study art."

Daphne listened, gratified that he was finally admitting the truth about her parents, but he was doing so as if reciting a prepared speech, and there was a hint of resentment beneath the rehearsed words. "I deemed it for the best."

Daphne folded her arms, giving him a hard stare. "Did you?"

The baron shifted uncomfortably in his chair at the cool contempt in her question, but Daphne was unmoved by his discomfiture. "Why did you then compound your wrong by refusing to acknowledge me? I know my father was an orphan with no family or connections, but he was a brilliant man, a good man, and your daughter loved him. He was a knight. You knew they had married. You knew that I was your granddaughter, yet you refused to acknowledge me. Are you ashamed of me that you have treated me thus?"

The baron was frowning at this rapid stream of words, looking displeased that such an attack was to be part of their first conversation together. But he did not speak in a tone that conveyed that displeasure. Instead, he forced away his frown and spread his hands in a gesture of bewilderment. "Daphne, it is not at all what you think."

"Is it not?"

"No, no." He gave another uncomfortable glance at Sir Edward and Lady Fitzhugh, but they remained silent and gave him no help. Lady Fitzhugh was embroidering, and Sir Edward stood idly stirring the fire with a poker. Neither seemed to notice the awkward silence in the room. Even the baron's slight cough did not cause either of them to look up.

With clear reluctance, he returned his attention

to Daphne, who was staring at him in stony silence. "Your father was in Durham, near my estates at Cramond, only a short distance away. He was giving a lecture on Roman antiquities to the Historical Society. My daughter chose to attend. They began meeting secretly, and a week later, they came to me and announced they intended to marry. Needless to say, I disapproved."

"Did you disown her?"

He denied it at once. "No, no. I was furious, for several reasons. Your father was an orphan of no family or connections whatsoever. He was nearly twenty years older than my Jane, and he scarcely had the money to support a wife and children. If they had intended to live with me, I could perhaps have been persuaded to forgive the match, but he intended to cart your mother off to some godforsaken place in the Mediterranean. Also, I did not believe any marriage of lasting happiness could be based on a week's affection. My daughter and I quarreled. She and your father eloped that night, and a few days later, they were on a ship out of Edinburgh, bound for Naples. I never saw my daughter again. My wife is gone, and I have no other children. Can you understand my feelings of betrayal and bitterness?"

"You say you did not disown her, but you did. You disowned her in your heart, and never answered any of her letters to you. Nor did you answer mine."

He winced at her blunt way of putting it. "I hope you can understand."

Daphne leaned back in her chair, still feeling no compunction to see his point of view. "No, I do not understand your actions at all, sir. Not only did you wrong your daughter, you have wronged hers as well. I wrote to you, and received a response from an attorney representing your interests. Shall I tell you what he said?"

He tried to respond, but she did not allow him that opportunity. "I was told in very explicit terms that I could not possibly be your granddaughter," she continued, "and that any attempt of mine to gain either money or connection to you would be futile. My father had just died. I was in the middle of the Moroccan desert, with no money, no family at hand to help me. I wrote to you from Tangier, and waited six months for your response to my letter, spending what little money I had, barely able to sustain myself. All the antiquities Papa had discovered at Volubilis had already been sold to the Duke of Tremore or to the museum in Rome, and most of the money from Papa's share had been spent for expenses."

She could hear her own voice becoming quavery and much too emotional, but she did not care. She wanted him to know just how devastating a wound his neglect had inflicted on her. "I was forced to sell Papa's books and equipment in order to eat and have a roof over my head, but I waited, hoping that as my grandfather, you would help me. You did not. You abandoned me, leaving me alone, with no money, no protection, and no means. It was only because the Duke of Tremore had hired my father and had sent billets of passage for us that I was able to journey to England. I went to Hampshire, and worked for the duke to support myself. You asked me if I understand why you did what you did. My answer is no. I do not understand, and I find it impossible to forgive—"

"You give your opinions far too decidedly for one so young!" he interrupted, his voice rising in anger. "I have come in good faith to right the wrong done you."

"Only because you believe I am about to marry a duke. There is no engagement. So you see—"

"Perhaps," Sir Edward's voice entered the conversation for the first time, interrupting what she had been about to say, "this matter needs to be discussed and settled between us, Lord Durand, for women, you must agree, are emotional creatures, and do not allow rational thinking to enter their speech at times."

Daphne made a sound of outrage, but Lady Fitzhugh put a hand on her arm, and when she turned to look at the other woman, Lady Fitzhugh mouthed the word, "Wait."

"Perhaps you are right, Sir Edward," Durand said.

"Capital! Shall we go into my study?" He gestured to the door of the drawing room, and the two men departed together, leaving the two women alone.

Daphne jumped to her feet the moment they

were gone and began to pace the room. "This is so humiliating! I know perfectly well it is only his desire for a connection to the duke that has impelled the baron to come forward and claim me as his granddaughter now. Horrid man! And how dare the duke go to Durand and speak of this? He knows I will not marry him, for my refusal was most emphatic."

"Daphne, sit down."

She looked over at Lady Fitzhugh, who was looking back at her with such a grave countenance that she returned to her chair at once and sat down.

"The duke did offer for you, then?"

"Yes." Afraid that Lady Fitzhugh was about to tell her to be sensible, she went on, "Please do not offer me counsel on the wisdom of my refusal. I—"

"No, no, Daphne, I would not be so indelicate as to inquire about your answer or your reasons. I respect your reticence in the matter and your choice. I only asked if he had offered because if he has, I would like to offer you a bit of advice, if I may."

Daphne looked at her with interest and a hint of dismay. She had a high regard for Lady Fitzhugh, and did not want to hear the other woman tell her she was being foolish to refuse a duke. "Advice?"

"Yes." She clasped her hands together in her lap and was silent for a moment, then she said, "But first, let me say that I have come to have a great deal of affection for you, my dear. You have been such excellent company for my daughters, for you are older than they, and therefore possess a good deal more sense because of it and are a steadying influence on them. But I am older still than you, and the wiser for my advantage in years, I hope. Please allow me to offer you my counsel, with the understanding that it is heartfelt and solely out of concern for you."

"Of course, you may offer me your counsel and advice. You have been so kind to me. You have taken me into your home, befriended me, and—" Her voice broke, and she waited a moment before going on. "Lady Fitzhugh, I am so grateful. You have treated me almost as a member of your family, and words cannot express—"

"Hush, now." She patted Daphne's hand. "Do call me Elinor, my dear. As for the other, well, I have come to regard you as a member of my family." She gave a wry smile. "Although you may not like me after you hear what I have to say."

Daphne steeled herself for the inevitable. "You are going to tell me I should be wise to marry the duke."

"No, no, you are a grown woman, and you know your own heart and mind. Besides, being a duchess would be an enormous responsibility, and I can understand your reluctance to take on such a role. I am not certain I would wish it even for my own daughters. No, my counsel to you concerns the baron."

"The baron?"

"Yes. Daphne, as much as I regard you as a member of my family, that does not alter the truth that the baron is your true relation. He is your grandfather. I appreciate your pride, for I possess a great deal of that quality myself, and I would feel just as indignant as you at his motives. No doubt it is the duke's interest in you that has compelled the baron to come forward after such shameful neglect. No doubt he values the possible connection that could come from an alliance with Tremore. No doubt he fears the censure that society will surely lay upon him for his refusal to support you and thereby force you to seek employment to support yourself. It is unconscionable, and his connection to Tremore would blunt his disgrace. Despite all his motives, I must advise you to allow him to do the right thing and allow him the pretense of being the benevolent grandfather, at least for the present."

Daphne started to speak, but Lady Fitzhugh laid a hand on her arm, and she fell silent.

"For your sake, Daphne," Lady Fitzhugh went on, "I must be so bold as to speak with you as if you were my own daughter. You are such a sensible woman in most respects, but in this matter, dear, you are allowing your pride to alter your judgment. If you are adamant about refusing the duke, he will eventually be made to accept that. If you allow Durand to acknowledge you now, he cannot take it back, even if your marriage to the duke does not come off. You will be given his support and protection, and you need not fear for your future ever again.

"From our conversation with him before you arrived, I came to the conclusion that though he is not a man of vast wealth, he does have a substantial and secure income from his estates, and would be able to support you quite adequately. My dear, you know from bitter experience how hard life can be. Do not allow pride to prevent you from having the security and connections your grandfather's position can provide. The duke, no doubt for your sake, has given the baron a chance to right his wrong to you. Allow Durand to save face and do so."

Daphne drew a deep breath, and let it out slowly. "You are right. He has repeatedly refused to acknowledge me, and when he came today, I was so outraged by his blatant and transparent attempt to curry favor with Anthony, that I blinded myself to the sensible course. To refute his acknowledgment would be folly."

"Anthony?" Lady Fitzhugh repeated the name, her voice so reflective and thoughtful that Daphne blushed. But Lady Fitzhugh was a tactful woman. "Perhaps a cup of tea would do both of us a bit of good," she murmured.

But the tea had barely been brought before the gentlemen returned to the drawing room. She and Lady Fitzhugh both rose to their feet, and Sir Edward came over to Daphne. Giving her a kindly pat on the shoulder, he said, "The baron has conferred upon me his acknowledgment of you as his legitimate granddaughter. Your future is secure, my dear."

Daphne turned to the baron, taking Lady

Fitzhugh's advice and allowing him to save face. "Thank you," she said politely. "You are very kind."

"We have also made all the arrangements regarding your situation," Sir Edward went on. "Lord Durand has agreed to allow you to remain with us, for he appreciates that Anne and Elizabeth are your friends, and he agrees with me that Lady Fitzhugh is an excellent chaperone for you. He is providing you with a pocket allowance of ten pounds per week, and you may use his name at all the shops for anything you might need."

"That is most generous of you, Lord Durand," Lady Fitzhugh added. "Whether she is to marry a duke or not, a young lady needs much in the way of clothes and other fashionable things. Daphne is a wonderful friend to my own daughters, and we are delighted to have her remain here. I shall see that she avails herself of your generosity wisely."

"Thank you." The baron turned to her with a little cough. "Daphne, I can only hope that once you have thought over the circumstances of your situation, your heart will soften toward me."

He bowed, she curtsied, and he departed.

The moment Mary had closed the door behind him downstairs, Anne and Elizabeth came racing up to the drawing room. "Well?" they demanded in unison.

"The baron is Daphne's grandfather," Sir Edward informed them.

They both gave cries of astonishment and turned to Daphne. "But why did you not tell us? Why were you having to earn your living for the duke if you are a gentleman's daughter?"

"The baron had not acknowledged me," Daphne said, still feeling a hint of bitterness as she remembered those frightening days in Tangier. "Now he has."

"Durand is allowing her to remain with us," Sir Edward told his daughters, "and he has provided her with an allowance, which I am sure the pair of you will be happy to help her spend as quickly as possible."

"Oh, yes, we shall!" Elizabeth said, laughing. "Lovely new gowns, bonnets, and all the other finery a young lady being courted by a duke will need. First a duke comes to call, then a baron. I am certain that by the end of the week at least one earl and a pair of viscounts shall visit us."

Daphne made a wry face. "It is only because he believes I am to marry the duke that the baron is being so generous. Now that my future is settled, I believe I shall go out and spend a bit of the baron's money this very day. May Elizabeth and Anne accompany me?" she asked Lady Fitzhugh.

"Of course, my dear," the older woman answered. "But where are you going?"

"DeCharteres'. I must send a reply to the duke for his gift of yesterday."

Anne and Elizabeth gave exclamations of delight at the idea of going with her to the florist and seeing for themselves what flowers she would use in her response, but Lady Fitzhugh's raised brows were her only indication of surprise. "Replying to his message in kind is a very sweet and gracious thing to do, my dear."

"Once he sees it, Elinor, I doubt he will agree with you."

Chapter 23

Anthony's London home in Grosvenor Square displayed none of the awe-inspiring opulence of his ducal estate. This home was one in which he spent a great deal of time, and it reflected his personal tastes to a much greater degree than any of his country houses. The chimney pieces were of a pale travertine marble, and the soft, thick carpets were of subtle colors and simple designs. It was described by some who dined there as a disappointment, intimate rather than imposing. To Anthony's mind, that was a compliment.

One of his soft, thick, subtly colored carpets was receiving some significant wear three evenings after his call upon Daphne in Russell Square. He was pacing back and forth in front of the fireplace of his study, growing more impatient by the hour.

When he had called at the Fitzhugh house, there had been no doubt in his mind Daphne would answer him. A game of flower language—a language in which she had once expressed such delighted interest—would surely intrigue her, and he had not yet seen her back away from a challenge. She enjoyed a game as much as he.

The first day after his call in Russell Square, he had gone about his usual business, certain his reply would be waiting for him by the end of the day, but there was no word from her.

By the end of the second day, he had still not received an answer, and he became a bit worried that this time, she would not accept his challenge.

By nine o'clock on the evening of the third day, both his confidence and his worry had been replaced by a deeper, darker feeling of uncertainty. It was still a new emotion to him, and one of which he was not particularly fond.

Now, he paced back and forth in front of the fire, hoping that her answer was not to provide him with no answer at all, and he began to think out his next move. Somehow, he had to convince her that marrying him was the only acceptable course. He had hoped the idea of a game and his claim of victory would challenge her to respond, but if not, he would have to think up something else. He was certainly not going to give up.

The door to his study opened, and Anthony stopped pacing the floor as Quimby, his London butler, paused in the doorway.

"Dylan Moore is here, your grace," Quimby informed him. The butler then stepped aside so that the composer might enter the room. Dylan was one of the few people who did not have to wait for ducal permission to pay a call. He was welcome anytime.

"Tremore, I must beg you to come out with me," he said without preliminaries. "I have had enough of petulant divas for one day."

"Problems with the new opera?" Anthony guessed, but his mind was elsewhere. He bitterly regretted his careless words to Viola all those months ago. He needed to convince Daphne that those remarks did not reflect the way he saw her now. Now, he saw that woman in the rain. He saw those gorgeous lavender eyes behind those gold-rimmed spectacles. He saw a round, adorably solemn face, a face that strove so hard to conceal from everyone what she truly felt, until it suddenly lit up with laughter or anger—though that anger was usually directed at him. He saw her in that godawful apron, looking at an erotic fresco and then at him in the most maddening, innocently seductive way.

"Not problems with the opera, dear fellow, but with the diva," Dylan was correcting him. "Elena Triandos is an excellent soprano, but she is Greek, and Greek divas are particularly maddening. When I remember it was I who insisted upon having her in the leading role, I . . ."

Dylan's voice faded into the distance as Anthony turned on his heel and paced back across the hearthrug, chewing on one thumbnail, thinking.

Daphne needed courting, and more than flowers seemed to be required. She had never been given an opportunity to enjoy the luxuries of life, and God knew she needed a few. The way her father had dragged her all around the East in the sands and dust, isolating her from any sort of good society, was appalling. Daphne deserved more pleasures than the few scented soaps, the box of chocolates, and one pink silk dress she had bought for herself. She deserved all the luxuries life had to offer, and he could provide them. By God, he would shower her with them. If only she would give him some sort of reply.

What if she sends me some polite, indifferent little note that refuses my suit? That might be worse than no reply at all.

He could feel doubt etching itself into his soul with every minute that passed without an answer from her. What if nothing he said or did was enough? He shook his head. No, he would not accept that. He would not believe it. He just had to hit upon the right thing to offer, the right words to say. He would not give up.

"What has you pacing back and forth with such feverish rapidity?" Dylan asked, watching him. "Political difficulties in the House of Lords? Problems with your museum? If so, they must be great indeed, for I have never seen you looking so worried as this."

Anthony cast his friend an abstracted glance as he paced, but he did not reply. If only he could get her alone. That might do the trick. He had already made his own feelings clear during his visit with Durand, and though he suspected Daphne would be quite put out about it, he had been impelled to do it. He knew that if society did not see her as one of their own and accept her, she would be the victim of even more vicious slanders. He could not keep his courtship of her a secret, no matter how discreet the Fitzhugh family chose to be. Anthony could just imagine the society papers tearing her to shreds for being some opportunistic gold digger attempting to ensnare a duke. Since everyone would soon believe they were engaged, it might be possible to get her alone. If he could just kiss her, touch her, tell her how beautiful she really was, inside as well as out—

"Damn and blast, Tremore, if you take one more turn across that rug without telling me what the trouble is, I shall throttle you!"

Anthony did not have a chance to reply, for at that moment, Stephens, one of his footmen, appeared in the doorway carrying a wooden crate in his hands. "From DeCharteres, your grace," the footman informed him. "Mr. Quimby knew you had been asking about any deliveries from there, so he told me to bring it up to you straightaway."

A wave of relief washed over Anthony, a relief so strong and so profound, that he had to close his eyes and take a deep, steadying breath at his own regained hope. *About damned time.*

He opened his eyes and gestured the servant into the room. The footman placed the wooden crate upon his desk and departed as Anthony walked around the desk to have a look. It did not matter what she had sent him. The fact that she had sent him anything from the florist gave him hope.

"DeCharteres?" Dylan moved to stand opposite him at the desk, interested, but eyeing the crate with doubt. "Is London's finest florist now delivering eggs to the nobility? Or is there perhaps some delicacy such as papaya plants for your famous conservatory hidden amid all this straw?"

Anthony was too preoccupied with pulling handfuls of that straw out of the crate to reply. He desperately wanted to see what she had sent. He lifted a potted plant from its tissue-paper wrappings, a pathetic-looking thing to be sure, its succulent leaves wrinkled and blackened. The plain clay pot in which it was contained was ice cold in his hands. Anthony burst out laughing.

His friend glanced at the plant and raised an eyebrow. "What the devil is it?"

"A gift from a young lady," he answered, still chuckling. *An ice plant*. No note was included, but none was needed. Trust Daphne to come up with something succinct, clever, and straight to the point.

"It is dead." Dylan pointed out the obvious as he touched one of its blackened leaves. "It is also frozen solid." He gave Anthony a curious look. "This is a gift from a young lady, and you find it amusing?"

"I do indeed," Anthony replied, grinning as he carried the plant across the room to the fireplace. He set the ugly, dead thing in a prominent place on the mantel. "More important than that, I find it encouraging."

He glanced over his shoulder at his friend, and added, "Since you are already dressed for an evening about town and begging me to distract you from maddening divas, you may come along with me."

"Certainly, but where are we going?"

"The Haydon Assembly Rooms."

It was Dylan's turn to laugh. "You are joking. The Haydon Rooms are a bit mundane for you, do you not think? The room will be filled with respectable country girls come to town to snare the sons of squires. What sensible man wants to meet respectable marriage-minded girls?"

Anthony turned around to face his friend. "We are going to see my duchess."

"Lady Sarah would never set one silk-slippered foot inside the Haydon Assembly Rooms. She would rather drink henbane. Nor can I believe she would send you a dead plant—" He broke off, and his eyes narrowed as he studied his friend. "You have changed your mind. You have chosen someone else. Pray, tell me it is so."

"It is indeed so."

"I am hearing angels sing, Tremore. Or have you been having a great joke at my expense all along? Either way, I am too relieved to care. So who is this new choice? What future duchess attends assemblies at Haydon Rooms and sends you dead, frozen plants? Not a country girl, surely?"

"You could say yes, although it would be more accurate to say a multitude of countries."

"You have intrigued me."

"Yes," Anthony said as he walked toward the

door with his friend following him. "I thought I might."

During her first public assembly in London, Daphne expected to spend much of her time in observation of the dancing rather than participating in it, but much to her surprise, she was asked to dance quite often. None of her partners tonight could equal the man who had taught her to dance in the first place, and she could not help making comparisons.

"How do you like London, Miss Wade?" Sir William Laverton asked her as they moved through the long, slow quadrille in which they were engaged. "Have you visited any of the museums?"

"Oh, yes," she answered, trying to keep her attention on her partner, but her gaze kept straying to the doorway of the Haydon Rooms. An ice plant meant a rejection of addresses, but she did not know if Anthony would accept that answer or not. She half expected him to come through the doorway any moment.

"Given your eminent father, Miss Wade, you will find the museums of London fascinating," Sir William went on, and she forced her attention back to him, trying not to yawn. Her partner was an agreeable enough man, but he did not spar or flirt with her or challenge her wits. He was not the sort of man who could tear her heart in half with a smile or burn her to the core with the touch of his hand. She ought to be glad of it.

The music stopped abruptly, bringing every person engaged in the dance to a halt. Her partner was staring at some point beyond her shoulder, and Daphne turned around. Though she was not wearing her spectacles, she did not need them to know the identity of the man standing in the doorway.

Voice after voice died away and the room became silent as the grave. Even those who did not know his identity would have been able to discern at once that someone of nobility had just entered the room. People began to bow, bending before him like young willows in a strong wind, but he seemed oblivious to them.

Though he was a blur to her eyes, Daphne felt his gaze light on her. She had enough vision to see him take a step toward her and stop again.

Another man followed Anthony through the door and paused beside him, a man dressed all in black, but for his snowy white linen shirt. The room was so quiet that the man's sigh was audible to all. "Really, Tremore," he drawled, "you spoil everyone's fun just by arriving." With a sweeping gesture, he went on, "They are struck all a heap. Do the customary ducal thing and tell them to get on with it. If you do not, I fear we shan't have a single dance with the ladies."

"That would be a great pity," Anthony replied, and she could still feel his gaze on her as he went on, "I have come to have a true fondness for dancing."

He looked away from her and acknowledged the entire room. "Carry on, everyone."

The music resumed, and Daphne's partner continued leading her around the floor. "The Duke of

Tremore," Sir William commented as they joined hands and stepped close to each other. "Our little assembly here cannot possibly interest him. I wonder what he is doing here."

"I cannot imagine," she lied as they both stepped back.

As Daphne moved with Sir William through the intricate steps of the quadrille, she kept her attention firmly focused on the dance, and it was not until the music ended that she caught sight of Anthony again. As she was escorted back to Sir Edward and Lady Fitzhugh, she saw that he and his friend had joined their party. She could not avoid him.

"Miss Wade," he said, bowing to her. "How delightful to see you again. May I introduce you to this gentleman?" He gestured to the man beside him. "This is Mr. Dylan Moore, an old and valued friend of mine. Moore, this is Miss Daphne Wade. You may, perhaps, have heard of Dylan, Miss Wade, for he is England's greatest composer."

"You exaggerate my talents, Tremore." The man in black bowed to her. "I understand you are quite the traveler, and have been in many exotic places, Miss Wade. Sir Edward here has been telling me of your adventures in the deserts of the East with your famous father. Have you truly ridden a camel?"

"Many times," she answered, trying not to look at Anthony. "But there is nothing exotic about it, I assure you. A single day's ride on a camel is enough to make one painfully aware of every muscle one possesses. It is as romantic an adventure as tooth drawing."

Everyone laughed, including Anthony, but as the musicians began to tune their instruments to the next dance, his amusement faded to a serious countenance. "I should like to hear more of the camels, Miss Wade. If you are not otherwise engaged, perhaps you would do me the honor of dancing the next with me."

"I do not think—" She broke off, but she was acutely aware of every person in the room watching them, and she knew she could not say no. Her refusal would be a slight to him and to his rank, and she could not do such a thing to him in front of all these people. "Of course, your grace," she murmured, forcing a disinterested politeness into her voice as he held out his hand to her. "I would be honored."

She took his hand and allowed him to lead her to the floor. She could feel the fascinated stares of everyone in the room as Anthony put his hand on her waist and lifted her other hand in his. She was sure she would stumble over his feet, and she looked down.

"Look at me, Daphne. Not at the floor."

She compromised, focusing her own gaze on the knot of his cravat, trying not to think of all the people staring at them. But her fear of making a public mistake proved unfounded, for when the waltz began, her body remembered all their hours of practice together, and she followed his lead with ease.

"I am delighted to finally have the opportunity of seeing the pink evening gown," he commented as they waltzed. "I remember how delighted you were to have acquired it."

Startled, Daphne looked up into his face. "You remember that?"

"Of course." There was something in his eyes, something so intense and passionate. "I remember everything."

She could feel herself shaking inside, so afraid. She was afraid of being his passion today, but not tomorrow, afraid of how much it would hurt in the future if she let herself believe him now.

"You look lovely in it," he went on. "Pink suits you."

"Don't!" she ordered in a fierce undertone. "Please do not give me these compliments."

"Very well. I shall change the subject and thank you for your unique gift. I received it only a few hours ago, and may I say I was never so gratified to receive anything in my life."

He did not even blink at her skeptical look or her humph of disbelief. "I speak truly, for you have been so cruel as to keep me on tenterhooks for three days, and I was beginning to lose hope of ever receiving a reply."

"It was never my intent to cause you such suspense," she countered. "The thing had to sit in an ice house for three days to ensure it was quite dead."

He gave a shout of laughter, and she glanced at the blurred faces of the people around them. "Shush," she admonished. "People are staring at us."

"Yes, I know." Still smiling, he said, "Words cannot express how happy I was to receive a dead, frozen ice plant. It shows me how much you care."

"Happy?" she countered. "I am disappointed, for I was hoping your feelings would take a different direction, toward futility rather than gladness."

"Not at all. Perhaps my reply tomorrow will be able to convince you that I live for any scrap of your favor and attention."

"Oh, stop this, Anthony! I do not like you this way."

"What way is that?"

"All these compliments and lavish expressions of sentiment. It smacks of insincerity, for it is so unlike you."

"I told you I always give my opinions honestly. I would not say it if it were not the truth. Not that I blame you for thinking compliments unlike me," he added before she could speak. "After all, I have not been the most articulate of suitors, to talk of duty and obligation, when I should have been talking of romance and passion and your beautiful eyes."

"Stop this! You are making me quite cross."

"You, Daphne? The woman who throws trowels at my head is cross? I do not believe it."

"I did not throw it at you on purpose," she reminded him. "And if I had, I would have exercised sufficient aim to actually hit you."

"I have no doubt of it."

She once again fixed her gaze on his cravat, pressed her lips together, and did not reply.

"Why are you angry with me, Daphne?"

She was not angry. She was trying to harden herself against him, but the tenderness of his voice was making her raw. She looked up at him, looked away, and looked back at him again. "You went to the baron and told him we were to marry. How could you presume such a thing when I have explicitly refused you?"

"Yes, I went to Durand. I did not tell him we were to be married. As he is your closest male relation, I told him of my desire to marry you, and I secured his permission to court you in honorable fashion. That is all."

"Knowing all the while he would entertain no doubt of my acceptance of your suit!"

"Well, yes," he admitted, trying very hard not to smile. "But I confessed to you long ago my abhorrence for the word *no*. I am hoping that at some point I will have persuaded you to overlook that defect in my character and that you will marry me in spite of it."

"I do not wish to marry you, and I have told you so. Why will you not accept that?"

"Because I cannot stop thinking of you. Of our dances and our conversations and the first time I ever heard you laugh. I cannot stop thinking of us, of that night in the antika," he said, his voice low and fierce and wrenching to hear. "I remember how your skin was so cold at first, but I could feel it warming as I touched you. I remember how you looked in the moonlight with your head tilted back and your breasts in my hands."

"Stop it." She was blushing under the staring eyes of a room of people.

"I remember how you said my name over and

over again as I touched you, of how I loved hearing you say it, of how you were filling my senses until I could not think."

She caught back a sob of pain and fury. "You are cruel, Anthony," she told him in a fierce whisper. "Cruel to say such things to me when we both know it is only your determination to have your way that impels you to say them."

"We both did what we hate to do, Daphne. We both lost control. I take all the blame, for I knew what the result would be, yet I could not stop myself from doing it anyway. You call me cruel? You will not even allow me to make up for the wrong I have done you. If I am determined, it is only to make you safe. It is you who are cruel, Daphne, to deny me that."

The dance came to an end, and the music stopped. As he returned her to her place beside Elizabeth, he defied the stares directed at them and whispered close to her ear, "I remember everything, and I cannot believe you have forgotten. If you have, I will make you remember. I vow on my life I will."

Chapter 24

Despite his accusation, Daphne had not forgotten their night together, nor anything else about him, and she could not believe he could think for a moment that she had. Memories of him were etched into her brain like carvings in stone, memories of how he had kissed her and made love to her, memories of the hard strength of his body, and the glorious delight of his hands and his mouth. And the act itself—the delight and pleasure of that experience never left her for a moment. She would never forget him, and even had she wanted to, the fortnight that followed their evening at the Haydon Assembly Rooms gave her no chance to do so.

The first day after their dance together, he sent her twelve bouquets of variegated tulips and rosemary to convey his admiration of her beautiful eyes and to signify his memory of the first time he had told her that. Each bouquet was in its own crystal vase banded with a ribbon knotted around a gold hairpin. Daphne fingered one of the dangling hair ornaments, remembering exactly what he wanted her to remember—of how he had taken down her hair that night and refashioned it himself.

A woman's hair can be a man's obsession.

Was he imagining her hair down, spread across his pillows?

That was the night he had admitted to her his awe of love, confessed his fear of it, recognized her defenses against it.

This gift was so lavish and expensive that the proper thing to do was send the whole lot—flowers, crystal vases, and gold hairpins—back to him. In the end, she kept the flowers, but she sent back the rest, with a note that reminded him she could not keep gifts, particularly such absurd, extravagant ones, for if she did, others would think them engaged, and they were not.

A few days later, twelve bouquets of dittany proclaimed his passion for her and his memory of their picnic, when she had described the hills of Crete to him, but they were tied with simple silk ribbons, and there were no gold hairpins or crystal vases with them.

After another few days, twelve more bouquets arrived. These were sprays of peach blossoms.

"You hold me captive," Elizabeth read from the book in her hands, then lowered it to lean forward and sniff one of the fragrant sprays in Daphne's bedroom. "It also means, 'I am in your power.' " With a sigh, she turned away from the bouquets on the windowsill and fell forward onto Daphne's bed. "I would fall in love with a man who told me that."

"He is talking nonsense," Daphne answered, squeezing the water out of her freshly washed hair into the bowl on her dressing table. " 'I am in your power,' " she repeated as she wrapped her head in a towel. "As if Anthony could mean anything so ridiculous."

She turned away from the dressing table, and her gaze caught on the flowers. She paused, pressing her fingers to her lips, remembering that night they had bargained over her spectacles.

Do you not see how much power you could have over me?

The same warm, aching sensation of anticipation and desire spread through her limbs as she remembered that night.

"But does it not soften your heart, at least a little?" Elizabeth asked.

Daphne jerked her hand down and frowned at her friend. "He does not mean it."

"You do not believe he is sincere?"

"I do not know!" she cried in vexation. "Let's not talk of it anymore."

Elizabeth did not mention it again, and the rest of the Fitzhugh family remained tactfully silent on the subject as well, although when twelve lime trees laden with fruit arrived, conveying the duke's undimmed intent to marry her, Sir Edward asked with amused exasperation whether these demonstrations of his grace's affection would extend to the next Christmas season, for if so, he feared they would be receiving an enormous quantity of partridges and pear trees.

In addition to the flowers sent to Daphne, they received stacks and stacks of cards and invitations. So many visitors came to Russell Square that the small drawing room could not always accommodate them all. Every person who called talked delicately of weddings and engagements, though none were so bold as to discuss the rumors about hers. No engagement had been announced, but Daphne's silence on the subject was thought to be motivated by an understandable desire for discretion rather than the unbelievable alternative that she had refused him.

The baron called on them numerous times during that week, making several such visits as well as some outings with him so that they might get to know one another. Daphne had no idea if her grandfather was coming to have a genuine concern for her, or was simply pretending his familial interest in her affairs. Whatever his reasons, Durand remained convinced that despite her denials, Daphne would soon be wed to the duke.

His conviction was reinforced by the pages of every society paper in London, for all of them seemed to take her acceptance of Anthony's suit for granted. Decorum prevented her from denouncing these rumors publicly, and she could do nothing but wait for the speculation to die down.

However, as the second week of this unusual courtship progressed, the speculation did not end, it only grew. Word of the lime trees got out, as did the news that Anthony was using the book of Charlotte de la Tour as the basis of his courtship. Soon London bookstores were depleted of every available copy and people of the ton found occasion to walk in the park of Russell Square quite often, hoping to see another of the duke's floral letters to Miss Wade pass through the doors of Sir Edward Fitzhugh's house.

There was a great deal of discussion in the papers about Daphne's background, which was so significantly lower than Tremore's. There was also some talk of her parents' elopement and the baron's desire to cover up such a scandal by claiming his daughter was in Italy with relations there. One or two hinted that her parents had not married at all, but such rumors were quickly refuted.

The most incredible statements about her life in Africa were bandied about, along with the news that she had been employed by the duke to do research on his antiquities and render the sketches for his museum.

Comments were made about her unprepossessing looks, her lack of a substantial dowry, and her connections, which though respectable, were hardly worthy of a duke. All of this pointed to her complete lack of suitability to be a duchess and led some papers to wonder if Tremore was quite right in the head.

Daphne did her best to ignore the hurtful things

that were being said about her in the papers and repeated to her by rumor-mongering acquaintances who "meant well." Harder to bear was the scrutiny. She could not go anywhere without being observed and discussed, and she truly began to appreciate what Anthony had told her about how smothering his life could be.

That did not stop him from adding fuel to the fire. The day of the Fitzhugh card party, another floral message from him arrived at the house in Russell Square.

"He is impossible!" Daphne declared, watching as two men maneuvered an enormous bouquet of flowers through the door, an arrangement in all the colors of the rainbow that filled the drawing room at once with the fragrance of its many flowers.

Lady Fitzhugh had a corner of the room cleared away to accommodate the thing, for it was at least three feet across, four feet high, and could not possibly fit in their tiny vestibule. Once this was accomplished, the two men who had delivered it departed, Elizabeth and Anne examined its flowers with exclamations of delight, and Daphne turned to Lady Fitzhugh in exasperation. "What am I to do?" she cried. "He will not take no."

"You are refusing him?" Anne cried. "Oh, Daphne, how can you be so heartless as that?"

The accusation stung, and Elizabeth must have seen it. "She should not have to marry him if she does not love him!"

"Do you not love him?" Anne asked, incredulous. "But why not?"

"Anne, that is enough," Lady Fitzhugh said. "It is not our business to inquire about Daphne's feelings. Now, girls, I believe we must depart for Lady Atherton's. It is nearly three o'clock. Let us allow Daphne some peace. Heaven knows, she is in need of it."

She gave Lady Fitzhugh a grateful look as the other woman ushered the girls out of the room, leaving Daphne alone with her latest present. She studied it for a long time.

Despite the dozens of flowers and plants in front of her that told of his passion, his attention to his duty, and his desire to protect and honor her, Daphne could not help but notice that there was no symbol anywhere in this enormous display that conveyed a declaration of love.

It hardly mattered. Anthony himself had deemed his feelings for her a temporary affliction, and even if a rose or a carnation or a spray of forget-me-nots had been tucked somewhere amid this vast quantity of flowers, it would not have convinced her he felt anything permanent for her. There was no flower, no gift, no words that could ever convince one's heart of anything.

Anthony knew there was no way to court Daphne without generating gossip. What he was not prepared for was his own anger every time he saw another snide comment about her in the society papers, an anger that burned all the stronger since he had once been as blind as that himself. During the week that followed their waltz together at the Haydon

Rooms, he did not call on her at Russell Square, hoping that would cause the gossip to die down.

Instead of Russell Square, he spent a great deal of time at his club. One night a week after the evening at the Haydon Rooms, he came into Brooks to find Dylan there, halfway through a bottle of brandy.

Anthony accepted Dylan's invitation to join him and sat down. He leaned back in his chair, noting the other man's drawn face and bloodshot eyes. "Every time I see you like this, I am grateful I do not have the artistic temperament," he commented.

"I do not have it either, it seems," Dylan said wearily. "I cannot seem to write two notes together, so I am occupying myself with a binge of alcoholic excess." He gestured to the bottle on the table. "Would you care to join me? From what I hear, you could use a drink yourself."

Anthony admitted nothing. Instead, he signaled for a glass. When it came, he poured a brandy for himself, ignoring his friend's amused stare.

"I hear the London florists are quite busy."

Anthony took a sip of brandy in silence.

"Perhaps I shall begin sending flowers to young ladies. That would be something new for me. How do you use flowers to ask a woman to share your bed?"

Anthony smothered a laugh. "You have already bedded so many, how do you keep count?"

"Not true," Dylan corrected. "I haven't bedded yours, much as I would enjoy doing so."

Anthony stiffened, his hand tightening around his glass. He said nothing.

Dylan leaned back in his chair and his brows rose with that mocking amusement. "The society papers call her plain, you know. They say her skin is a bit too tanned for fashion, her cheeks are too round, and her hair is an unremarkable brown. You would compare the color to honey, no doubt."

Anthony was in no frame of mind for Dylan's mockery. "Are you trying to provoke me?"

"I confess I am. I would like to see the ducal hauteur come down for once. D'you know, in all the years I have known you, I have never once seen you lose your temper? Not once. But let us leave your character for another day, and talk of the charms of Miss Wade." He took a swallow of brandy. "They say her vision is very poor, for she wears her spectacles nearly all the time. All the women of London are baffled by how such a dowdy thing has claimed your heart, but I—and I think there are plenty of other men who would agree with me on this—see something quite appealing there."

Anthony picked up the copy of *The Times* that lay on the table and folded it back to the political pages.

"She has a luscious figure," Dylan went on. "I saw that straightaway, for I always notice the most important things first. Now, the papers may have a point about her face, for it is a bit too round to be truly pretty, but sweet enough to look at for all that. It is not a face to give much away, is it? I watched as you danced with her, and I might have thought she didn't care tuppence for you. And as for her eyes, God, what a color!"

Anthony slapped the paper back on the table. "Do not push me, Moore, for I am not in the mood for your satiric comments tonight."

"You in the agonies of unrequited love *is* a satire. In fact, watching this romance from a distance as it unfolds has become my most entertaining amusement. Lime trees, Tremore? No one to touch you for folly. Miss Wade does not seem to share your passion. How do you feel? Frustrated? Wounded? Outraged that the gods have thwarted you?"

A muscle ticked in Anthony's jaw. "Go to the devil."

"I already have, my friend." Dylan refilled his glass and lifted it. "Here's to hell," he said, and knocked back the brandy. "Now that both of us are there."

He shoved back his chair and rose as if to depart, but before he did so, he leaned toward Anthony, resting his palms on the table. "I believe I shall compose a piece in Miss Wade's honor," he said in a low voice. " 'Daphne of the Violet Eyes,' or something like that. Who knows? I might succeed with a sonata where your flowers have failed."

A blackness came over Anthony like a curtain going down, and the next thing he knew, his greatest friend was on the floor with a bloody lip, a bone-jarring ache was in his fist, and other members of Brook's had seized his arms to hold him back.

Dylan touched his hand to the corner of his

mouth. He glanced at the smear of blood on his fingertips, then raised his gaze, confronting Anthony's rage with a rueful smile. "You see, my friend?" he murmured. "Madness comes to us all. Even you."

Chapter 25

As he had promised Lady Fitzhugh, Anthony accepted the invitation to her card party, though he knew it would only inflame the already rampant gossip.

He wanted to see Daphne. He wished propriety did not prevent him from seeing her privately, but seeing her amid a group of people was better than not seeing her at all. When he arrived at the house in Russell Square, however, he received exactly what he had been hoping for—a chance to be alone with her.

The usual flutter of excitement the arrival of a duke created was followed by introductions to the other guests, and resulted in the inevitable awkward silence. Lady Fitzhugh cleared her throat and turned to her husband. "Perhaps we should begin?" she suggested.

Sir Edward concurred at once. "Yes, yes, capital idea, Elinor. Let us start the play. A pair of us will have to make do with piquet, I fear, instead of whist. Mr. Jennings has developed a cold, and his wife sent word late today that they would not be able to attend, so we are two short for whist."

Daphne turned to Anthony. "Perhaps your grace would prefer chess to cards?" she suggested, gesturing to the doorway that led into an adjoining room.

The silence that followed was not awkward, but deafening. For some reason, Daphne wanted a private interview with him, and though he doubted it was for the same reasons that motivated him, he was quick to take advantage of it.

"I love chess, Miss Wade," Anthony said. "I would be honored."

"Excellent." She strode into the adjoining room, where the chessboard had been moved out of the way for the card party. He bowed to the other guests and followed her. When she sat down, he took the opposite chair.

"Your grace," she began without preliminaries, "you have to stop—" She broke off, frowning at the smile on his face. "Why in heaven's name are you looking at me like that?"

"Because by tomorrow everyone in London will know we are engaged." He gestured to the board. "A lady makes the first move."

"What are you talking about? We are not engaged." She frowned as she shoved a pawn two spaces forward in an abstract fashion. "And I do not care in the least what people think."

"In front of everyone else in the room, you have invited me to be alone with you," he pointed out, moving his own pawn. "The inevitable conclusion is that we are engaged. If I had known it would be this easy, I would have maneuvered you into chess days ago."

Daphne shot an impatient glance at the doorway and slid another pawn forward. "This is ridiculous. We are not alone and the doors are open. Lady Fitzhugh can see us perfectly well from where she is sitting."

"It doesn't matter. We have moved into another room, and we are now having a private conversation. No couple not engaged are allowed this sort of liberty." He moved his knight, and looked at her, still smiling. "When you were looking up rules in etiquette books, did you miss that one?"

"Anthony, you must stop this. The fact that I even need etiquette books proves what an inadequate duchess I would be."

"You will be wonderful at the job once you get the gist of it. Everything you do, you do well."

"That is not true, and it is not the point anyway. I am not going to marry you."

"So you keep telling me, but I can only hope that one day, you will see my torment and take pity on me." He pointed at the board. "It is your move."

"Why do you do this?" she demanded, caring nothing for the game. "Because I am a temporary madness? When this madness has passed, what will take its place? Will this Marguerite return to your bed? Or some new mistress perhaps? How many mistresses have you had, anyway?"

"More than one. Less than a dozen."

"Have you—" She paused and looked away, and Anthony felt a glimmer of hope as she asked, "Have you seen that woman?"

She cared. She must, or she would not be asking these questions. He told her the truth. "Yes. Once, on the Row. I saw her from about seventy feet away. I had already sent her a letter and ended our arrangement." He reached across the table and cupped Daphne's chin, returning her attention to him. "Are we playing Twenty Questions now," he asked gently, "instead of chess?"

"No, but—" She pulled free of his grasp and glanced around, as if trying to think how to put what she wanted to say. "You once said I am a mystery, but it is you who reveals nothing. Since that dinner with the Benningtons, I have told you many things about me. My life, my work, my father, my . . . my feelings for you. Yet, you have told me only the smallest things about yourself. I do not know you well enough to marry you."

"What would you like to know? Ask away. I shall interview for the post of husband."

"I am not interviewing you for a post! And this conversation is making me appreciate more and more that nothing I would ask could be satisfied in words. Or flowers either, for that matter. You do not love me. You offer me your name only because you are determined that honor be satisfied, and because you are so damned obstinate and arrogant and—"

"And you say you do not know me well enough to marry me?"

She made a huff of pure vexation, and stood up. Turning away from him, she crossed the Persian rug to the fireplace. He glanced at the other room and observed that Lady Fitzhugh was fully occupied with her cards. He got out of his chair and followed Daphne to where she was gazing into the fire. He halted behind her and leaned close to whisper in her ear.

"You know me better than you realize, Daphne," he said. "No one knows me better than you do. No one ever will."

She started to speak, but he forestalled her. "Listen to me. All week I have been trying to tell you and show you how much I desire you. I know words are inadequate to make you believe me, but I do not know how else to do it. What else can I do, Daphne?" He put his hands on her waist and pulled her back against him. "Could I say it with my body?"

She closed her eyes, but something changed in her. Something fluttered, softened. She lifted her hand, clenched her fist around air. "Don't, Anthony, don't."

He pushed his advantage. "You desired me. Only a few weeks ago, in the antika." He pulled back just a little. "Have you forgotten that?"

"I haven't!" she answered in a fierce whisper.

"Nor have I forgotten I am not the one you wished to wed."

"But I never desired her the way I desire you," he said. It sounded so lame, but it was the truth, and he was desperate. "It is you who no longer wants me."

She shook her head, her eyes still closed, her lips pressed tight together as she made a tiny sound of dissent.

"You deny it," he went on, "but you deny yourself so many of the pleasures in life. Why, when I can give you them all?"

A tiny moan escaped her lips as ran his hands up her ribs to her breasts. "I do want you," she admitted in a whisper. "It isn't that. It was never that. I always—"

"Prove what you say, then." He glanced over his shoulder at the door and pressed a kiss to her ear. "If you want me, spend the remainder of the night with me. We can go to my house. All the guests here will have gone by midnight and everyone will be in bed and asleep by half past one. Wear something to conceal your face. I will wait for you behind the mews with my carriage and have you back before dawn. Meet me there."

"I won't."

"I will wait all the same." He kissed her cheek. "You see, Daphne? Honor is not my only motivation, for I feel quite dishonorable at this moment. I want you more than I have ever wanted anything in my life."

* * *

He did not think she would come. The three hours that had followed his illicit suggestion to her had been excruciating for both of them, as they pretended to play chess and pretended to enjoy supper, Madeira, and small talk at opposite sides of the table. By the time the party ended, he thought that she would surely have changed her mind.

But no. A few minutes after the church clock nearby had chimed half past one, he saw a cloaked, hooded figure emerge from the stable into the alley where he sat in his carriage. He opened the door and she climbed inside. When she pushed back the hood of her cloak, there was barely enough light to see her face, but it was enough. "Are you certain about this?" he asked.

"Yes."

That was good enough for him. Time enough later to learn why she had changed her mind. Just now, he did not care. He pulled down the window shade, tapped the roof with his walking stick, and the carriage lurched into motion.

With the last shade down, it was so dark inside the carriage that he could see nothing of her. Over the sound of the carriage, he could not hear her breathe. She did not speak. The scent of gardenia was the only thing that told him she was there.

That night in the antika, he had seen her only in the dimness of moonlight. This time, he was going to light all the candles he could find. This time, he was going to see her while he made love to her, see the perfect curves of her breasts and hips, see the tapering length of her legs, see the expression on her face as she climaxed.

Anthony leaned back, concentrating on the sound of the carriage wheels, striving to drive away the hungry, aching need of his body. The carriage ride to Grosvenor Square seemed to take forever.

He took her through the stables and into the back of the house, for there were always carriages going in and out of the square at this hour, taking people home after parties such as the one they had attended, and even with a hood to cover Daphne's hair and shadow her face, he did not want to take the chance of anyone recognizing her.

Holding her hand, he took her up the back stairs, and through the dark rooms and corridors that led to his own suite. He went into the dressing room, woke Richardson, told him to fetch a footman to light a fire, and explained that he would not be needing anything further until morning. His valet departed, with only one quick glance at the hooded woman by the bed with her back to him.

When the footman came, Anthony ordered every candle in the room be lit along with the fire. When the servant departed, he turned the key in the lock. At last, he thought, drawing in a deep breath, then letting it out slowly. At last they were alone.

Anthony turned around. So did she.

She pushed back the hood of her cloak, and he studied her bathed in the soft light. He was reminded of the first moment he had ever seen her, for she looked much the same now as she had then. No straw hat, but the same solemn, baby-owl face and a cloak, not a tattered and dusty one this time, concealing her body. Light reflected off of her gold-framed spectacles and kept him from seeing her eyes. She was much the same in all the superficialities, he supposed, but so different in a way much harder to define.

Tonight, all he wanted was to show her what he felt when he looked at her, not just what he saw. As he had told her earlier, if words and flowers would not suffice, he would use his body. He just hoped he could keep himself in check. Arousal was coursing through him like anarchy, but the next few hours were not for him. They were for her.

He moved to stand in front of her. He reached out and removed her spectacles, then placed them on the bedside table. He pushed her cloak off her shoulders. She wore no sensible dress of dun or beige cotton now, but instead the evening frock of midnight blue silk she had donned for the party. The neckline skimmed the edges of her shoulders, and the color made her skin look like pale gold in the candlelight. He traced her collarbone with the tips of his fingers, then cupped her cheeks and tilted her head back as he brought his mouth closer to hers. "Daphne" was all he could manage before he kissed her.

Beneath his, her lips parted at once, soft and lush and tasting of Madeira. Her eyes were closed, but he kept his open, for he wanted to see every nuance of feeling he could pull out of her with his hands and his mouth. He slid his hands up into her hair, grateful she had not become so fashionable as to want all those silly ribbons and silk flowers so many other women seemed so fond of. There were no pins, either, only combs, and as he pulled them free, her hair fell in a thick, heavy wave down her back. The combs fell to the floor, and he tangled his hands in her hair, reveling in the feel of it, warm and satiny in his fists. He deepened the kiss, tasting the hot sweetness of her mouth.

She made a tiny, smothered sound of desire and wrapped her arms around his neck, pressing her body closer to his and igniting his raw hungry need to be inside her, the need he was striving to keep at bay.

To buy time, he tore his lips from hers and trailed kisses along her shoulder to the pale blue ruching at the edge of her dress and back again. His hands left her hair and slid down to her waist. He wanted her out of all these clothes, but he forced himself to wait, containing his moves until her body told him the next one to make.

When she was quivering in his hold and making hushed little moans against his shirt front, he took the next step. His hands left her waist and moved up her back. He pulled back enough to look into her face as he gathered her hair and brought it forward over one shoulder. Then he began to undo the buttons down her back.

Her eyes were closed, her lips parted and her head tilted back, but as he pulled the dress down from her shoulders, she opened her eyes, and he felt her stiffen slightly, just a hint of resistance, but enough to give him pause.

She looked into his eyes. "Is this sort of thing usually done with candles lit?"

"Oh, yes. Most definitely." He slipped the dress down her shoulders, but by the time he freed her arms, by the time the dress was down around her waist and he could see the soft white cambric bodice of her princess petticoat, she was pushing against his shoulders to stop him.

"Anthony, I think we should put them out."

"Why?" He bent his head to kiss her neck. "I want to look at you. Do you not want to look at me?"

"I can't see anything," she whispered. "You took my glasses. Again."

He chuckled, blowing soft breath against her neck, and he did not move for a long moment. "Daphne," he finally said, "I want to see you naked on my sheets. I want to see your hair spread across my pillow. I want to look at your face while I touch you because you are so lovely to me now and because I want so badly to know how you feel." He paused, wondering if he was talking like a complete idiot. "But if you would be more content with the dark, if you want me to put out the candles, I will."

She did not reply. Instead, she lowered her gaze and bit her lip, fingering the lapels of his evening coat. After a moment, she began pulling his coat away from his shoulders. "No," she said. "Leave them."

Anthony stood still and let her take away his coat and his waistcoat. He let her unbutton his shirt, then he pulled it off. He waited, forcing himself to stand utterly still, as she caressed his bare chest with her hands and pressed kisses to his skin. He waited, shuddering with pleasure as she pushed him to the very edge of his wits. When he felt the flick of her tongue against his nipple, he stopped her.

"God, Daphne, enough," he groaned, and his hands tangled in her hair, gently pulling her back as he took a deep breath. "I believe you enjoy tormenting me."

She looked up, a long, appraising glance. "I could get used to it."

"I have no doubt." He rested his hands on her bare shoulders and touched the edge of her neckline. "Lace on the bodice?" he said, taking deep breaths and attempting a bit of conversation while he regained control of the lust that threatened to overwhelm him. "Daphne, I am astonished at this extravagance."

"Mrs. Avery told me a princess petticoat for evening had to have lace, though since it is hidden from view, I hardly see the point of it."

"I do," he said fervently as he reached behind her to unfasten the buttons of the delicate cambric garment. "I only ask that you never take to wearing corsets."

"But it would keep my posture perfect when walking, would it not? Why, I believe it was you, your grace, who advised me to wear one."

"I changed my mind. Corset hooks take too damned long to unfasten." He grasped the lacy edges of her princess petticoat and pulled the garment down her arms, revealing her breasts. So luscious, cream and pink in the candlelight. His throat went dry.

He cupped her breasts in his hands and heard her gasp. He lifted his gaze, watching a beautiful delight wash over her face as she closed her eyes and leaned back against the wall behind her, and he did not think he had ever seen anything lovelier in his life. He gently closed the thumb and forefinger of each hand over her hardened nipples, relishing the little whimpering sounds of pleasure she made even as he felt his self-control slipping.

Reluctantly, he slid his hands away from her breasts to grasp the folds of silk and cambric that were caught on the flare of her hips. He pulled the dress and petticoat down her legs as he knelt in front of her, keeping his gaze fixed firmly on the thick, willow-green rug and his lust reined in.

His body was burning by the time the garments reached her ankles. She put a hand on his shoulder for balance and stepped out of them.

He pulled off her heeled silk slippers and tossed them aside, then his hands curved behind her ankles and moved slowly up her calves. He caressed the backs of her knees, and smiled when he felt shivers run through her. He untied her garters and pulled them down with her stockings.

Only when she was completely naked did Anthony dare to look up again. But he did it slowly, over long, straight shins and taut, tapering thighs, thighs that had a sleek, outside plane and an oval hint of muscle above each knee. Strong legs, lean and taut, more beautiful than all the plump, fleshy limbs of other women he had seen. A man's most insane dreams could not conjure up legs like these. "God, Daphne, I—"

He couldn't go on. Anthony ran his palms up the outside of each of her thighs, then grasped her bare hips in his hands. He pulled her toward him and pressed a kiss to the soft brown curls at the apex of her thighs, inhaling the scent of gardenias and feminine arousal.

That kiss was too much for her. She gave a strangled, startled cry, and her hands came down on his shoulders to keep herself from falling.

He stood up and lifted her in his arms. Turning around, he laid her on the bed, then sat on the edge beside her as he removed his boots. Standing up again, he looked at her as he began to unbutton his trousers, and found that her gaze was fixed on his hands. He watched her face as she watched him slide his trousers off his hips, and when her lips parted with a soft, startled oh and a smile of pure approval, he wanted to laugh with exultation.

The mattress dipped with his weight as he moved to stretch out beside her on the bed. Leaning on one elbow, he gazed down at her for a moment, then he reached out to touch her. He flattened his palm across her stomach, then moved lower, and slid his hand between her thighs. He slipped the tip of his middle finger inside her.

She was wet, aroused, panting, as he encircled her clitoris gently with the tip of his finger. He barely moved, watching her face as her hips rocked frantically against his hand and she approached her climax. Nothing she felt was suppressed or hidden from him now; there was exquisite joy in every plane and curve of her face as she let out the soft, keening wail of feminine ecstasy. Anthony felt the tiny, convulsive shudders of her body as she wrung the last few pleasures of her orgasm from him, and he was more pleased by what he had just witnessed than by any other sexual experience of his life.

He withdrew his hand and moved on top of her, his weight pressing her deeper into the mattress. He entered her, and he wanted to move within her slowly, bring her to ecstasy one more time, but she was so tight, and the feel of her surrounding him was so exquisite that his good intentions went straight to hell.

He heard his own visceral groans as he felt the tension within him rising, thickening until it was unbearable. No way to be gentle now, or hold back. He quickened the pace, thrusting into her with the rough, frantic motions of his own passion finally unleashed. He came in a rush, the sensations exploding inside him with all the flash and heat of fireworks.

Afterward, he stilled on top of her, his hands sliding beneath her back as he watched her open her eyes.

"My goodness," she whispered, trying to catch her breath. "No wonder the Romans painted all those frescoes."

He laughed, the sound ringing through the room loud enough that it probably woke the dozing footmen out in the corridor. He rolled onto his back, taking her with him.

Her hair fell all around his face and he kissed her, not knowing if this woman made him feel more like a Roman god or the greatest lover in all of England. Either was more than he had ever dreamed of.

Chapter 26

"And that is how we came to be in Morocco," she summed up. She had been lying here beside him, naked, with the sheets flung back, giving him a detailed account of her life as if she were a travelogue. It was not the most romantic aftermath to lovemaking, she supposed, but it was so nice to lie here beside him and watch his face watching hers with such avid interest.

"I envy you your travels, Daphne," he said after a moment, "but I do not understand your father. What was he thinking? Wandering around the deserts of Africa, with you working your fingers to the bone. That should not be a permanent life for anyone, especially for a woman. I cannot help but condemn your father's thoughtlessness."

"No, no, you do not understand. He was not so thoughtless as you think, Anthony. It was my insistence to remain." She turned her head on the pillow to look at him. "Papa wanted me to have a better life. He wanted me to go to England, he wanted to reunite me with my mother's family, but his letters, like mine, were rebuffed. The baron had disowned my mother, even going so far as to pretend she was dead, and he would not be moved to relent. Papa suggested sending me here for school, but I refused to leave him, and I could not allow him to give up his work and come here with me. He was so lost when my mother died, he needed me so desperately. I would not leave him, I could not. So we stayed together, and I assisted him. I loved him, and I helped him. His work and I were his purpose in life, and both of us were happy."

"Your father was stronger than mine," he said, turning his head to stare at the ceiling. "Perhaps because he had you."

She rose up on her arm. Resting her weight on her elbow and her cheek in her hand, she looked at him. "Your father had you, Anthony, and your sister."

"I sent Viola to relations in Cornwall." He turned his head to look at her. "I was not enough to ease his pain."

"I doubt that." Daphne reached out to touch his cheek, wishing he would open up to her about himself. "What happened to your father?"

He sat up, rolled his legs over the side of the bed, and stood up. "Dawn will be here soon. I should take you back."

Daphne watched him, her heart aching. "Why will you not tell me about this? I should not care if he had gone mad, if that is the reason you keep silent—"

"You should get dressed," he interrupted, bending down to retrieve his linen. "If the servants at Russell Square wake up and find you have gone missing, everyone will know where you are. Or they will think we have eloped."

Daphne did not move. "Why won't you tell me about him?"

"Because I do not want to discuss it, Daphne," he said as he dressed. "Ever."

She got out of bed and went to him, wrapping her arms around his waist. He felt as rigid as a statue. "Anthony," she whispered, staring at his back. "You press me at every turn to be more forthcoming about myself, to share what I feel and think and believe, yet you refuse to do so with me. I find it as hard as you to talk about my deepest feelings, but I have done so with you. Somehow, you have become my dearest friend. Despite all my efforts to keep you from seeing my many insecurities, you pull them out of me. I think that is because deep down, under all my fears, I want you to know who I am. I have come to trust you more than I have ever trusted anyone."

He did not move. He did not reply.

She pressed her lips to his back, feeling the fine weave of his linen shirt against her mouth and the hard muscles of his body beneath. She let her arms fall away, and she took a step back. "Anthony," she said to his back, "I know you are a very private person, but you want me to be your wife. I have opened my heart to you more than once, told you things I would die before revealing to anyone else. If you cannot open up to me and do the same, even if it is only a little bit at a time, we have no chance of happiness. I love you, but until you can begin to share yourself with me, I will not marry you."

He did not reply, but she knew that was not out of coldness. It was out of fear, fear just like hers. She got dressed without another word, and the carriage ride back to Russell Square was silent. It seemed there was nothing more to say.

Daphne did not go to the museum opening on the following day. Instead, she went out with Elizabeth and Anne to make calls, and their talk and laughter was a welcome distraction.

When they returned to the house just before six o'clock, Mary had barely opened the door for them before Lady Fitzhugh came out of the drawing room above with a cry of delight.

"My dears, I am so glad you are back." She came rushing down the stairs, a happy smile on her face. Her daughters and Daphne paused in the vestibule, stunned that the normally sedate Lady Fitzhugh was actually running down the stairs.

"Mama!" cried Elizabeth. "What has happened?"

"Something good," Anne put in. "How you are smiling, Mama!"

Lady Fitzhugh pointed to the calling-card table

behind them, and all three of the younger women turned around.

On the silver tray atop the table was a single, thornless red rose. Beside it was Anthony's card.

"Another flower for Daphne," Anne said, laughing. "This is the reason you have a smile on your face as wide as the Thames, Mama? Because of a rose?"

"It's a thornless rose," Elizabeth said ecstatically. "And it's red. Oh, Daphne, at last!"

"What does it mean?" asked Anne.

"Love at first sight," Lady Fitzhugh told her, and turned to Daphne, putting a hand on her arm. "I am so ashamed of myself, my dear, but I had to look it up in your little book, for I could not wait. He left the museum—and it is the opening day, you know—to bring this to you himself. He was devastated, my dear, simply devastated that you were not here when he called."

"Daphne?" Elizabeth stared at her. "You are so quiet. Surely you do not doubt his feelings now?"

She did not answer. With a trembling hand, she picked up the rose, staring at it in bewilderment. She had been waiting for him to make the next move, but what did this mean? She vividly remembered her painful confession to him in the antika of how she had fallen in love with him the first moment she met him. Was he trying to tell her he remembered that, too? Or was he making a genuine confession of love? But that did not make sense, for he had certainly not loved her at first sight. She was not even really sure he loved her now.

She didn't care. She loved him, and he was taking another step toward her. Odd how one simple thing could put everything else into place. This time, she was going to take a leap of faith all the way to him. This time, she wasn't going to be afraid of getting her heart broken. This time, she wasn't going to worry about making a mistake. She snatched the flower off the tray and ran for the front door, flinging it open to leave the house once again.

"My dear, where are you going?" Lady Fitzhugh called after her.

"The museum," Daphne called back over her shoulder. She grabbed up her skirts with one hand, held her rose with the other, and raced toward the entrance to the square, oblivious to the incredulous stares of those strolling in the park. She ran through the gates and up the street, scanning the carriages for an available hansom as she went. It took seven blocks before she finally hailed one. The church clock was striking seven o'clock as she gave the driver the address of Anthony's museum and climbed into the carriage. Once inside, she fell back against the seat, breathing hard, holding the rose to her cheek, and hoping with all her heart that the position of duchess was still open.

She did not come. Though surrounded by people every hour, Anthony watched for her, glancing at the doorway of his collection room every few seconds, scanning the faces in the crowd constantly as the hours of the afternoon dragged by, but she did not come.

The opening of his museum would be hailed as a triumph. Twenty-seven collections of Romano-British art and architecture, including his own, were on display, and those who waited until the opening day to purchase tickets found that none were available for any viewing at any hour until mid-July. But Daphne, so much a part of this project, did not come.

His extraordinary and controversial decision to have the museum open to all who wished to view the antiquities would continue to be debated for decades, and the ha'penny tickets for morning views had been among the first to disappear, but he could not share that gratifying news with Daphne, for she did not come.

He ordered the doors kept open an additional hour, but when everyone had left and he was alone, she still had not arrived. Yet he walked around his museum, his footsteps echoing on the stone floors. And he waited.

Anthony knew he had been a fool not to tell her last night what she wanted to know, but God, he had never told anyone about his father. He never discussed it, not even with Viola. People gossiped about it, and servants whispered about it, but no one really knew what it had been like.

There was so much he would say if she came. He would tell her every secret he had, shout them from the Whispering Gallery at Saint Paul's, if only she would come.

So hard to reveal himself, but Daphne understood. Like no one else, she understood.

Anthony heard the front door open, heard it thrown back with a bang. Then footsteps crossing the stone floors through the main gallery. And there she was, breathing hard, with the rose in her hand and her bonnet askew, looking disheveled, windblown, and utterly lovely.

"What does this mean?" she asked him as she walked toward him, twirling the flower in her fingers. "What are you telling me?"

"My father killed himself."

She stopped. The rose stopped twirling in her hand. She stared, her beautiful eyes wide with shock at the abruptness of his statement.

"One night, three years after my mother died, he drank four bottles of laudanum. He missed her so much, you see. She was everything to him, and he loved her down to the depths of his soul, and she died. He did not want to live without her, and he killed himself. I found him."

So hard to say these things, even harder than he had thought they would be, each word a world of pain, and he felt as if he were twelve years old all over again. "I thought it was a blessing. God help me, I did. I was glad."

She did not say anything, but simply stood there, listening as the words began pouring out of him. "Can you imagine what it is like to see your father sob for hours at a time? He talked about her with me, and with Viola. I had to send her away, for she was only six years old, and she did not understand. Daphne, he talked to the servants as if she were still alive, giving orders to them about how she wanted a cup of tea sent up to her room, or sending them on some other such errand for her. He would wander the halls at night, calling her name. He sat at the dining table and talked to her. Entire conversations every night with an empty chair."

Oh, God. Daphne put her hand over her mouth. The words were pouring out of him so rapidly, she could hardly understand what he said. She knew some of it already, but it was harder to hear him speak it. He had been a boy then, only a boy. Once she had foolishly thought she knew what a broken heart was like. So wrong, for it was only now that it was breaking, breaking for the man she loved, who had been a boy watching his father go mad.

"I was twelve when he died, but I really became the duke when I was nine," Anthony went on. "I had to. He could not make a decision for the life of him. He would stare at documents for hours, but never sign them. The land steward started coming to me. All the duties began to pile up, and by the time my uncle came to be my father's regent, I had already been running things for several months. With my uncle's assistance and advice, I did everything. I had to assume the power at once. I knew that."

"I remember you told me," Daphne murmured. "That day of our picnic."

"My poor father could not manage to add two numbers together. He was incoherent. He could not converse on any subject but my mother. He refused to allow his valet to shave his face, because he was waiting for Rosalind to do it. She had always done it—it was a sort of intimacy between them."

Daphne saw his face twist with pain, and it was almost unbearable. She took a step forward. She wanted to tell him to stop, that he did not have to explain any more. But she steeled herself to wait and let him finish.

"I had to lock him up, Daphne. He started to do things, like load his guns and fire them into the walls. He could have killed someone. He could have killed himself, so I had him locked in a room upstairs." His voice broke. "I do not know how he got the laudanum. The doctor, I suppose, though he denied it."

Anthony straightened and looked at her as if remembering she was there. He must have seen something of her horror in her eyes, for he said, "Now you know my deepest fear. I never want to be my father."

He turned away. His back to her, he said, "His madness might not have been caused by his grief, only brought out by it. I cannot say it is not hereditary. I knew you were entitled to know all this when I proposed, but God help me, Daphne, I could not tell you."

She did not know what to say. How could any words suffice? She started to walk toward him, but even as she did, he was walking away from her.

"I will not pursue you any longer," he told her over his shoulder. "All I ask is that if . . . if there is a child after last night, you let me do my duty in that, at least."

Daphne halted a few feet away from him. She gave a little cough. "Thank you for telling me, for sharing that with me. But I really came because I heard you were looking to fill a position on your estate. What are the qualifications of being a duchess?"

He stiffened, and did not speak for a long moment. Then he drew a deep breath and let it out slowly. He turned around. "Are you applying for the post, Miss Wade?"

"I thought I might, but I have concerns about the position, for I know it is an arduous one. What does a duchess do, exactly?"

He took a step toward her. "Love the duke. Love him with all the passion she hides within her, love him each and every day of her life."

Daphne nodded with no change in her expression. "I already do that. What else?"

"She would need to rid herself of any fashionable notion of ever sleeping in her own rooms, unless of course he takes to snoring."

Daphne tilted her head to one side, her heart pounding so hard she believed she could hear it echo off the dome overhead. "I believe I could manage that, even the snoring, for if one can sleep through a sandstorm, one can sleep through anything. What else?"

"She must run his household, at whichever estate they are in residence. She must be discreet, for the duke is a private man, and she would need to always behave with restraint no matter what her inner feelings, for she will be constantly observed by others and gossiped about."

Daphne tapped her fingertip to her lip several times, then nodded. "I believe I am rather good at that part."

"However, she must learn not to conceal her true

feelings from the duke himself, who only wants to make her happy. She must give many fêtes and country house parties, run a vast number of charities, be able to entertain dignitaries—kings and such—and try to look down her nose at everyone else and convince them she is far better than they are. She might have difficulty with that part."

"I can learn."

"She would need to treat servants with all her diplomatic kindness, smoothing over any feathers ruffled by the duke, who is known to be an impatient man, difficult to satisfy, and not always thoughtful of the feelings of those who work for him. Pleases and thank yous and things such as that are difficult for dukes to manage, you know."

He smiled, and her heart began to soar. He took another step toward her. "She has to learn how to spend the duke's money with absurd extravagance, especially on follies for herself, such as beautiful clothes, jewels, and presents for her friends. She must never, ever, allow herself to run out of gardenia-scented soap, for dukes are known to be quite partial to gardenias. And should she and the duke have children, she has to love them. She has to lavish upon those children all the attention and care that the duke and duchess's own sets of parents were never able to lavish on them."

"I could do that," she whispered.

He took another step, and halted a foot in front of her. He reached out and wiped her tear away with the tip of his finger. Only then did she realize she was crying. "She has to stop being afraid of getting hurt, for the duke will surely hurt her again on many occasions during their long marriage, but he will never do so with deliberate intent, for he loves her more than anything on earth."

She caught back a sob and started to speak, but he gestured to the flower in her hand, stopping her. "I sent you this because it is the truest expression of my feelings that I am able to give you." He took a deep breath. "I fell in love with you that day in my gardens, when I saw you standing in the rain. I have loved you since first sight, Daphne, for that moment when I saw you standing in the rain was the first time I ever truly saw you."

"Oh, Anthony!" She threw her arms around his neck. "I *was* afraid," she cried, her voice muffled by his shirtfront. "I could not believe that you were sincere. I kept telling myself I did not love you anymore, but I knew I was deceiving myself and had been for such a long time. I love you. I do not know when I fell in love with you—the real emotion, I mean, and so much stronger and deeper than what I felt before—but I did fall in love with you."

She sniffed and took his offered handkerchief. "Now, what were those twenty questions you wanted to ask me?"

"Only one." He cupped her cheeks in his hands, loving her face and all the subtle nuances of feeling conveyed in her expression. "How much time do I get in exchange for that rose?"

"For the rose, a short engagement. For the speech, you get a lifetime."

"I can live with that," he said, and kissed her.